The Fairytale Curse

MARINA FINLAYSON

FINESSE SOLUTIONS

Cover design by Karri Klawiter
Editing by Larks & Katydids
Formatting by Polgarus Studio

Published by Finesse Solutions Pty Ltd
2016/4/#01

Author's note: This book was written and produced in Australia and uses British/Australian spelling conventions, such as "colour" instead of "color", and "-ise" endings instead of "-ize" on words like "realise".

National Library of Australia Cataloguing-in-Publication entry:

Finlayson, Marina, author.
The fairytale curse / Marina Finlayson.
ISBN 9780994239143 (paperback)
Finlayson, Marina. Magic's return; bk. 1.
Fantasy fiction.
A823.4

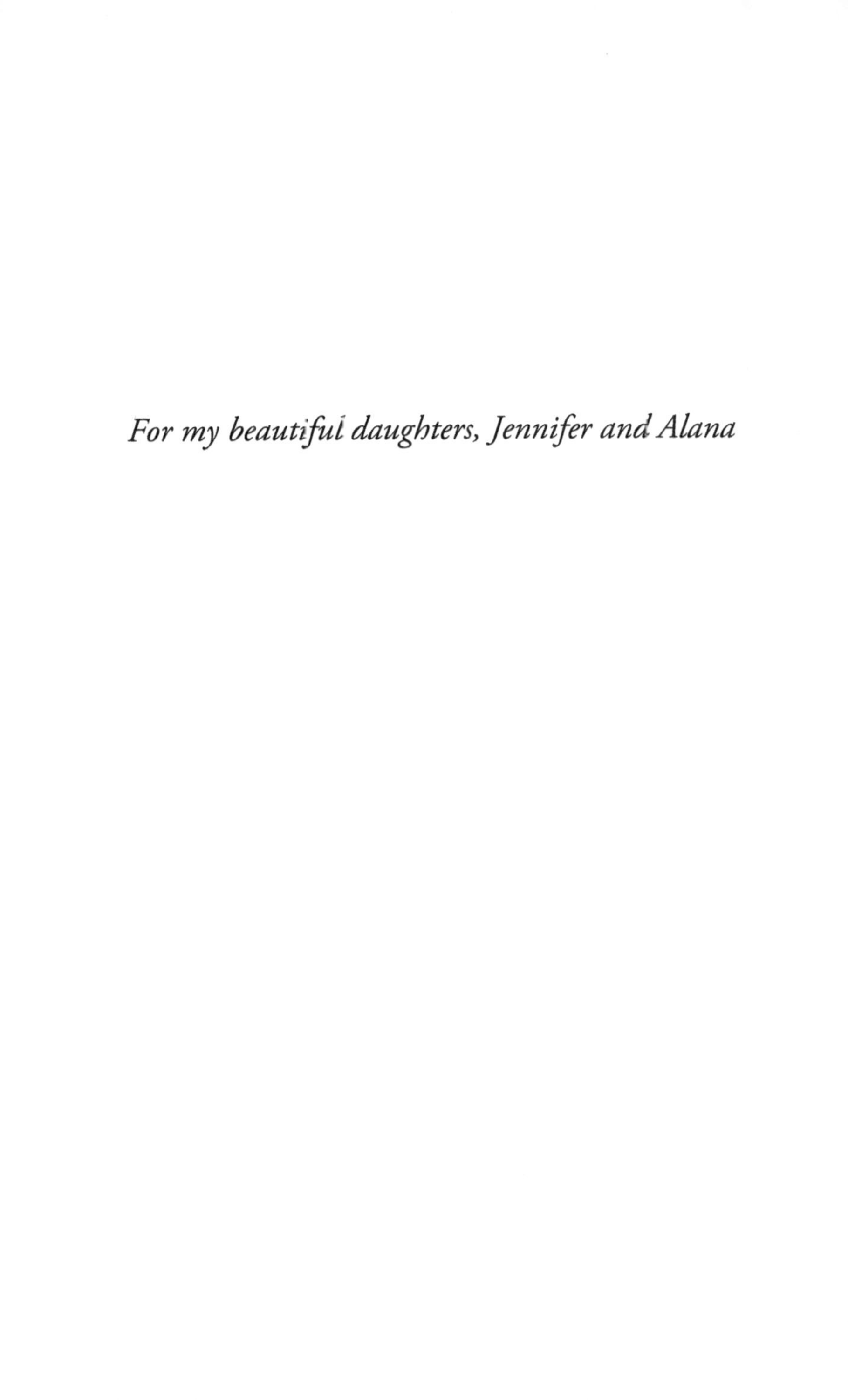

For my beautiful daughters, Jennifer and Alana

Chapter One

The girl on the TV wore a long white dress, as if she'd been on the way to her wedding when she decided to lie down in a glass coffin instead. Her skin had a healthy glow; her cheeks were a rosy pink and her lips bright red. She certainly didn't look dead. I almost expected her eyes to flutter open as I watched.

"Janey!" Dad never took his eyes off the TV. "Come and look at this."

Mum came in with a *this better be worth it* expression on her face. She didn't approve of watching TV at breakfast time. Whenever Dad picked up the remote, she'd roll those sharp green eyes of hers and sigh in that *I'm so disappointed in you* way. Not that Dad took any notice. You'd think she'd have gotten used to it after twenty-one years of marriage, but every morning it was the same old same old. It always ended with her huffing off to another room as soon as her cereal was done, where she made as much noise as possible until the TV was turned off again.

The footage was wobbly, as if it had been taken with a mobile phone, and only lasted a few seconds. The camera panned around a small clearing in what looked like dense forest. And not the kind we have in Australia, either. This was forest straight out of Central Casting, dark and foreboding. Huge pines towered over the scene, leaning in as if whispering secrets to one another. In the centre of the clearing, in the gloom beneath the pines, stood a massive marble platform. How the hell it got there, I couldn't imagine, since there didn't seem to be any gaps in the trees big enough to drag a huge lump of stone like that through. On top of it rested the glass coffin.

The girl inside was laid out like royalty at a state funeral. Her dark hair fanned neatly across the pillow, and her hands were clasped precisely on her chest. Whoever had put her there had obviously taken a great deal of care. They'd even tucked a single red rose into her hands, its colour a perfect match for the lipstick she wore.

"The unidentified girl was found early this morning in the Blue Mountains west of Sydney, not far from the popular tourist destination of the Three Sisters." The camera zoomed in on the girl's still face as the reporter spoke. She could have been anything from sixteen to twenty-six. "This footage was taken by the hiker who discovered her. Despite appearances, she isn't dead. Emergency services took her to hospital where doctors found her to be in a deep coma, though apparently healthy. There is no visible sign of trauma, and police are appealing for anyone who can shed any light on the mystery of the Sleeping Beauty to come forward."

Dad snorted. "Sleeping Beauty, my foot. Idiot doesn't know his fairy tales."

And Dad did? He was more comfortable with gadgets than

books; I would never have suspected him of an interest in fairy tales.

The picture changed to the reporter standing in the same clearing. The coffin was gone, but the platform remained, cordoned off with police tape. Good luck shifting that sucker.

"I'm here with a local resident, who's lived in the area for the past fifty years."

The camera pulled back to reveal a grizzled old bloke who could have claimed to have lived there for the past hundred years and I'd have believed him. He had the leathery look of someone who'd spent a lot of those years outdoors.

The reporter turned to him with an encouraging smile. He was probably afraid the old guy would drop dead on national TV from the excitement.

"You were telling me before that there's even more to this mystery than first appears."

"That's right." The old man nodded vigorously. "I was a park ranger before I retired, and I know this area like the back of my hand. I've probably walked this trail more times than a young bloke like you's had hot dinners."

The reporter chuckled. "And what can you tell the viewers about this spot where we're standing?"

"It doesn't exist, son. At least, that's what I'd say if I *wasn't* standing in it, if you see what I mean."

Hmm. Old guy wasn't making any sense. Maybe he had dementia, and the reporter was about to make an idiot of himself live on camera. Mum and Dad were staring like three-year-olds hypnotised by a Disney movie. I'd never seen Mum pay that much attention to "that idiot box" before.

The old guy waved a bony hand at the trees looming over the clearing. "These trees here, they look pretty established, don't they? Forty, fifty years old, maybe. But I'm telling you, they weren't here last time I came down this track, and that's only a couple of years ago. Maybe weren't even here yesterday, you know what I'm saying? The main trail's only twenty metres that way, and this whole section is nothing but gum trees and other natives. Not a pine tree for miles."

"But the clearing was here?"

"Nope. Well, I mean—just look at that grass."

The camera swung to focus on the grass, which didn't look all that sinister to me. It was just grass.

"What's wrong with it?"

"It's thick and green. Looks freshly mowed, doesn't it? More like a putting green. Grass doesn't get like that on its own, you know. You've got to take care of it. You seen anybody standing round the middle of the national park with a hose and a lawn mower?"

"So how do you explain it?"

The old man shrugged. "It's got to be a hoax, hasn't it? Probably one of those reality TV shows."

The camera zoomed in on the reporter. "And there you have it. A mystery girl in a mystery clearing."

The reporter signed off, and Mum reached for the remote and started flicking channels. Cooking shows and cartoons flashed past, but there was no other news. She turned it off, and for once Dad didn't complain.

"What do you make of that?" he asked. "Did that girl look familiar to you? I feel like I've seen her before somewhere."

Mum said nothing. Her forehead was creased into her thinking frown. No point talking to her when she got like that. She probably hadn't even heard him.

"Do you think that guy was right about it being a hoax?" I asked. "Is this the kind of crap they get up to in Sydney?"

Dad seemed to have forgotten all about his cornflakes. They'd gone all soggy in the bottom of the bowl. "Snow White in the Blue Mountains? Either that or a serial killer, I suppose."

"But she's not dead."

"Not a very good serial killer then."

I refused to laugh. I was still mad at him for dragging us down to Sydney, just when things had been going so well in Townsville. We'd been there nearly two years, the longest time we'd ever stayed in one spot. "Snow White, is it? I didn't know you were such an expert on fairy tales."

He grinned. The corners of his eyes crinkled up when he smiled, making him look like a mischievous kid. It was hard not to smile back, but I wasn't giving in. "Hidden depths, my darling. Hidden depths."

A thunder of feet on the stairs announced CJ's arrival. She was always running late in the mornings—probably because she spent so long in the bathroom doing her makeup.

"Have you seen my black hairband?" She shot me an accusing look.

"As if I would dare borrow anything of yours without asking." My twin wasn't big on sharing. At least not me sharing her stuff. Her sharing mine was apparently just the natural order of things.

"Good morning, darling daddy, I hope you slept well," said

Dad, watching her bang around the kitchen getting breakfast.

She snorted, but dropped a kiss on the top of his head before flopping into the seat next to his. "Morning."

She, at least, wasn't holding the move against him. She'd been hanging out to get to the big city for years.

Breakfast was at the small round table in the meals area off the kitchen. The dining room was still piled with the last boxes from the move. After two weeks, the unpacking was nearly done, but there were always a few odds and ends it was hard to find a home for in a new place. Like photographs, or Christmas decorations. Or our baby clothes that Mum had been carting around for the last seventeen years and ten houses. Every time we moved she and Dad went toe-to-toe about throwing them out. Again.

"Have you seen it since we moved in?" I asked.

"Wore it on Wednesday," she mumbled around a mouthful of cereal.

"Well, I haven't got it. Besides, you're only allowed to wear accessories in school colours."

She rolled her eyes. "Yeah, right. Like I'm going to wear ribbons in a lovely shade of cat vomit."

"Caramel, please, Crystal," said Mum, suddenly tuning back into the conversation. "Not cat vomit."

"Whatever. I liked our old uniform better. The blue matched my eyes."

Mine too, but that was about the only thing we had in common—we both had Dad's blue eyes. Most people couldn't believe it when we told them we were twins. CJ was about ten centimetres taller and three cup sizes bigger, so everyone assumed she was my big sister. She could easily have passed for twenty, though we'd just turned seventeen.

Me, I'd gotten my height from Dad—which was to say, I had none. CJ not only had Mum's height, but she'd gotten her beautiful sleek dark hair too, not to mention the skin that tanned golden-brown the minute she even thought about going outside. She looked like a younger, blue-eyed version of Mum, whereas everyone could tell at a glance I was Dad's daughter—short, with pale freckled skin that never *ever* tanned, and a mass of orange-coloured steel wool that passed for hair.

The uniform of our new school was a gross mustard brown, but it looked good on CJ. Everything did. Somehow it made her skin glow even more golden, and the blue of her eyes fairly leapt out of her face. In the same dress, I just looked washed out—also pretty common, given that my skin was so pale the veins in my arms stood out like a road map.

"Well, you know what they say," Dad said. "A change is as good as a holiday."

I shot him a look sharp enough to cut him to ribbons. Him and his stupid sayings. "Probably the people that say that haven't moved *quite* as many times as we have. I don't need any more holidays like that, thanks very much."

Mum's face was an odd mixture of sympathy and guilt. "I know you haven't been very happy about this move," she began.

"This move? When have I been happy about any of them? Would it be so much to ask if we could just stay in one place for more than two seconds at a time?"

This was our fourth high school, and I was getting kind of sick of making new friends. It hardly seemed worth the effort any more. I'd just start to get comfortable, then Mum and Dad's stupid job would uproot us and dump us on the other side of the country. Again. They worked for the military, some top-secret hush-hush thing.

"I promise you this is the last one for a while," she said.

Like that was supposed to be comforting. "How long is a while exactly? Six months? A year?"

"I'd tell you," said Dad, "but then I'd have to kill you."

I rolled my eyes. Like I hadn't heard *that* one before.

"That kind of information is classified, Violet," Mum said. "Curiosity killed the cat, you know."

Yeah, I did know, because she'd been telling me that since I was knee-high to a grasshopper. It was one of her favourite ways of shutting down a discussion.

"Doesn't your bus come soon?" Dad asked, one eye on the clock.

In Townsville we'd lived close enough to walk to school, but not any more. Everything in Sydney was bigger, further away, and more crowded. Welcome to the big city.

"Yeah." Guess that was the end of *that* conversation. It made me crazy how they'd never give you a straight answer if it involved their stupid work. I stomped into the kitchen to pack my bag.

"We might be late home tonight," Mum said, changing the subject with her usual skill. "There's lasagne in the freezer if you get hungry."

"Don't worry about us." CJ crammed in the last of her breakfast and grabbed her school bag. "We'll be fine. Come on, Vile. You don't want to be late in your second week, do you? Might make a bad impression."

"I'm only ever late if I wait for *you*, Cryssie."

'Bye, Violet. Have a good day." Mum was the only person who called me Violet. She called CJ Crystal too—she said she couldn't see the sense in giving someone a perfectly good name and then never using it.

I shoved my lunch in my bag without replying. The chances of having a good day were pretty damn low, all things considered, though I doubt she really cared.

I looked back as we reached the door. Mum had turned the TV back on to the news channel. Well, that was a first. Was the girl in the glass coffin really that interesting? It was probably just some stupid advertising stunt.

Chapter Two

Ashleigh Redmond was waiting at the bus stop, and she hugged CJ as if it had been three years since she'd last seen her, instead of only yesterday. I only got a grunt, but that didn't bother me. I'd seen enough of the Ashleighs of the world to know the type. Appearances were everything to girls like that, and since CJ was the most beautiful girl she'd ever seen, they were clearly destined to become Best Friends Forever.

Ashleigh's friends, all as bubble-headed as herself, clustered around CJ like bees to nectar, and she was soon knee-deep in a conversation that seemed to be mostly about the best colour bikini to show off your tan. CJ, of course, had an opinion on that—CJ had an opinion on everything—but I stood off to one side and tried not to yawn. Bikinis and my skin type just didn't mix. Nobody needed third-degree burns on their stomach.

Eventually CJ noticed I was doing my loner thing again and tried to get me to join in. "Hey, Vi—the girls are going bikini shopping on Saturday. Want to come?"

Ashleigh shot me a look that said clearer than words *over my dead body and why does someone like CJ even have a sister like you?*

"Sure." Even to impress CJ Ashleigh couldn't fake any enthusiasm. I'd heard more emotion from robots. "That would be great."

I thought about winding her up but it just wasn't worth the aggravation. "Maybe some other time."

"Suit yourself." Ashleigh didn't bother hiding her relief.

The bus arrived and we piled on. Naturally Ashleigh's crowd sat down the back with the cool kids. She took the seat next to CJ, and shot me a look of triumph. She was like a dog peeing on my sister to mark her territory. I shrugged and sat in front of them. Did she think just because we were twins we always had to be together?

I passed the time staring out the window, letting their mindless chatter swirl around me. All of them were in a frenzy about the Year 12 formal next week. The after party was everyone's favourite topic, closely followed by dresses, hair, and makeup, plus which boys were going with which girls.

"You're lucky you came when you did," Ashleigh said to CJ, "otherwise you might have missed the whole thing!"

Yep. What a shame *that* would have been—no chance to celebrate the end of school for a bunch of people in the year above me that I'd never met. Colour me devastated. But a helpful office lady had pointed out to Mum that the day we enrolled was the last chance to pay for the formal, so we were all paid up and ready to rock.

"Did you manage to find a dress yet? You poor thing, only having two weeks to shop! I had fittings for months. Wait until you see it. It's so beautiful!"

"I'm sure I'll find something. Maybe we can look this weekend."

"Oh, yes! I know the perfect shop, it sells these gorgeous labels …"

That was about when I zoned out and stared out the window. That was another difference between me and my so-not-identical twin. She loved shopping; I hated it.

The houses rolled past, all jammed up tight against their neighbours on their tiny little blocks. There weren't many big trees, though everyone had neat gardens and cute little brick walls. That was the trouble with new developments—no trees. No history. Everything looked like it had just been plonked down yesterday, and could just as easily disappear tomorrow. A bit like me, really.

"Did you ask your parents?" Ashleigh's voice was a whiny little buzz-saw, slicing into my thoughts again.

"Oh, they won't mind," CJ said airily. "We go to lots of parties."

Maybe in Townsville, where we knew everyone. She hadn't mentioned any party to Mum and Dad that I'd heard of. What were they talking about?

"Fantastic!" Ashleigh gushed. "He put it on Facebook. Everyone's going. You should see his place—it's a mansion! He's got a pool and a jacuzzi and like *ten* bedrooms! It's going to be awesome."

I swung round and gave my sister a hard look. "Whose party's this?"

"Some guy called Josh."

Ashleigh laughed. "Some guy? Only the hottest guy in the

school. Josh Johnson." She got this gooey look on her face when she said his name, like it tasted good. "He's the school captain, in case you haven't noticed."

I hadn't, but then I wasn't in the habit of paying much attention in school assemblies. I don't know when else I could have discovered who the school captains were. It's not as if they walked around with flashing signs above their heads.

At the next stop a dark-haired girl got on. She was in Year 11, like us, but I didn't know her name. The bus was pretty full that morning, but the seat next to me was empty, so she tramped down the aisle and stood swaying next to me, a friendly smile on her face.

"Mind if I sit here?"

I shrugged. Why did people ask questions like that? She was obviously going to sit down whatever I said.

"I'm Sona. You're new, aren't you?"

"Yep."

Her skin was a deep warm brown. Next to hers, my arm was so pale it practically glowed.

"What's your name?"

She was certainly persistent. Either that or my *leave me alone* vibes needed work. "Vi."

"Vi? Is that short for something?"

"Yeah, but we don't need to go there."

"It can't be that bad. Did you know there's a girl in our year called Dream? Her parents must have hated her."

She was grinning at me, ready to share the joke. I sighed. Here we go again, making friends at a new school. Did I really want to go through this again? What was the point, when we'd probably be moving on in a year or less, whatever Mum promised? But she had such a friendly face, it seemed rude to just ignore her. "Parents are weird sometimes."

"I know, right? Mine named me after some Indian actress."

"Are you Indian?"

She laughed. "Me personally? No. True-blue Aussie. Mum and Dad are. They came out about twenty years ago and I was born here. My grandparents back in Delhi think it's a scandal that I can't speak a word of Hindi. Every time they visit they jabber away at me and then get shocked all over again when I don't answer. Poor Dad gets into so much trouble."

She had the biggest brown eyes I'd ever seen, and now they glinted with mischief. I kind of liked her, but who knew if we'd even be sitting the HSC at this school? And that was only a year away. I'd lost count of the number of times I'd gotten attached to people, only to have them ripped away by Mum and Dad's stupid jobs.

I looked out the window, hoping she'd get the hint, but apparently she didn't do hints.

"Is that your sister?" She jerked her head at CJ.

"Yep."

"She in Year 12?"

"No, Year 11, same as me. We're twins."

Her eyebrows shot up. "Right. And she's the ugly twin?"

Now that sounded like my kind of person. A smile twitched at my lips. "Obviously."

She grinned. "Sucks to be you, huh?"

I liked the way she thought. "Got it in one."

"Eh, could be worse. My brother's at Sydney Uni, studying

to be a doctor. My parents think the sun shines out of his butt. *And* he speaks Hindi. All I hear is *why can't you be more like your brother, Sona?*"

"Bummer."

"Yeah. Hey, Zac!" Suddenly distracted, she poked a boy sitting on the other side of the aisle. "You coming to robotics club today?"

He turned around, an angry frown on his face, but when he saw who'd poked him he smiled and pulled his earphones out. "What'd you say?"

He was tall and tanned, and had brown hair that flopped in his eyes. Might be time for a haircut. If he hadn't smiled I wouldn't have looked twice, but his smile lit up his whole face, and the cutest dimple peeped out. I took a deep breath; I was a sucker for dimples.

"Are-you-coming-to-robotics-club?" Sona repeated, as if speaking to a very small and rather stupid child.

"You don't have to sound like a robot just because you're talking about robotics, you know," he said.

She pulled a face at him. "So helpful, Zac."

He threw her a mock salute. "Always happy to be of service."

His eyes slid sideways, checking me out. They were a warm, delicious brown that made me think of dark chocolate. Mmmm. Chocolate.

"So are you?"

"Sure. You?"

"As long as I get my maths homework finished at recess." She turned to me. "What about you? Are you interested in robotics?"

I shrugged. "Some."

They'd die if they saw Dad's workshop—so many tools, so many gadgets. Some of them I'd made myself. It *would* be kind of fun. Dimple-boy smiled at me, and my heart skipped a beat. *No, don't be stupid, Vi. What's the point of getting all excited about new people, even if they do share your interests? You'll only have to leave again.* But robotics … I'd never been in a robotics club before.

"When is it?" I wasn't committing to anything. Just asking.

"Lunch time." Sona grabbed my arm in excitement and squeezed. "Oh, my God! Another girl in the robotics club. Someone sensible to talk to! This is going to be so great!"

Well, *she* seemed to think I was committed. We'd see. Gently I extracted my arm as she continued to talk, flitting from subject to subject with what I was beginning to realise was her natural enthusiasm.

"Did you hear about that girl in the mountains?" she asked.

"What girl?" Guess there was no breakfast TV allowed at Zac's house.

"The one that was found in the glass coffin. It's like she's a fairytale princess, just waiting for her prince to come and wake her up. So romantic." She frowned. "Not that we approve of princesses lying around snoozing and waiting to be rescued, of course."

"Of course," Zac agreed.

Oh, my God, that dimple was *killing* me. How could a smile make such a difference to a person's face?

"What happened when she woke up?" Zac asked.

"That's just it. She hasn't. They say she's in some kind of a coma."

"So why was she lying in a coffin?"

"Nobody knows."

He folded his arms, and I couldn't help noticing the muscles move beneath his tanned skin. Sometimes it seemed as though everyone in Australia had a tan except me. And Dad, of course.

"Who puts someone in a coffin when they're in a coma? That's just sick."

You tell 'em, Zac. The world was full of weirdos.

'I know, but isn't it strange, that it's just like a fairy tale? Imagine if magic was real, and fairy tales did come true."

"I don't know if that would be so great," he said. "Don't most people in fairy tales get cooked in a witch's oven, or eaten by a giant, or something? It's not all princes and glass slippers, you know."

She screwed up her face at him. "God, Zac. My *cat* has more imagination than you."

He shrugged and slipped his earphones back in as the bus pulled up outside school. There was a thunder of feet as we piled off, and Sona waved as she walked away.

"Don't forget robotics! Lunch time in Room D27."

Maybe, maybe not. I waved back and headed for the library. Once I was out of CJ's sight I pulled her black headband out of my pocket and put it on.

Chapter Three

I hadn't lost my locker in days, and I was feeling quite proud of myself. Though small by Sydney standards, this was the biggest school I'd ever been to, and I'd been to a few. There were four massive main buildings spread out among the gum trees. Each one was built in a rectangle around a central courtyard. They were all two storeys, with a balcony-style walkway running around the inside of the top storey, so each classroom opened into the fresh air. On rainy days everyone hugged the wall trying to keep dry as rain slanted in over the railings. At least on the bottom level the overhanging walkway kept you relatively dry.

Then there was the canteen building, which also housed the change rooms and an indoor basketball court, plus half a dozen portable classrooms scattered around the grounds to accommodate the school's growth. The final building was a school hall that was only just big enough to fit all the students inside.

Lining the lower levels of all the buildings except for A block and the canteen were lockers painted in rainbow-bright colours which would have suited a preschool better than a high school, but whatever. Mine was in E block, a violent red. I was ramming my maths textbook into it at the start of lunchtime when someone opened the bright yellow one two lockers away.

"Hi again," said a deep voice.

It was Zac.

"Oh, hi." I hadn't realised his locker was so close. I'd never seen him use it before. It was one of the lower ones, and he had to crouch down, his long fringe falling forward over his eyes as he extracted something from its depths with great care. He looked so cute. Why had I ever thought he needed a haircut?

The thing seemed to have gotten stuck. "You need a hand there?"

"No, I'm fine."

He tugged, and something broke off and skittered across the concrete to finish up against my shoe. I picked it up.

"What *is* that?"

In his hands was some kind of machine, roughly egg-shaped, with three small wheels. He tucked it under one arm and slammed his locker shut with the other.

He grinned, and the dimple peeped out again. "This? It's my demented chicken."

"Really?" I handed back the little piece of metal that had fallen off. His definition of "chicken" must be fairly fluid, even allowing for the "demented" part.

"It's an automatic vacuum cleaner I'm building in robotics. You coming?" He strode off, and my legs just started following without my brain having any input at all. What happened to not making new friends? But he had such a cute butt.

Oh, well, that *was a good reason for changing your mind. Well done, Vi.*

He looked back and I felt my cheeks flush with heat. Hopefully he hadn't caught me staring.

"Slow down," I said. "Your legs are longer than mine."

He waited for me, then matched his stride to mine. *See? He's a nice guy. It's not all about the looks.*

"So tell me more about this vacuum cleaner. Why do you call it a demented chicken?"

"That was Sona's idea. It sorts small objects out from dirt, but it's still a bit wobbly. She says it looks like a chicken pecking up crumbs."

"What sort of small objects are we talking? How big?"

He grinned, and my heart did a little flip. *Oh, for God's sake, what are you, twelve? You've met cute guys before.*

"Lego-sized. My little brother keeps complaining that every time Mum vacuums he loses another piece of Lego, so I said I'd invent a vacuum cleaner to fix the problem."

"Has he tried not leaving them on the floor?"

"He's six."

"Fair enough. I guess the demented chicken is the way to go, then."

"Anything's better than stepping on bits of Lego in your bare feet."

"Ouch." I winced in sympathy. We'd never had Lego at home, being more of a Barbie household, but I'd experienced that particular treat at other people's places. Not exactly fond memories. "Remind me not to take my shoes off at your place."

Oh, God, had I really just said that? I hardly knew the guy.

Now he was going to think I wanted him to invite me over. We were walking past the canteen. Maybe I should suddenly remember I had to buy some lunch. The urge to run away nearly overwhelmed me. That telltale warmth flooded my cheeks again. Great. The truly *wonderful* thing about being so fair-skinned was that there was no hiding it when you blushed.

"Don't worry," he said. "I'll make sure to deploy the chicken before you arrive."

I could hardly look at him, but there was warmth in those dark brown eyes.

"Scout's honour," he added, holding up his free hand as if taking an oath.

There was something suspicious about that grin now.

"Were you ever a Boy Scout?"

"Do we really have to go into the details?"

I laughed. I liked a guy with a sense of humour. "You weren't, were you?"

"Maybe not. But I bet I would have made a great one. All that knot-tying and cookie-selling and ..."

"And?"

"And ... whatever else they do. Okay, so I don't know much about it."

"I believe they go camping." We left the dazzling sunshine of the playground and entered D block. A large tropical-looking garden sprawled in the centre of the courtyard, basking in the spring sunshine. There was an almost identical one in B block, which had caused some confusion in my first couple of days last week. "And hiking."

Someone was hanging over the railing of the upper floor,

overlooking the courtyard. All the buildings were like this, with open-air walkways outside the classrooms instead of enclosed hallways. That someone began to wave madly when she caught sight of us. Sona.

"Hey, you brought her!" she called to Zac. "That's great!"

We started to climb the stairs, our footsteps echoing in the empty stairwell. "Is she always so …?"

"Enthusiastic? Well, she *is* the only girl in the club, and some of the guys are … how shall I put this? Great at robotics, not so great at conversation. And Sona does like to have a chat."

"Yeah, I'd noticed that."

"You do like robotics, don't you? You're not just coming because she pressured you?"

With those dark eyes full of concern, it suddenly seemed impossible to tell him that I'd only planned to come to check it out. As we reached the classroom I reassured him that I loved robotics.

"In that case, welcome to the robotics club." He took my hand in a firm handshake, then his solemn expression dissolved into a grin. That dimple peeped out again.

Sona threw an arm around my shoulders. "Come on in and meet the gang."

I went with her, my hand still tingling from Zac's touch.

I got out the lasagne at six. Mum and Dad weren't home but I couldn't wait any longer. I was starving.

"Dad makes the world's best lasagne," CJ said.

I would have agreed, but I was too busy shovelling it into my face to talk.

"Did you leave some for Mum and Dad?" she asked.

I wiped my mouth. "If you wanted to play Mother, you could have defrosted and served it yourself, instead of lying on the lounge watching TV. It's a bit late to be concerned when you've already eaten half of it."

She waved her hand. "Dad usually takes care of it."

"Yeah, it must be so nice to be you, always being waited on."

She considered me for a moment, dark head tipped to one side, then sighed. "You always get like this when we move. The minute I open my mouth you jump straight down my throat. Could you *please* try to remember that moving wasn't my idea?"

"I do *not* always get like this." Even to me, that sounded defensive. "And I'm not *like* anything."

"Starting over sucks. I get that. You can always hang out with me and my friends if you get stuck."

I bit back a nasty comment about her taste in friends. She was trying to be nice. "Thanks."

"So how did it go today?"

I shrugged. "My physics teacher doesn't know his arse from his ankle, but otherwise it was all right. I joined the robotics club at lunch."

"Full of boys with no social skills?"

"Actually there's one girl. Sona. She sat next to me on the bus. She seems okay."

"The Indian girl with the beautiful hair?"

Trust CJ to notice that. My sister wasn't *at all* obsessed with personal appearance.

"Yeah."

"Her plait is so long she was actually sitting on it!" Her eyes filled with a brief longing. "Ashleigh says she's just a brainiac, though."

I bristled on my new friend's behalf. "Oh, well, if *Ashleigh* says! Guess I'd better dump her then, if Little Miss Forked Tongue doesn't approve."

"Oh, for God's sake, don't be so prickly. I didn't say I believed her." She pushed her empty plate away and leaned back with a satisfied sigh. "What are you going to wear to the party tomorrow night?"

"The one the school captain's throwing? John or James or whatever his name is?"

"Josh. Josh Johnson."

Uh-oh. Her voice had that same sickly sweetness as Ashleigh's had when she said his name.

"Who said I'm going? The guy's a jerk. Why would you want to go to his party?"

"Because it's a *party*? You know, somewhere you go to have *fun*? And you need to get out and meet people so you can stop being so bitter and twisted. I heard he's going to have a keg."

"Yeah, right. As if his parents would let him have a keg when the party's going to be full of under-eighteens."

She grinned. "That's the best part. His parents are in Europe. Anyway, who says he's a jerk?"

I rolled my eyes. "Didn't you see him this morning, capering round that statue like a caveman who's just discovered fire?"

There was a large, vaguely humanoid but very ugly statue in front of the admin block. It had been donated by a past Year 12 as a farewell present to the school. Obviously they'd all hated their time at school and the statue was their idea of revenge. This morning we arrived to discover the current Year 12 had wrapped the thing in toilet paper and sprayed it with whipped cream as part of their muck-up week celebrations. It looked like a giant misshapen mummy and smelled as rank as you'd expect from the combination of dairy and hot sun.

Josh and a group of his mates had been posing in front of it taking selfies and carrying on like three-year-olds. They couldn't have been prouder of themselves if they'd invented a cure for cancer—instead of which they'd left a giant mess for a bunch of unfortunate Year 7s to clean up.

As we'd streamed in from the bus, the group had caught sight of CJ, in her extra short uniform. I swear she took the hems up when Mum wasn't looking. They started whistling and shouting at her.

"Where've you been all my life, babe?" Josh called.

So original.

CJ had ignored him, but I could tell from the way she tossed her hair over her shoulder that she liked the attention.

"Don't break my heart, gorgeous!" He clutched at his chest with great melodrama, while his friends whooped. "Come to my party on Saturday and I'll show you a good time!"

Yep. Those pick-up lines definitely needed work. I guess a good-looking guy like him didn't usually need to try too hard. He was your classic blonde-haired, blue-eyed surfer dude. There wouldn't be too many girls knocking him back.

"Well," CJ said now, "at least the caveman has good taste in women."

"You mean because he likes you? What does that prove? Everyone that's got a pulse likes you. Hell, I bet there are even dead people who like you."

She snorted. "Gee, thanks. Just call me queen of the zombies. You make it sound like a crime to look good."

"Please. Not the 'it's not my fault I'm gorgeous' speech again."

Tall. Gorgeous. Popular. Everything I wasn't. Smart too. Not that I wasn't smart. It was just that somehow she often seemed to get just one little mark more than me in assignments, though I worked just as hard. Scientific studies had proven that beautiful people were better liked than us plain Janes. I couldn't help feeling that science was on to something there.

She stuck out her already full bottom lip. "Well, it's not. I just happened to win the genetic lottery. Nothing to do with me."

"Fine. Whatever."

There was no point trying to persuade her that her charmed life really was extraordinary. She'd gotten the star treatment from everyone since the day we were born. To her, being the special one was just the normal state of existence.

"You know, you're not exactly ugly, Vi. Lots of girls would kill for hair your colour. If you tried to talk about things that normal people are interested in once in a while, you'd have lots of friends."

"I don't need to be worshipped by the Ashleigh Redmonds of the world." Who wanted a bunch of airheads following them around? "I have plenty of friends."

"Oh, yeah? Like who?"

"Sona," I said. "And there are heaps of nice guys in the robotics club."

One in particular. She didn't need to know about Zac yet,

though. Maybe I'd imagined that look in his eyes when he'd smiled at me. Too soon to be sharing secrets with my twin.

"Right. Well, you have fun with the nerds in the robotics club."

Whatever else she'd been about to say was cut off by the phone ringing. While she flounced off to answer it, I put the plates in the dishwasher then settled myself on the lounge to watch TV. Friday night was a night for unwinding, not studying.

CJ came back in and dropped into an armchair. "What are you watching?"

"Nothing. Just some quiz show."

"That was Mum on the phone. She said they won't be back until Sunday night."

Maybe I could spend the whole weekend not studying too. "Did you ask her about the party?"

She threw me a pitying look. "Are you serious? Why would I ask her? They're *away*, doofus. We can do what we like."

I turned back to the TV. I was sick of arguing with CJ, but that didn't feel right. It was one thing to slack off and not study when your parents were away. Sneaking off to a party you knew they wouldn't approve of was a whole 'nother ball game, and guess who'd get the blame when they found out. Not perfect little CJ.

A newsbreak came on and CJ picked up a magazine with a bored sigh. They replayed the footage of the girl in the glass coffin.

"They're still calling it the Sleeping Beauty case," I said. "Dad would be so cranky."

"Why?"

"Because Sleeping Beauty fell asleep for a hundred years in her own bed in a castle, surrounded by all her sleeping family and servants. Remember? And the hedge of thorns grew up to hide the castle? It was Snow White who fell into a death-like sleep after she ate the poisoned apple. The seven dwarves thought she was dead but they couldn't bear to bury her, so they left her in a glass coffin in the woods, then the prince came by and kissed her awake."

"And Dad knew the difference? I thought the only things that interested him were his gadgets."

"Apparently not."

The girl was still in her weird coma, and no one knew how or why she'd ended up in that coffin. Basically nothing new had happened, so they were just showing a couple of official-looking black cars arriving at the Three Sisters carpark and talking about the ongoing investigation.

A face appeared at a car window. Only a brief flash.

"Was that—?"

"What?" CJ looked up but they'd cut to another story.

"Nothing. Never mind."

It couldn't have been Dad.

Chapter Four

Ashleigh's dad dropped five of us at the party. A lot of the Year 12s could drive, but most of us in Year 11 were still on our Ls, so we had to suffer the shame of being dropped off by mummy or daddy like five-year-olds, while the cool kids turned up with their own wheels.

I'd been kind of hoping we wouldn't be able to get there, but of course CJ organised a lift. We were barely speaking. She'd insisted I needed to get out of my shell and meet some new people, but the thing had *disaster waiting to happen* written all over it. I was only there to keep an eye on her, because guess who would have to explain it all to Mum and Dad later if she did something stupid? My sister had many fine qualities, but common sense wasn't one of them.

We could hear the music before the car even turned into the street, the bass beat throbbing over the dark neighbourhood. The house was lit up like a Christmas tree, and it was *huge*.

"Nice little place," CJ said as we walked up the drive. Even the driveway was over the top, swirling round a central fountain in a giant circle, as if any minute they were expecting a fleet of stretch limos to turn up and disgorge a pack of movie stars.

We followed the excited PARTY THIS WAY!! signs around the side of the house and through a tall gate into the backyard, where a scene from a Hollywood movie met our eyes. A tennis court strung with fairy lights doubled as a massive dance floor, and a live DJ was set up there, pumping out something that had about half of Year 12 dancing. Across an immaculate lawn was an enormous pool, complete with palm trees and a waterfall. At the moment it had a net strung across its middle, and a boisterous game of volleyball was going on. The other half of Year 12 was watching, alternating jeers with encouragement.

The deck at the back of the house was covered in sun lounges. Taking pride of place in the centre was a large jacuzzi full of girls holding champagne glasses. My heart sank a little, and then I noticed the garbage bins full of ice lined up along the edge of the deck and it hit rock bottom. I could tell from here that there wasn't much soft drink in those suckers.

"This is a bad idea," I said, but I might as well have saved my breath.

"This is *great*," CJ breathed, her eyes shining as she took it all in.

"Hey, girls!" a voice called from the pool.

Josh heaved himself out of the pool and strode across the lawn dripping. Behind him his friends groaned and called out, "aw, come on man, we were winning!", but he ignored them.

Damn, but he was hot. Drops of water gleamed on pecs so hard you could have bounced a ping-pong ball off them. He wore boardies slung low on his hips, and the six-pack had to be seen to be believed. He could have made his fortune as an underwear model.

The collective IQ of our little group plummeted as he approached. They all looked at him with one thing on their minds—and didn't he know it, strutting like he was already on the catwalk.

"Stop drooling," I hissed at CJ. "It's undignified."

"Shut. Up."

"Glad you could make it," he said to CJ. His gaze slid past me, standing next to her, and dismissed me as unimportant. He turned a megawatt smile on my twin.

"Nice party," she said, keeping her cool. True, he was gorgeous, but CJ had had her pick of gorgeous plenty of times before. Indeed, she assumed it was her right. He might find it harder than he thought to win her over.

"Thanks. Help yourselves to drinks, ladies. Whatever your little hearts desire." He waved an expansive hand towards the ranks of alcohol-laden bins. He stepped closer to CJ and dropped his voice. "Join me in the spa later?"

"I didn't bring my bikini."

His smile broadened. "Even better."

That set the other girls twittering like starlings. With a little wave he strode back to the pool and dove into the middle of the volleyball game.

I glared at his smarmy blonde head bobbing in the water. "Let's dance."

"In a minute," CJ said. "I want to get something to drink first."

"Soft drink."

"Oh, lighten up, Vi. Live a little."

She swept the whole flock of them off with her. I watched them helping themselves from one of the bins and turned away, almost getting knocked down in the process by a big guy who was weaving unsteadily across the grass.

"You all right?" I asked.

He stared at me, still swaying. He seemed to be having trouble focusing on my face. "Don't feel so good."

And then he doubled over and heaved his guts all over my sandals.

"Oh, *great!*" I jumped away, but it was too late. I could feel it, hot and disgusting, oozing between my toes. I kicked off my sandals and wiped my feet frantically on the grass, ignoring the guy, who was now on his knees. The smell was horrendous. My own stomach heaved in protest. There was nothing quite like the stink of fresh vomit.

I hurried over to the pool, leaving my sandals where they dropped. I was *not* touching them again. I'd rather buy new ones. Standing on the top step with water up to my ankles I watched a little chunk of carrot float away. Guess I wouldn't be going swimming either.

Barefoot, I padded across the grass toward the tennis court dance floor. This was going to be a long night. No Sona to keep me company. Her parents didn't let her go to parties unless they knew the family well. She hadn't even bothered asking.

I scanned the crowd jumping and heaving to the music. As usual, it was mainly girls dancing while the guys stood around the edges looking self-conscious, though this time with added booze, which helped with the self-consciousness, I guess. Looked like it had worked its magic already on a few guys who were in the thick of it, bobbing around with beers in hand. One girl sagged against the wire fencing of the tennis court, looking like a rag doll that had been dropped there. Her friend had a sympathetic hand on her back. Another chunder in the making, by the looks of it. Geez, it was only nine o'clock. How drunk could you get in an hour? More than a few of these people were obviously working hard at it.

I caught sight of a familiar figure lounging against the fence on the other side of the dancers. Zac smiled as I made my way across to him. He had a can in his hand, but it proved to be only Coke.

"You not drinking?" I asked. "Everyone else seems determined to get smashed."

"Nah. I'm driving. Got my Ps last month. Dad would kill me if I damaged the car."

I stared meaningfully at him.

"Apart from the fact it's illegal to drink on your Ps, of course," he added hastily.

"Of course. Glad to see someone's being responsible."

"Can I get you something to drink? Something soft and responsible, I mean?" The dimple peeked out. He was so cute when he smiled. Shame he was so tall, though—without shoes I felt like a midget standing next to him. I'd need to stand on a box to kiss him.

"No, thanks." *Stop thinking about kissing him! You hardly know the guy.* "I'm going to dance for a while. Want to join me?"

He glanced down at my bare feet. "I think your feet will be safer if I just stay here and hold up the fence a bit longer. Dancing's not really my thing."

Probably safer for my libido too. "Suit yourself."

I pushed my way through the press of hot bodies until I found CJ and her group. They were all swigging from bottles of cooler as they danced.

"Having fun?" CJ asked. She had to shout to be heard over the thumping music.

"Yeah, it's great. Some arsehole threw up on me."

Her pretty nose wrinkled. "Hope he has the world's biggest hangover tomorrow."

I grinned. He probably would. Him and half the people here.

The DJ was good. He kept the rhythm going, one good dance track after another. I shook my head when he put on YMCA, but what the hell. Sometimes it's fun to be daggy. I yelled the chorus and did the stupid arm movements along with everyone else. I even caught a glimpse of Zac throwing his arms around on the edge of the crowd, which made me laugh. He was right; he couldn't dance, but even guys who can't dance can manage to make like an air traffic controller. That song was just irresistible.

I danced my way through the crowd to his side.

"Having fun?" I shouted.

"Sure!" The other guys from the robotics club were staring at him as if he'd grown an extra head, but he didn't seem to care. Now that he'd decided to dance, he threw himself into it, and we were both laughing by the time the song finished.

Something slow came on to replace it, and all around us couples formed out of the crowd. Zac opened his arms and I moved into them, mouth suddenly dry. The world narrowed to the smell of his skin and the feel of his body warm against mine. My head came up to his shoulder. Maybe I wouldn't need a box after all. I hid my hot face against his chest so he wouldn't see me blushing, and listened to the steady beat of his heart. His arms tightened around me.

Someone behind me dropped their can, and beer splashed everyone's legs. We sprang apart.

"You okay?"

I missed the feel of him already, but the song was ending and the moment had gone.

"Yeah. I'll just go and … ah … find something to wipe this off with."

I left him there and headed for the deck, past a girl on a sun lounge who seemed to have passed out. The party was getting louder and more frantic. Drunken shouts and laughter rose over the pounding music. I checked my watch. Eleven thirty. How much longer till the neighbours started calling the police?

CJ and Ashleigh staggered up the stairs to the deck, both unsteady on their feet.

"We're going to find the ladies'," CJ said. "Wanna come?"

"No thanks."

They wobbled their way into the house, arms around each other, probably for support, given the way they were walking. Note to self: if getting drunk is on the agenda, don't wear heels. I grabbed somebody's towel and dried the backs of my legs, then took a soft drink. All that dancing had given me a thirst. I looked around for Zac, and found him chatting to a couple of the other guys from the robotics club. He glanced up toward the deck but didn't see me. Maybe when CJ got back I'd ask him to give us a ride home. I didn't like the way she was swaying.

Time passed as I sipped my drink and watched the party swirl around me. Should I go back to Zac? It was just a dance. It probably hadn't meant anything, and I didn't want to look like I was chasing him. Because I wasn't, however hard my heart pounded when he smiled. Definitely not.

Josh was in the spa now with a group of Year 12 girls who were squealing like five-year-olds in a jumping castle. No one was swimming in the pool any more, though a couple of guys were floating around on lilos drinking beer while their friends shot them with water cannons from the edge. The robotics club seemed to have called a meeting in the shadows behind the palm trees—half a dozen of them had their heads together over there, including Zac, all talking intently. Probably about something involving circuitry.

I finished my drink and began to get restless. It was ages since CJ and Ashleigh had disappeared inside. Surely it couldn't take that long to go to the toilet. Time to send out the search party.

I stepped into an open-plan kitchen/living area that was nearly as big as our whole house. Acres of white tiles stretched away in front of me. Not as clean now as they probably usually were, though. There were a few spills and I felt sticky patches beneath my bare feet. Empty cans lay everywhere. One guy dropped a cigarette butt on the floor as I watched and left it there, grinding it out with a lazy foot. Pig. Another time I might have had a go at him, but right then I was focused on finding my sister.

There were plenty of people in the house too, and the noise level was almost as high as outside. Someone had turned on the stereo, and now Katy Perry at full volume competed with whatever the DJ was playing on the tennis court. The lights were dimmed or not on at all in many of the rooms. I pushed through the crowds, stepping over trash and people and a few trashed people, searching for CJ's dark head in the gloom.

I ran into one of Ashleigh's friends.

"Have you seen CJ?" I had to shout it three times before she could hear me, but then she shook her head.

I covered the whole ground floor. There was white carpet in the formal lounge room. Well, it had started out white. I shuddered at the state it was in. Josh Johnson's parents were *not* going to be happy with their little boy when they got back from Europe.

At the bottom of the stairs I hesitated. Maybe I should go back outside and check? We could have missed each other in the crowds. It didn't feel right to go poking around people's bedrooms.

But the bathrooms would be up there. I shrugged and started up the grand curving stairs, feeling like an extra from *Gone with the Wind*. These people had serious money.

There were party-goers sitting on the stairs too. I had to step over them on the way. At the top the sound of girlish laughter led me down the hallway to the master suite, where a group of girls from my English class were primping in front of an outsize mirror in what was probably known as the "powder room" or something posh like that. Or maybe "the room for people who really like staring at themselves". There were mirrors on every wall.

"Have you guys seen CJ?" I asked.

"Sorry."

I went the other way, and found the queue for the main bathroom.

"Anyone seen CJ?" I asked. "Or Ashleigh Redmond?"

"Ashleigh just went downstairs," said one girl. "She was looking for CJ too."

Damn. Time to try the bedrooms.

The first door I came to was locked. I pounded on the door, yelling to be heard above the noise from downstairs.

"CJ! Are you in there?"

"Get lost!" yelled a girl's voice. Not CJ's. I moved on.

The second door I tried was *not* locked, but definitely should have been. I caught a glimpse of naked bodies before I slammed the door shut.

"Sorry!"

I could feel heat rising in my face. *Please let me find CJ soon.*

I opened the next door more cautiously, but the people inside were fully clothed—and one of them was CJ. Unfortunately the other was Josh Johnson, and this was evidently his bedroom. Though why any boy his age needed a king-sized bed, I didn't know. And now he was lounging on it with my drunk sister. Colour me unimpressed.

I shut the door behind me and folded my arms over my chest. "Time to go home, CJ."

"Can't go now, Vi. Josh's got a special drink for me."

Josh held up a bottle. "Absinthe. The green fairy. Fancy some?"

"That's the one with crushed beetles or something equally gross. The one that kills people."

He poured a small glass and held it out to CJ. "Not any more. That was years ago."

Something about him seemed off. Maybe he was drunker

than he looked. An odd smell lingered in the room—not marijuana, something sweeter. It reminded me of making toffee as a kid and overcooking it until it burnt and stuck to the pan. Could they have been smoking something?

I didn't like the avid way he watched as CJ tipped her head back and downed the glass in one go. His eyes shone like a cat's in the dim room. Somehow he seemed more adult, more dangerous now than he had outside.

"Whoa!" She swallowed a cough and shook her head. "That's got a real kick to it."

I advanced on the bed. "Okay, now you've had your drink, let's go."

"So soon?" She lay back against Josh and pouted. Her pupils were huge. There was hardly any blue left in her eyes. "The party's just getting started."

"That's right, gorgeous," said Josh. "And now that you've drunk up like a good girl, I'm going to give you a present."

I bristled. "No offence, but she doesn't want anything *you've* got."

He smiled, idly stroking CJ's bare shoulder. It wasn't a friendly smile. "Saying 'no offence' doesn't stop an insult from being offensive, you know."

I smiled back, poisonously sweet. "I know."

"I'm happy to give you a present too. In fact, I know just the thing."

I pretended to consider. "Gosh, let me think … *no*."

CJ made impatient shooing motions at me. "Go away, Vi. You're spoiling the fun."

"Yes, go away, Vi, there's a good girl."

His tone was lazy, but there was a dangerous glitter in his eye. My opinion of him, never flattering, hit rock bottom. He'd invited a girl he hardly knew, who was obviously drunk, into his bedroom and now he was filling her with more alcohol. What a douche. He looked so smug, with CJ's woozy head pillowed on his shoulder, stretched out on his bed like king of the heap. As if he just had to snap his fingers and everything he wanted would fall into his lap. As if I was powerless to stop him.

Leave my sister alone with this creep? I don't *think* so.

I pulled out my phone and snapped a photo. "Smile!"

CJ sat up. "What are you doing?"

"Taking a picture to send to Mum. I'm sure she's still awake. She'd love to see what her darling little Crystal Jane gets up to when she's away."

"Vi!"

I've never seen anyone get off a bed so fast. She made a drunken lunge for the phone, but I danced away, back to the door.

"You wouldn't!"

I grinned. "Actually, I think I would."

I took off down the hall and back down the staircase, CJ in hot pursuit. Well, she tried hot pursuit, but it wasn't up to her usual standards. For one thing, she was wearing heels and I was barefoot. For another, and more importantly, I was stone cold sober and she—well, let's just say she was not in a good way. I looked back as I got to the bottom of the stairs just in time to see her trip over the leg of someone sitting on a step and nearly go arse over apex. She managed to catch herself, but it wasn't dignified. She sprawled against the bannister, legs every which way. The onlookers thought it was the funniest thing they'd seen all night.

That's right, you jerks, laugh at the poor drunk girl. I bet you'd think it was hilarious if she fell and broke her neck.

I waited for her to limp her way to my side. She winced every time she put her weight on her right foot.

"What the hell is your problem? You've ruined everything!"

"You've got to be kidding me. That guy was using you, CJ." I was glad to be out of there. That nasty little grin of his had been weirding me out.

"Don't send that text." She made a drunken grab for my phone.

"As if I would. Where are you hurt?"

"My ankle."

"Okay. Let's get out of here. Lean on me."

The fact that she didn't argue told me she was hurt worse than she was letting on. Her anger seemed to have fizzled out already. We went back to the deck, me looking for a spot to park her while I went to find Zac. My gaze roved across the jacuzzi and I did a double take.

Josh was in the spa, with the same group of Year 12 girls as before. Cuddled up all cozy and bubbly. What the—? He couldn't have got there so fast. He'd been lying on a bed fully dressed upstairs a moment ago, and he hadn't passed us on the way down. Yet here he was, comfortably ensconced in the arms of half a dozen other girls in the spa.

For that matter, hadn't I seen him in the spa with these same girls just before I went looking for CJ? Yet his hair was dry when I saw him moments later in the bedroom with my sister—and they certainly looked as though they'd been there a while.

"Has Josh got a twin?" I'd never heard he did, but it seemed the only explanation.

CJ followed the direction of my gaze and frowned. You could almost hear the gears grinding as she tried to think through a haze of alcohol, but she got there in the end.

"How did he get there so fast?"

"Don't know."

Didn't care either. I'd be happy never to see the creepy bastard again. The important thing was to get CJ home. I spotted the dark head I was looking for lurking by the palm trees with the robotics crew.

"Wait here," I told CJ. She leaned against the railing of the deck, her face paler than usual. Her ankle must be pretty bad.

I hurried across the lawn and tugged on Zac's arm.

"Oh, hi!" He grinned down at me. For once the dimple failed to work its magic on me. My emotions were too mixed up between anger and worry over CJ. "Come to join the social outcasts?"

"Actually, I need to ask you a favour."

Instantly the grin was replaced by concern. "Sure. What's up?"

"My sister's hurt herself." I didn't mention she was also falling-down drunk. He'd probably be able to smell that for himself once he got close. "Would you mind giving us a ride home?"

"No problem. Where is she?"

Thank God not all guys were like Josh Johnson. We went back to CJ. Zac raised his eyebrows at me when he saw the condition she was in, but said nothing. He let her lean on him and ended up half-carrying her out to his car.

When we had her settled in the back seat, he turned to me. "If she throws up in my dad's car, you are going to *die*."

"I promise she won't." I got in the front seat next to him. "Or at least, if she does, I'll clean it up so beautifully your dad will never know. Scout's honour."

He laughed. "Oh, very nice. Were you ever a Scout?"

"No."

"Thought not. Strangely, I find I'm not reassured."

It was only a couple of kilometres. I sat in the dark and watched him drive, wishing that our house was further away, that I could sit here with him all night. His long, clever fingers held the wheel firmly, and he made sure there were no sudden bumps or stops, so we made it home with the contents of CJ's stomach still where they were supposed to be.

As soon as we pulled up CJ flung the back door open and staggered out.

Hand on my own door, I turned to him. "Thanks so much. I owe you one."

"Do you need help getting her inside?" He leaned closer. Something in his eyes made my palms break out in a sudden nervous sweat.

"No, we're good." CJ would just have to manage without me for a moment. My hand fell away from the door handle. I couldn't have gotten out of that car if I tried. Was he going to—?

"I had fun." He reached out and brushed a corkscrew curl out of my face. "Maybe we should do it again some time."

"Go dancing, you mean?"

The dimple peeked out, and my heart did the by-now

familiar flip-flop. His hand settled on the back of my seat, so close.

"I was thinking more like movies or something. Less potential for embarrassment. And for stepping on your feet."

That hand was playing with my hair again. A shiver ran through me.

"I'd like that."

His mouth was closer. I couldn't take my eyes off it. Gravity seemed to have changed direction, because I was falling into him, and I didn't want to stop. His breath was warm on my face, his lips so close …

And then CJ convulsed like a cat with a hairball and spewed into the gutter in front of the car.

"Oh, my God." We sprang apart, and I flung open the door. "Sorry. I've got to go."

My heart was still pounding, and I felt like a fool. *Thanks for nothing, CJ.*

"That's okay." He looked a lot calmer than I felt. Maybe he hadn't been going to kiss me at all, and I'd imagined the whole thing? "See you Monday."

I dragged my sister out of the gutter. Didn't bother being too gentle, either. He waved, and the car pulled away from the kerb. I watched its tail lights disappear down the road.

Monday? I didn't think I could wait that long.

Chapter Five

It was nearly ten-thirty when I woke next morning. The house was quiet—no surprises there. I hadn't exactly expected CJ to be bounding out of bed at the crack of dawn after the night she'd had. I peeked into her room as I headed down the hallway to the bathroom, suddenly taken by the thought that she might have drowned in her own vomit in the night, but the snores proved she was still in the land of the living.

Of course she might wish she wasn't when she woke up—bet she'd have a cracker of a headache. She was sprawled face down under the sheet, with the pillow over her head, so I closed the door and left her to it.

Downstairs I grabbed a bowl of cereal and flopped on the couch in front of the TV to eat it, thoughts of Zac—and what might have happened if it wasn't for my drunk sister—floating through my mind. This morning I didn't feel so bad about the way the almost-kiss had ended, and I couldn't wait to see him again. If only I had his number. But phone numbers had been the last thing on my mind once the vomit started flying.

I found an old black and white movie that had just started, and settled down to watch. I dozed off a couple of times, so I lost the thread of it, but the guy got the girl in the end, so I didn't care. I loved me a bit of Happily Ever After.

The movie had finished and I was starting to think about lunch when CJ finally made an appearance. Just as I'd expected, she looked like hell, with dark circles under her eyes and an unhealthy pallor to her skin. The urge to say *I told you so* was almost overwhelming, but I bravely resisted, limiting myself to an inner smirk at her expense.

She hobbled down the stairs, the limp still quite noticeable.

"How's your ankle?"

As I spoke, I felt the weirdest tingle in my throat, and two little green drops fell from my lips. What the hell? I didn't normally spit when I talked. One of them landed on my leg, and I looked down to see the green droplet expand like a soufflé rising in the oven.

Only this soufflé was frog-flavoured.

Oh. My. God. A little green frog, no bigger than my fingertip, was sitting on my leg. Its bright green back was speckled with raised yellow dots. Adrenalin jolted through me as my heart started to pound. Its tiny orange feet were almost translucent, as if they were made of jelly. They felt real enough pressed against my skin, but they couldn't be, could they? I stared down at the frog, panic rising in my throat. It stared back out of bulging eyes whose irises were an even brighter orange than its feet, not the least fazed to find itself there.

My heart pounded. Where the hell had it come from? What was happening?

Frozen in shock, I couldn't move. Its long, delicate toes tickled my leg as it shifted, then it pushed off with powerful back legs and hopped down to join its friend, who'd sprung into existence on the couch where the other droplet had landed. There was a flash of purple when it jumped, as it exposed the undersides of its skinny legs.

"Shit!"

Horrified, I felt the tingle again, and another droplet burst out with the word. This one was brown, and grew bigger and uglier than the cute little frogs. I scrambled back against the arm of the couch, released from my paralysis, as a hideous toad, all warty and nasty, hopped across the carpet towards CJ. This was insane.

She shrieked. "Oh my God! What the hell is that? Did that just come out of your *mouth*?"

Then she clapped a hand to her own mouth, but it was too late, the drops had fallen, and now something lay scattered at her feet. Not frogs, though—something that winked with reflected light.

Toad forgotten, she knelt to gather them with a shaking hand, then held them out to me.

"Are they diamonds?" I breathed, forgetting until—too late—the terrible tingle reminded me. Two more little green frogs hopped off to join their brothers, flashing the purple undersides of their legs.

"Violet! Will you shut *up*." She squeaked and flinched away as one of the frogs got too close, but three more diamonds fell from her lips. "Oh my God, there are frogs everywhere. What is going *on*? Where are these things coming from?"

I opened my mouth.

"Don't answer that!"

I got up and fled to the bathroom, where I leaned on the sink, trembling with shock. What was happening to me? To us? I still looked the same. Shaking, I tipped my head from side to side, trying to see into every part of my mouth. Nothing looked different. How could this be happening? It was insane. My eyes filled with tears, and I dashed them away angrily.

Was this some kind of joke? Was I still asleep and dreaming? I slapped myself hard, and watched in the mirror as the pink imprint of my fingers appeared on my cheek. Well, that hurt. Guess I wasn't dreaming, then.

"Hello?" I whispered, my voice shaky. I sounded like a little kid who'd just woken up from a nightmare. How did I wake up from this?

A lone droplet tingled its way from my lips and landed on the sink. In seconds a tiny green frog looked up at me. It blinked its orange eyes once, very slowly, almost in apology.

If this was a joke, I sure wasn't laughing.

The damn frog looked just as real as I did. Kind of cute, even, with its bright green skin and long, delicate froggy fingers. Moving slowly, so as not to frighten it, I reached out, half-expecting it to disappear as strangely as it had come, but it let me cup my trembling hands round it and pick it up. It felt real too, its skin a little moist but not slippery, its tiny body almost weightless. It croaked once, then settled, quite comfy in my hands. I carried it downstairs and outside. I could hardly leave it in the bathroom if it was a real frog, could I? I nestled it in the garden among the maidenhair ferns. It was almost a perfect match for the ferns' bright green leaves.

'Leave the door open," CJ said as I came in. I thought she'd been pale before; now her skin was paper-white, and she had her arms clutched around herself as if that was the only thing holding her together. "You've got to get the rest of these frogs outside. I can't stand them."

A dozen or more diamonds dripped from her lips as she spoke. Why did she get diamonds and I got frogs? How was that fair? Then I saw how she was shaking and felt guilty for thinking like that. Either way, this was horrendous.

I went over and put my arms around her. Her breath still reeked of alcohol but hangovers were the least of our problems now Tears welled up in her eyes as she stared at me.

"Please, Vi. That horrible fat one's gone under the couch. I can't bear it."

I nodded—and then gripped her shoulders hard.

"You ..." Just one word, just to see.

No frog. I breathed out a great shuddery exhalation of relief.

"You just spoke and nothing came out. *And so did I.*"

She clapped her hands to her mouth. "So I did."

We stared at each other, all tears and stupid grins, the toad forgotten in its hiding place.

"But why?"

I stepped back, letting my hands fall away from her shoulders. I gestured for her to speak. Better to have more diamonds than more frogs.

"You think—" A diamond fell out, and she stopped. I grabbed her hand and motioned for her to continue. "You think it's because we were touching?"

"I think that just proved it." Once I held her hand the

diamonds had stopped, and though she'd flinched when I started speaking, no frogs had appeared either. I took a deep breath, my racing heartbeat beginning to slow at last.

She sank down onto the couch, feet curled beneath her, and buried her face in her hands. I tried to shoo the remaining frogs out the door to the patio, with only partial success. They were so tiny and hoppy. Three went outside, but two bounded off to the kitchen. Another zigged just as I zagged, and nearly got turned into frog jam. He leapt away in alarm and went to join the toad, which still lurked under the couch.

I gave up frog hunting and sat on the other end of the couch, knees drawn up. I couldn't shake the feeling that I must be dreaming. Had we *both* got drunk last night? So drunk that I didn't remember it? But I remembered everything else so clearly. Josh Johnson being all weird and creepy, Zac dancing to YMCA, then in the car with Zac …

Oh, God. Zac would never kiss me now. Not with frogs coming out of my mouth every time I opened it.

I made sure my feet were touching CJ.

"Are you okay?"

She lifted her head long enough to give me a withering look. "No, of course not. Are *you*? I have the world's worst headache, my mouth tastes like the bottom of a birdcage, my ankle hurts— oh, and I have *diamonds* falling out of my mouth every time I speak."

"Could be worse," I said, stung. "You could have frogs coming out instead."

She looked at me for a long moment, apology in her eyes. "True. Why is this happening, Vi?"

Her voice trembled like a frightened child's.

"I don't know. It's not possible, is it? It's like … it's like magic."

I felt like an idiot for saying it, but CJ didn't laugh. How else could we explain this?

"If magic is real, why can't we have three wishes or find a pot of gold or something? This is the suckiest magic in the whole history of suck! Although …" she stopped, struck by a sudden thought. "We do have diamonds …"

I looked at the sparkling stone as she held it up to the light. "Do you think it's real?"

"How should I know? Do I look like a diamond expert? But the frogs seem pretty real."

I had to agree with that.

"Do you think it was the absinthe?" she asked.

"The *absinthe*? Don't be ridiculous. It may be freaky bad alcohol, but it doesn't work magic. Besides, I didn't have any, remember?"

"Well, I wasn't sure." She looked defensive. "I don't remember that clearly."

I snorted. "I'm not surprised. You were wasted. That reminds me—you'd better hose out the gutter before Mum and Dad get home and find your lovely pile of vomit from last night."

"They won't know it was me."

"One look at you and I think they'll be able to put two and two together."

"You didn't send Mum that photo, did you?"

"Oh, you remember that part, do you?" Funny, my sister getting drunk had seemed like such a big deal last night. Now we had much bigger problems. "No, of course not."

"You'd better delete it."

"Why? I thought I might put it on Facebook."

"Don't you *dare*."

She hit me with a cushion, and I scrambled away, laughing almost hysterically, though nothing about this morning was funny. The minute I lost contact with CJ I felt the tingle again, and two more frogs bounded away across the carpet. My laugh finished up more like a sob, and CJ slid her foot over to touch my leg. We gazed at each other, panic barely suppressed.

"What are we going to do? We can't go round like Siamese twins for the rest of our lives!"

What a horrific thought. I loved my sister, but there were limits.

"Never mind the rest of our lives. What about school tomorrow?"

Oh, God. We only had two classes together, Maths and English, and we weren't even allowed to choose our own seats in English. What about the rest of the day? And what the hell was I going to say to Zac?

"I'm going to Google it," CJ said. "Maybe there'll be something."

Oh, sure. Even Doctor Google wouldn't have an answer for this one.

"You get the rest of these things outside," she ordered, disappearing upstairs to find her laptop.

Funny. I'd never realised my sister was so squeamish. Frogs didn't bother me at all. Apart from the fact that they were falling out of my own mouth, that is. That sure as hell wasn't right. I was still shaking. Now, if it had been *spiders*—well, that would have been a different story.

These little guys were cute, with their big orange eyes and delicate splayed toes. The yellow spots on their backs looked liked someone had dotted them with the world's tiniest paintbrush. They were so small, not much bigger than a decent-sized cherry, but they could fit a lot of hop in those little legs. Catching them was quite the challenge. It took a good twenty minutes before I had them all settled among the maidenhair, and CJ was well into her Google search, though not having much luck, judging from the grim look on her face.

That just left the toad. Him I didn't feel quite so comfortable about handling. There was just something about that big ugly warty body with its stumpy brown legs that put me off. Why did I get that one gross toad among all the cute little green frogs? Had I said something different? I tried to recall—had I sworn?

Surely that couldn't be it—just my luck, to get a sucky magic curse that had morals. I felt a hysterical giggle threatening and sucked in a deep breath, trying to stay calm. What was a girl supposed to say when frogs started exploding out of her mouth? *Gosh, what a surprise?*

Only one way to find out for sure. I looked down at my froggy audience and took another deep breath.

"Shit."

Sure enough, the drop that fell onto the pavers was a nasty brown colour. I watched the thing expand into another toad, just as ugly as the first. It gave me a mournful look.

"Ribbit," it said, its voice much deeper than its tiny cousins', and hopped away under the azaleas.

In the spirit of experimentation, I dropped a few more choice words, and soon had a collection of toads. I shuddered. QED: theory proved.

Then CJ noticed the toads.

"What the hell are you doing?" she shrieked.

Oh, *that* was fair. She could say "hell" and get a ten-carat diamond, but when *I* tried it I got a big fat toad. Nice one, sucky magic.

I stomped back in and leaned on her shoulder. "Any luck?"

"All I could find was this."

She turned the laptop so I could read the screen.

"*Toads and Diamonds*—a fairy tale? Seriously?"

"Read it."

She shoved the laptop at me, so I settled on the lounge with it.

There was once upon a time a widow who had two daughters …

It was pretty short. One daughter was beautiful and good, but the mother didn't like her because she was just like her father; the mother favoured the daughter who took after herself. So the good daughter has to do all the work, just like Cinderella, and one day she goes to draw water from the distant well, and an old lady asks for a drink. Naturally, it being a fairy tale, the old lady's really a fairy in disguise, and when the girl is all sweet and helpful and gets her a drink the fairy rewards her by making flowers and jewels come out of her mouth every time she speaks. So when the mother finds out what's happened, she sends the mean ugly sister off to the well, with instructions to be nice to any old ladies who happen to be lurking there.

I looked up at CJ. "This is such a pile of crap."

She flapped her hands impatiently. "Read the rest of it."

The disagreeable sister turns up, but this time there's no old lady, but a fancy rich woman. It's the same fairy, of course, but the mean sister is stupid as well as mean and doesn't realise, so when the woman asks for a drink the mean sister tells her to get it herself, she's not her servant.

And abracadabra, this sister gets the gift of snakes and toads instead of diamonds. When the mother finds out what's happened, she blames the pretty girl and drives her away. The girl hides in the forest, where the king's son finds her. Having his eye on the money, he promptly "falls in love" with this jewel-making machine, and marries her. Yeah, right. Pretty convenient romance. No chance *at all* that he only loves her for the money. And in true fairytale fashion, the toad sister dies alone and miserable, having been abandoned because of all the grossness coming out of her mouth.

I snapped the laptop shut and glared at my sister. "And your point is …? Be pretty and get rewarded for it? I think we already learned that lesson. Being your twin is just one long lesson in the benefits of being beautiful. Are you saying I'm the ugly sister? That I'm so mean and stupid and vile I *deserve* to be spitting amphibians for the rest of my life?"

"No, of course not. The point is it's a *fairy tale*."

I was too angry to listen. *Of course* my beautiful sister got the diamonds. When did anything ever go wrong in her perfect life? "And who was the one who got drunk and disgusting last night? Who was the good sister then, huh? Where would you have ended up if I hadn't dragged you away from that sleaze who was trying to get into your pants? You didn't earn those diamonds, sweetheart. You should be the one spitting toads."

"Vi! Calm down. Don't take it so personally."

"Don't take it *personally*? How am I not supposed to take it personally?" I dropped the laptop on the carpet, surprising a croak out of the toad still lurking under the couch.

"Because it doesn't matter who got what."

"Easy for you to say."

She stared at me intently. "What *matters* is that it's a fairy tale come to life. Doesn't that remind you of anything?"

"What do you—? Oh. Snow White."

The girl in the glass coffin. The clearing in the bush that never existed before, the one that looked more like it belonged in a European forest—or a fairy tale—than in the Australian bushland.

Smart girl, my sister. Sometimes she surprised me.

"You think this is like that? How is that possible?"

She let her head fall back against the cushions with a groan. "I don't know what to think. The Snow White thing seemed like some kind of weird prank—but it looks pretty suspicious now, doesn't it? That girl won't wake up, and they don't know why. Wanna bet if they find some prince to kiss her she'll be jumping out of her skin?"

"But … fairy tales aren't real."

She removed her foot from my leg. "Ya think?"

She spat a diamond into her hand and threw it at me. Yeah, it was kind of hard to argue with that. I turned it over in my hand, thinking. I should be working on my Ancient History essay. Or writing up that Physics experiment. That was real. This stuff was just crazy.

Yet, unless we were both suffering from the same weird

hallucination, I had to accept that this was real too. And this diamond was no hallucination, hard and cold in my hand. I just had to adjust my expectations of reality to allow for some new and unusual manifestations.

I heard the car before really registering what it was. CJ leapt up, panic all over her face.

"Oh, my God, Mum and Dad are home!"

The noise of the automatic garage door grinding open came next, and we both stared at the door leading from the kitchen into the garage with horror. The car drove in, the engine stopped, and the outside door started up again, while we stood there, frozen.

Then I shoved her back onto the couch and scooped up the diamonds she'd scattered. The TV was still on.

"Sit down! Look like you're watching TV."

She sat bolt upright in the corner of the couch. I stretched out and put my feet in her lap.

"Relax! Look natural."

She shot me a panicked look, but slouched a bit just as the door opened.

Dad breezed in. "Hi, girls! Did you miss me?"

"Hi, Dad."

He came over and gave us both a kiss.

"You two look cozy there," Mum said, coming in behind him.

"How was work?" I asked.

"Busy," she said. "Don't I get a hug?"

I held my arms out. "Don't make me walk all the way over there."

She shook her head and muttered something uncomplimentary about teenagers, but came over to give us both a hug. While she was bent over CJ the toad decided to add to the moment by croaking loudly.

"What was that?"

"I think the springs might be going," I said, bouncing violently to produce a few squeaks from the couch.

"That's a shame. I thought we might get a few more years out of it yet."

Mum headed upstairs to unpack.

"Fancy a cup of tea, love?" Dad called after her. "I'll put the kettle on."

Behind his back, the toad emerged from under the couch and hopped across to the round table where we ate our meals.

"I'll do it!" I said brightly. "You go upstairs and help Mum."

I rushed into the kitchen, willing him to go away before the damn toad moved again.

"Thanks, sweetheart." He smiled at me, then looked at CJ. "You're very quiet this morning. Feeling all right?"

She nodded.

"Cat got your tongue?" he teased.

She jumped up and came into the kitchen to help. Out of sight behind the bench she stretched her foot out to touch mine as she got two cups out of the cupboard.

"Just a bit tired," she said.

He frowned. "Are you limping?"

"She's fine." *Go away, Dad.* I didn't dare look at the toad. "Just slipped on the stairs last night.

"I'll see if I can find a bandage. You should be resting it if it's that sore."

"I'm okay, Dad, honest. Don't fuss."

He smiled. "Well, look at you two—so domesticated. I'll just duck upstairs for a minute and then you can tell me all about your weekend."

"Sure." I kept the grin plastered on my face until he disappeared around the bend in the stairs. Then CJ let her head drop on to the bench with a thump and I dived under the table.

I had to get rid of that toad.

Chapter Six

I spent the rest of the day on the internet, reading all I could about magic. Maybe I could find someone who actually knew enough about this crap to help us, though most of the "magicians" I found were the kind who did children's parties. I didn't give up looking, though; I had to find some way to lift this curse. In the *Toads and Diamonds* fairy tale the fairy had called it a gift, but maybe fairies had a different definition of that word than the rest of us mere mortals. It certainly didn't feel like a gift to me. Even CJ's diamonds, now I'd had a chance to calm down, were no picnic. How could we have any kind of normal life like this?

The only people I found who seemed to be able to do "real" magic were illusionists like David Copperfield. I'd never believed it was real before, but maybe it was time to be a little more open-minded. Wouldn't it be cool if their tricks were all true? What else might they be able to do? Most of the famous ones were running shows in places like Las Vegas. How were two seventeen-year-old girls supposed to get themselves halfway around the world to meet someone like that?

We played the antisocial teenager card and hid from Mum and Dad in our rooms, only emerging for dinner, and then it was easy enough to make sure our feet touched under the table. I'm not sure Mum and Dad would have noticed if one of us had slipped up, to be honest. Mum looked exhausted, and they both seemed preoccupied. They left for work so early on Monday morning neither of us was even out of bed.

"So far, so good," I said to CJ as we left the house. I had my hand on her shoulder as she locked the front door behind us. "But how are we going to handle school?"

Our new school had a draconian roll call system—students' names were checked off at the beginning of every lesson, and parents were contacted the minute someone didn't show up for school—so hanging out at home all day wasn't an option.

"Well, we can sit together for Maths and English," she said, as if that answered the question.

"No, we can't. Maths maybe, but Mrs Harcourt won't let us change seats in English. You know she insists on splitting up the boys and making them all sit with girls. Besides, we couldn't talk in two classes and refuse to speak in all the others. How would we get away with that?"

The bus stop was just around the corner from our house. We stopped on the footpath and looked at each other.

"We'll just have to keep quiet all day, then."

I laughed. "You? Not speak? What if a teacher asks us a question? You can't not answer."

"We'll tell them our throats are sore. Well, not *tell* them, obviously. Mime it or something. We can pretend we've got laryngitis."

I'd been hoping she'd come up with something brilliant, but laryngitis looked like the only answer—apart from convincing our parents we were both deathly ill, which had been my preferred option, only they'd left home so early I hadn't been able to put that plan into action.

I'd have to check how long laryngitis lasted. There was only a week left until the holidays, so if we could stretch it to three days, we'd only have to skip the last two days of term. Hopefully we could convince Mum and Dad we were sick. Then there was just the little matter of finding a way to get rid of this curse … So far my research hadn't turned up anything useful, but that was a problem for the holidays. We could go check out that mysterious clearing in the Blue Mountains, see if there were any clues that might help us. But first we had to make it through the last week of school.

Ashleigh and the girls crowded around CJ with their usual exuberance at the bus stop. They were like a litter of puppies, falling over each other and wagging hysterically. All they could talk about was the party, but they soon ran up against CJ's silence.

"What's wrong?" Ashleigh asked, her last question hanging in the air while they all waited for CJ to answer. "Can't you talk?"

CJ patted her neck and mouthed the words *sore throat* until they got the message.

"You've got a sore throat? Have you lost your voice?"

CJ nodded violently.

"Oh, you poor thing! When did this happen?"

Ashleigh looked at me for the answer, so I had to go through the same patting and mouthing routine. Her eyebrows drew together in a suspicious frown.

"You've *both* lost your voices? Really?"

More violent nodding from both of us, but I could see she wasn't a hundred per cent sure we weren't pulling her leg. Which we kind of were, I guess.

On the bus I was fine until Sona got on. Despite convincing her I couldn't talk, she insisted on firing off questions about the party.

"So how was it?"

I held my hand out flat, then wobbled it from side to side.

"Only so-so?" Her eyebrows flew up. "I stayed at home and studied algebra! You get to go to the biggest party of the term— of the year, maybe—and you think it was only so-so? What a waste! Did you dance?"

I nodded.

"Who with?"

I pointed to myself. Even if I could have found a way to tell her I'd danced with Zac, I didn't want to say anything until I saw him again. Maybe that moment in the car hadn't meant what I'd thought it did. Better to play it cool.

"By yourself? Well, you're no fun. Couldn't you find a nice boy to dance with? Wait—did you kiss anyone?"

I rolled my eyes. *God, don't blush now, you idiot!*

"Oh, this is too frustrating. Zac!"

Zac had just got on. He lurched down the aisle as the bus set off again and took the seat in front of us. He was even cuter in the flesh than I'd remembered, and his dark eyes were warm as they smiled at me.

"Hey. How was the rest of your weekend?"

"Tell me about the party," Sona demanded. "Vi's lost her voice, and I want to know *everything*."

Thank God she'd saved me from going through the whole miming a sore throat thing again.

He was still smiling at me, and I couldn't help smiling back.

"It was good," he said.

She waited, but there was nothing more.

"Oh, come on, Zac. Details, man, details!"

He shrugged. "It was just a normal party. Lots of music, dancing—"

"Did you dance?"

"A little."

I grinned and started forming the letters Y-M-C-A with my arms.

He laughed. "Hey, I said I couldn't dance."

"Did he really have a keg there? Did you drink?"

"*I* didn't. I was driving. I'm a responsible Boy Scout. A few other people did, though." He looked at me. "How's your sister?"

I gave him the thumbs-up, but Sona was staring in shock.

"Did CJ get drunk?" she hissed.

I mimed throwing up and her dark eyes grew so huge she looked like an Indian Bratz doll.

"Wow. I wish I'd been there."

"You probably wouldn't have enjoyed it," Zac said. "A lot of idiots got drunk and made a lot of noise. I spent most of the night talking to the guys from the robotics club." That was all true, but it wasn't the whole story. Guess the rest of it was our little secret. "You would have been bored."

She gave him a pitying look. "I don't *think* so."

We got off the bus and Zac walked with me to our lockers.

An awkward silence stretched between us without Sona to fill every moment with chatter. Stupid bloody frogs. If only I could speak to him!

I sneaked a glance up at his face and found him looking down at me.

"So," he said, "I was wondering … if you wanted to meet up after school."

Oh, no. Of course I wanted to meet up with him, but …

I grimaced and patted my throat, trying to ignore the blush I could feel creeping up my cheeks.

"Oh. Right. Maybe when your throat's better."

I nodded vigorously. I didn't want him to think I was trying to give him the flick. Then I opened my locker and hid my hot face inside. He opened his too, and I could hear him rummaging around inside.

"Damn! Where the hell is it?"

I peeked around my locker door.

"Can't find my calculator," he said, "and I've got a maths test in period 2."

Wordlessly I took mine out and offered it to him. His face lit up.

"Thanks! I'll get it back to you at lunch."

The bell rang and we split up. First period for me was English with Mrs Harcourt. I used to like English at my old school, but Mrs Harcourt was quickly changing my mind. We were studying *A Midsummer Night's Dream*, but so far her idea of studying it was to have us read the whole thing aloud in class. Given that some of the Einsteins in our English class seemed to have a reading age of two, it was pretty slow going.

Today she chose people for the parts and the torture resumed as normal.

"Tarry, rash wanton—am I not thy lord?" Rob Burke read, stumbling over every word longer than one syllable. "What's a wanton, miss? Aren't they those Chinese things like spring rolls?"

At least Bottom wasn't in this scene. Every time he appeared most of the boys collapsed in helpless sniggers. Apparently body parts were just as funny at seventeen as they'd been at three. And the fact it was all about *fairies* with stupid names like Puck and Peasblossom —well, the laughs just never stopped.

Julie Lee was his Titania today. She read well, but in such a tiny little voice that Mrs Harcourt kept bellowing at her to speak up, which only made her more mouselike.

I was bored, but congratulating myself on having made it through, when Mrs Harcourt stopped the readers.

"Thank you, everyone. Okay, now we'll have Violet as Titania and Eric as Oberon. Rob, you read Puck."

I shook my head, but she ignored me. Eric read his lines and then it was my turn. Titania had an enormous speech. Mrs Harcourt waited, giving me the evil eye.

"Well, Violet? From *These are the forgeries of jealousy*, please."

I patted my throat and pulled faces of terrible pain. A couple of the boys laughed.

"I think she's got laryngitis, miss," someone said.

Her overplucked eyebrows disappeared into her fringe. "Is that true, Crystal?"

CJ pointed to her own throat as more of the class started laughing.

"She's got it too, miss!"

"I see. I assume you have a note from your parents explaining this sad state of affairs."

Damn. Should have thought of that. I could have forged one before school. Too late now. I had to shake my head.

"In that case, you can both spend lunch in detention." She fixed me with an icy stare. "Unless you feel a miraculous recovery coming on, Violet? No? Very well, report to E23 at the start of lunch, please."

She picked someone else to read and the class settled down. CJ shot me a disgusted look, as if it were all somehow my fault. Hey, at least it solved the problem of lunch time. No one was allowed to talk in detention anyway. Maybe we should just aim for detention all week.

It wasn't a good start, though. First period and already teachers were suspicious. How long could we get away with this laryngitis thing? If only we could hide in the girls' bathroom all day. But Mrs Harcourt would notice if we didn't show up for detention. And then there was that stupid mark-the-roll-in-every-period thing.

Next period was Maths. I kept my head down and the class passed without any unpleasantness. In Physics Mr Dunkley talked about force and vectors of acceleration in his usual dry way. I could see people's eyes glazing over.

"And who remembers the unit of measurement for force?" he asked brightly.

Silence. My arm twitched, but I remembered in time that I couldn't speak.

"Violet?" he asked.

Even in the short time I'd been in his class he'd discovered he could usually rely on me to know the answer. This one was so easy I hated to look like an idiot, but I shook my head and he moved on. Nevertheless I was glad when the bell went for the end of the period.

I grabbed my books and hopped down off the lab stool—and walked straight into the corner of the bench.

"Ow!"

Oh, hell. A little green frog puffed into being on the benchtop, his orange toes spread out like fingers. I looked around, but everyone was busy shoving to be first out the door to recess. Mr Dunkley had his back to the room, cleaning formulae off the board. No one noticed my frog.

I hesitated. Should I take it outside and sneak it into the garden?

"You coming, Vi?" my lab partner called from the door.

Hastily I shielded the frog from view with my body, but she was already turning away. *Sorry, little guy.* It was too risky. I didn't want anyone catching me with him. If someone saw him here they'd probably assume he'd escaped from a biology class. That mightn't end well for the frog, but what could I do? I hurried after her, leaving the frog to his fate.

Of all the days to have double English, it had to be today—the one day in a fortnight of timetabling. Last period saw us back in Mrs Harcourt's class for more interminable reading. Fairies had never been so dull. If Mrs Harcourt was trying to instil a lifelong hatred of Shakespeare in her class she was doing a fantastic job.

I knew I was in trouble the minute we opened our copies of *A Midsummer Night's Dream* and her eyes fell on me.

"This time I think we shall hear from Violet as Helena, and you can read Hermia, Crystal."

"But they've got laryngitis, miss," said some helpful soul.

"I don't think so. It's time to stop this stupidity, girls. Isn't one detention enough for you?"

CJ stared at her desk. I looked at Mrs Harcourt, trying to appear innocent, but she was in no mood to be fooled.

"Begin reading, please, Violet."

I looked down at my book, but said nothing. The room was still, as everyone waited for the explosion. Watching someone else get into trouble is always entertaining.

Mrs Harcourt slammed her book down on her desk, making everyone jump. "Right! I've had enough. You can take yourself off to the principal and explain this stupid prank to her."

I stood, my chair shrieking across the wooden floor, and walked down the aisle between the desks. Just as I passed, that moron Rob Burke stuck his foot out and I tripped and staggered, nearly ending up flat on my face.

"You jerk!"

Oh, no! I clapped my hand to my mouth, but it was too late. The whole class was staring straight at me, and they all saw two green drops fly out and turn into two little frogs sitting all innocent on Rob's desk.

Rob, who'd been swinging his chair on its two back legs, nearly fell off in his scramble to get away. There were squeals of horror from every girl in the immediate vicinity.

"Miss!" Rob's voice was hoarse with shock. "Vi's got *frogs* in her mouth."

The screaming rose to new heights.

"Ewww, gross!"

"That's disgusting!"

Half the class were scrambling onto their chairs, craning their necks to see the frogs. Mrs Harcourt yelled for silence but no one was listening.

One of the frogs hopped onto the next desk, which happened to be Julie Lee's. That quiet little Chinese girl, who rarely spoke above a whisper, let out the loudest scream I've ever heard—and that was it. The room descended into complete chaos.

Three boys leapt up to try to catch the frogs. Every girl in the room—including CJ—was either standing on a chair squealing, or pushing towards the door. I stood in the middle of it all and glared at Rob Burke. Jerk face. This was all his fault.

One poor frog, probably terrified out of its froggy wits, hopped my way, trying to evade the frog hunters, whose numbers had grown. One of the more enthusiastic hunters ploughed straight into me and sent me flying.

"Watch what you're bloody doing!" I snarled, sprawled among the overturned furniture.

Oh, dammit. When would I learn? Three more frogs and a dirty big toad joined the mayhem. I should have just stayed in bed this morning. How could this day get any worse?

Silly question. As soon as I looked up I knew how. At least three iPhones were trained on me, capturing every last damned frog that spewed out of my mouth, ready to be uploaded to someone's YouTube channel.

"Vi! Are you all right?"

CJ was down off her chair, pushing her way through to me. Her sisterly concern was touching, but OMG did she have to pick that moment? Couldn't she see people were recording this whole disaster?

I lunged for her hand.

"Shut *up*," I yelled, but it was too late.

Rob Jerk-Face Burke scrabbled on the floor at her feet, and came up with a look of mingled awe and greed on his face.

"Look at this!" He held something sparkly up to the class. "It's a diamond!"

The stampede to the door reversed itself, and thundered back our way. We backed up against the wall, ignored by our classmates while they pushed and shoved to be first to find a diamond. Some found frogs instead, and the crowd rippled and eddied around those spots like some great heaving screaming animal. Mrs Harcourt roared for silence the whole time, but no one paid the slightest attention until a deep male voice bellowed from the doorway.

"WHAT IS GOING ON IN HERE?"

It was the English head teacher, whose office was next door. He waded into the room, manhandling boys up off the floor, pushing bodies back into seats, until some semblance of order was restored. Then he stood at the front of the room with a face like thunder, letting the silence stretch to ominous lengths.

"I would expect a display like that from Year 9, perhaps, but not from Year 11. You are supposed to be setting the standards of behaviour for the rest of the school, not acting like a pack of wild animals. My *dog* is better behaved than you."

No one laughed. No one dared.

"But, sir, there were frogs—" Jerk Face didn't know when to keep his mouth shut.

"Silence!" Mr Ormond shot Jerk Face a glare so icy he was lucky not to get frostbite. "When I want to hear from you I will rattle the pig bucket. Mrs Harcourt, I assume I will be seeing some of these boys in my office shortly?"

Boys always got the blame. Of course, that was because ninety-nine per cent of the time they deserved it.

Mrs Harcourt gave me a chilly glare. It needed work; it was nowhere near the standard of the English head teacher's. "Actually, Mr Ormond, it's Violet and Crystal Reilly who are the troublemakers here."

The toad hopped out from under her desk. All the girls in the front row squealed. Mr Ormond recoiled from the ugly thing.

"What is *that* doing in here?"

"I'm afraid you'll have to ask Violet about that," said Mrs Harcourt. "I believe it belongs to her."

A scream and a sudden relocation of students down the back of the room revealed three of the toad's more attractive friends.

Mr Ormond turned that cold stare on me. "How many of these things are there?"

How should I know? I was too busy bashing elbows and knees on the furniture at the time to do a headcount. I returned his stare in silence.

"You boys!" He picked the two nearest. "Collect those poor creatures and take them outside before all this screaming bursts their eardrums. And *you* two—" CJ and I got the death stare. "You come with me."

Chapter Seven

I caught Dad watching us in the rear vision mirror as we drove home. The car was deathly quiet: this was a new low for us. In all the schools we'd attended over the years, our parents had never been called to the school to discuss our behaviour before. That they'd both come surprised me: I knew how busy they'd been at work lately. Obviously Mr Ormond's garbled story of frogs and mayhem had been sufficiently impressive to make them drop what they were doing and drive straight over.

In Mr Ormond's office they'd seemed inclined to brush it off as some kind of acting out. As if I always threw frogs around when I was angry at having to start over at a new school.

"The girls were very reluctant to leave Townsville," Mum had said, leaning forward with an earnest look on her face, as if to take Mr Ormond into her confidence. "They were both so happy there, it was a bit of a wrench for them. I think Violet in particular was hoping to finish her schooling there."

I'd stared at the floor, angry that they were discussing us as if we weren't even in the room.

Mr Ormond's gaze rested thoughtfully on me for a moment. "I can certainly understand the difficulties the girls have faced, and continue to face, due to the peripatetic nature of your work. You say this is their fourth high school?"

Mum nodded.

"Nevertheless, much as I might sympathise with their feelings, Violet's way of showing them is quite unacceptable. Bringing frogs to school and causing such disruption in the classroom will not be tolerated."

I could tell he hadn't believed Mrs Harcourt's story that the frogs had actually come out of my mouth. He was probably a very good teacher, but he had no imagination. Sadly, that didn't stop him from laying the whole story before our parents anyway.

Mum's face paled at the mention of frogs bursting from my mouth. She and Dad exchanged a worried glance, which Mr Ormond caught.

"But as you can see," he said, smiling to reassure them that he didn't believe any such nonsense, "she's not spitting frogs out any more. I suppose she had them in her pocket all along, and some of the eyewitnesses have become a little excitable. Isn't that right, Violet?"

"Yes, sir."

The four of us were crammed into his small office, arrayed in a tight semi-circle in front of his desk. My knee pressed up against CJ's.

"Maybe you should suspend us, sir," I suggested.

He frowned. "This is not a joke, Violet. I'm sure, once your parents take you home and you have time to think about your behaviour, such extreme measures won't be necessary."

Well, it was worth a try.

Then he'd shaken hands with Mum and Dad and sent us on our way. The last bell rang as the interview finished, and we got swept along in the usual tide of kids rushing to leave school.

Only today the tide seemed to swirl around us full of whispers and pointing fingers. Word had spread already.

"Give us a diamond, CJ!" yelled one boy.

Funnily enough, no one seemed to want a frog. I heard the word enough, though, along with *disgusting* and *gross* and *freak*. Never had so many people looked at me with such revulsion. I stuck close to Dad and tried to ignore them all, but by the time we got to the car I was almost in tears.

I'd expected the lecture to start as soon as the engine did, but neither of them said a word all the way home. Guess they were saving it up.

We trooped in from the garage and Dad pointed at the couch in the family room. "Sit."

We did, though I made sure to sit close. CJ's leg was warm against mine. Mum sat in an armchair, but Dad remained standing, leaning back against the kitchen bench with his arms folded. If he was going to rant I wished he'd just get it over with. The suspense was killing me.

"Okay, young ladies. I want the truth now."

No, you don't, Dad. You really, really don't. Now I knew we were in for it. Last time he'd called us young ladies we'd been grounded for a month and scrubbing the shower with a toothbrush.

"And don't bother looking at each other like that, trying to get your stories straight. I'm perfectly happy to interview you separately if that's what it takes."

"You don't have to do that." Immediately I tried to look cooperative, but I must have overdone it.

He looked at Mum and she nodded. "Violet, come with me while Dad talks to Crystal."

"No! Can't I stay? I won't say a word."

Mum's gaze hardened. She did a death stare even better than Mr Ormond. "Get up."

I sighed and stood up. I guess trying to keep it from them was a pretty forlorn hope anyway. She crooked her finger at me and I walked to the door with her.

"Before you go," Dad said, "answer me one question. Where did you get the frogs?"

I hesitated.

He quirked an eyebrow at me. "Well?"

Fine. If you really want to know. We needed help. If we were going to fly to Las Vegas to see an illusionist, we'd need Mum and Dad on board with the idea. "Out of my mouth."

We all stared at the three little green frogs on the carpet. They stared back, blinking their bulbous orange eyes as if surprised to find themselves the centre of so much attention. Mum drew her breath in sharply as they appeared, but Dad didn't bat an eyelid.

"And the diamonds, CJ? The same place, I suppose?"

"Yep." She caught the diamond as it fell and held it out for his inspection.

He sighed heavily and sat at the table, waving me back toward the couch. "Fine. You can sit down again. We don't really want to be overrun with frogs. Being together suppresses the effect, I take it?"

I nodded and resumed my seat. How had he figured that one

out so fast? And why was he so calm? My heart was pounding, but he seemed to be lost in thought, gazing off into space while his fingers tapped an absent rhythm on the table top.

"You're taking this better than I thought you would," I said.

Mum sighed. "It wasn't entirely unexpected."

"It wasn't?" CJ stared open-mouthed. "Do you know what caused it? How do we get rid of it?"

"The Hendrix counter, I think," Dad said to Mum. They both ignored CJ's questions.

She nodded and left the room. Okay, this was getting weird—weirder still when she returned a moment later with a box no bigger than a paperback. It had a couple of dials on the side, but the main feature was a clear glass tube mounted on the front of the box. She knelt on the carpet and held it over the frogs. One hopped away but the other two sat patiently. As she adjusted the dials the glass tube began to glow a soft pink.

Then she brought the box to us.

"What is that thing?" CJ asked.

"A Hendrix counter."

The tube flushed bright red as she held it out to CJ.

"For counting Hendrixes?" I joked, uneasy now. What was going on?

I edged away. I didn't want that thing anywhere near me.

"Sit still," Mum said. "There's nothing to be scared of."

"I'm not scared," I said at once, but as the tube began to glow red that wasn't exactly true. "What are you *doing*?"

Mum looked at me calmly. "It's called a Hendrix counter because it was invented by a man named Hendrix. It measures the presence and intensity of aether, the raw stuff of magic."

I laughed, but she didn't crack a smile. "Seriously? Mum, you're freaking me out."

"You have some other rational explanation for why frogs are suddenly jumping out of your mouth when you speak? If you remove all impossible explanations, then the only possibility you're left with has got to be the answer, however unlikely."

"But magic's an impossible explanation too," said CJ.

"Says the girl dropping diamonds with every word," Dad said.

"And where did you get this Hendrix thingy?"

Mum pulled out a chair and joined him, putting the Hendrix counter on the table between them. It looked rather like an old-fashioned radio. We faced each other, them together on one side of the table, the two of us on the edge of the couch across the room. It felt like being back in Mr Ormond's office, only with more space.

Dad must have seen something of what I was feeling in my face.

"You're not in trouble, girls," he said, "but I need the truth. Obviously something has happened while we were away that we need to get to the bottom of."

How could anyone get to the bottom of this freakiness? When I'd been a little girl Daddy had always been able to fix everything. Sadly, I was too old now to be reassured by his calm assumption that he could fix this. Although … the fact that he knew about magic, and even had a gadget to measure it, suggested that we weren't the only ones in the family who'd been hiding secrets.

"Have you met any strangers lately?" Mum asked.

CJ rolled her eyes. "We just started at a new school, Mum. Of course we have."

"Suspicious ones, then. Anyone who asked you for a drink, for instance."

The image came to me from *Toads and Diamonds* of the old lady at the well asking the pretty girl for water. Is that where she was going with this?

"Why are you asking? We're not part of some fairy tale."

"I think you are, sweetie," Dad said.

What had gotten into them? I glared at the stupid Hendrix counter, glowing now with nothing more than the sunlight streaming in the sliding glass door. If I hadn't seen that shining all pink and red I'd think they were both smoking something funny.

"Who did you see on the weekend?" Mum asked. "This is serious, girls."

CJ glanced at me. I could feel an *I told you so*, bigger and uglier than any toad, trying to burst from my mouth. That stupid party. Why couldn't she have asked them about it? *Maybe you should have asked them yourself*, came the guilty little whisper. Imagine the tantrum if I had, though, and they'd said no. CJ wouldn't have talked to me for a week—and she would still probably have gone. *So you took the easy way out even though you knew better.*

To her credit, CJ didn't try to hide the truth. She might have broken the rules now and then, but she was no liar.

"We went to a party on Saturday night. Half the school was there."

"Really?" Dad's eyebrows drew together in a scowl. "Did you know about this, Janey?"

Mum shook her head, such a look of disappointment on her face that my heart sank. "No, I didn't. Was this your idea or Violet's?"

"Mine." CJ lifted her chin, but I knew she hated that look of Mum's as much as I did. Being yelled at was far better than earning that reproachful *but I thought I could trust you* look. "Vi said we should ask but I didn't think you'd let us go, so …" She shrugged. "I just really wanted to hang out and make some new friends."

Ooh, low blow. She knew how guilty Mum felt about dragging us around the country all the time.

"Never mind," said Dad. "We can discuss your choices and their consequences another time. Right now we need to know about that party. The truth, CJ. Did anyone ask you to give them something? A drink, a kiss, a lock of hair, anything?"

"No."

"What about gifts? Did anyone give you both something?"

If you counted drunken boys offering to show us a good time, yes, but I didn't think that was what Dad meant. There was Josh Johnson, of course, giving CJ absinthe, but I hadn't had any, so that didn't count either. Although …

"Josh Johnson talked about giving us presents, but he never actually did."

"Josh Johnson? Who's he?"

"The school captain," CJ said, shooting me a quick *why-did-you-have-to-mention-him?* glance. "The party was at his house."

"What sort of present?" Mum asked.

This was tricky. I didn't want to mention the absinthe.

"He didn't say. I just assumed he was … umm … you know,

being suggestive." And if saying something like that to your mother isn't awkward, I don't know what is. It had been pretty awkward at the time, too. There'd been something almost frightening about that moment in the bedroom. Josh had seemed sharper, harder somehow than his usual *look at me, I'm God's gift to the world* self.

And also …

"I don't know if it means anything, but something kind of weird did happen. I saw Josh in the spa with some girls one minute, and the next minute I saw him somewhere else, fully dressed."

"That's right," said CJ, clearly relieved to turn the conversation away from absinthe territory. "And when we came outside again, he was back in the spa, as if he'd never left. I wondered how he could have changed and got there so quickly."

Dad frowned. "That does sound odd. What does this Josh boy look like?"

"I can show you a picture of him," I said.

The look on CJ's face was priceless. I almost laughed, despite the seriousness of the situation. She didn't know I'd taken two photos that night—the one of the two of them lying back on the bed, and then another straight after of the look on Josh's face.

"I'm pretty sure you deleted that photo," she said, her eyes boring into me. *Take the hint or I swear I will kill you*, those eyes said.

I pulled my phone out of my pocket. "No, it's still here." I flicked through the photos until I found the right one, and held it out to Dad. "This is him."

Dad took the phone and showed it to Mum. "Why is he pulling that face?"

"He has red eyes," Mum said.

"That's just the flash."

"I don't think so. Not if you saw him in two places at once."

She shared a troubled look with Dad. I was getting sick of this whole unspoken conversation they were having without us.

"What do you mean? Sure, it was weird, but maybe he got changed really quickly."

Mum sighed and handed the phone back. "They rely on that, you know—that people will talk themselves into disbelieving the evidence of their own eyes. That person in the picture—that's not Josh Johnson."

"Sure it is," said CJ. "No offence, but you haven't even met him."

"I don't need to meet him to know that that creature's not human. That's a Sidhe."

"He's a she? What are you talking about?"

A hint of a smile flickered across Mum's face. "Not *she*. S-I-D-H-E—it's pronounced *shee*. The Sidhe are—well, I suppose you'd call them fairies."

"I think it's time we told you two what we do for a living," said Dad.

I was too busy boggling at Mum to look at him. Did she really just say fairies?

"You work for the military," CJ said. She looked pretty dazed too.

"No. That's just what we tell people. It's easier than the truth."

"Which is—?"

"That we're really prison wardens."

I don't know what I'd been expecting, but it wasn't that. Prison wardens didn't sound too magical. What was the big deal?

"For a very special kind of prisoner," said Mum. "Actually, it's a special kind of prison too. To keep the Sidhe from our world. To keep their magic locked away where it can't do any harm."

Whoa. Okay, that was a pretty big deal. I wanted to say I didn't believe it, but those frogs weren't my imagination. Magic was real. And my parents knew all about it. I didn't know which one was crazier.

"Only now, magic is leaking through the walls, appearing in our world as pieces of fairy tales," Dad said. "The girl in the glass coffin was the first—Snow White in the middle of the Australian bush. I knew something was terribly wrong the minute I saw it on the news. That's where we've been the last two days, trying to get to the bottom of it."

I knew that was Dad's face I'd glimpsed on TV!

"We actually know her. I thought I recognised her on the TV. She's the sister of one of our colleagues."

"What's wrong with her?"

"We don't know. We've never come across anything like this before. There's been no change in her condition since we found her."

"And now you two." Mum's face crinkled into worried lines. "This changes everything."

"How do you mean?"

"Before it might have been an accident. Now it's starting to look like an attack."

Chapter Eight

At least we didn't have to pretend to have laryngitis any more. Dad spent the next morning running experiments on us. Most of them involved bits and pieces of weird gadgetry like the Hendrix counter, that beeped or spat out incomprehensible printouts while Dad muttered to himself.

The only test that made any sense was when he was trying to establish just how connected CJ and I had to be to nullify the Frog Effect. He tried us holding the ends of all kinds of things: a length of steel chain from the garage, various items of clothing, glass bottles (both empty and full), jewellery of gold and of silver. None of them worked. We had to be in direct contact.

Pretty early in the experiment we moved outside. Frog production was in overdrive with all the talking I was doing, and the little devils were hopping everywhere.

"Why don't you just make CJ talk?" I complained. "At least diamonds are worth something."

"To address your first point," Dad said, looking up from his laptop, "what kind of scientist only tests one side of the equation?

One of these things might stop the frogs without affecting the diamonds. We'd never know if CJ is the only one talking. And secondly, I hope you girls aren't dreaming of riches, because these diamonds aren't worth anything."

CJ looked crestfallen. She'd most certainly been making big plans. "What do you mean? They're real diamonds, aren't they?"

"Oh, they're real enough to fool any jeweller, all right. They just won't last long. There's not enough aether in the world any more to sustain them."

"I should have taken some to a jeweller on Sunday, before they got home," CJ whispered to me. "They would have lasted long enough to make me rich."

"Oh, that wouldn't have looked suspicious at all," I whispered back. Honestly, sometimes I wondered about my sister. She was smart enough, but had no more common sense than a flea. "A teenager wandering into a jeweller's with a handful of massive diamonds. You would have got yourself arrested."

To Dad I said, "What's aether?"

"Aether is the raw material of magic. There's barely any left in the world any more. Or at least, there shouldn't be. Only enough to power some of our devices, like the Hendrix counter, and we keep that safely locked away. There's aether in the tube, and when a current is passed through it, it reacts to the presence of aether in the vicinity. That's why the tube glows when it's near you two."

I couldn't believe this was my father talking. He looked the same as always; kind of balding, a bit daggy. But apparently he was an expert on magic.

"Were you ever planning on telling us any of this?" An expert on magic, but all these years he'd let us think he worked for the military.

He frowned at his computer screen and said nothing.

"We're not kids any more, you know." I could understand keeping secrets when we were little, but now? Considering the sacrifices we'd made for their careers, it would at least have been nice to know *why*.

"It would depend entirely on the results of your tests."

"What tests?"

Dad sighed and ran a hand over his face. "Everyone with the blood is tested in childhood, and again at eighteen. If they have enough latent affinity for magic, they become a part of our organisation. We have a web of people all over the world. Web …" He broke off, and I could tell from the look on his face that his mind had veered off down a completely different path. "Spider-silk's a marvellous conductor of aether. We should try regular silk." He bounded inside and came back with an old scarf of Mum's. "I should have thought of that before. Most of the High Sidhe's garments are made of silk."

He handed one end to me and the other to CJ, and looked expectantly at us.

"Who are the High Sidhe?" I asked.

"Bingo!" Dad actually clapped, but I got no more answers.

With the scarf in our hands, we could speak freely even without touching. I tied one end around my wrist, and CJ did the same. It beat holding hands all day.

Mum's car came into the garage, and soon Mum appeared, looking flustered. "Did you know there's a TV van parked outside?"

"Really?" CJ ran to peek out the front window, so I had to go, too. A bored-looking guy lounged against the side of the van, but he straightened when he saw us at the window and gestured to his companion, who pointed a camera our way.

"Come away." I grabbed a handful of silk and yanked. I did *not* want to be the light relief story on the news tonight, squeezed in after all the wars and politics, just before the weather, where they usually had the story about the performing dog or the crazy small-town fundraising idea. The human interest story, where the newsreader was finally allowed to crack a smile after pulling their serious newsreader face for half an hour. I wasn't a performing seal, and the attention I'd already drawn at school was more than enough to convince me that a life in the limelight was definitely not for me.

Mum came in and closed the blinds. "Let's not encourage them. Come and have some lunch."

We sat at the kitchen table, watching her make sandwiches. I tried a few questions, but she was just as tight-lipped as Dad. Being given the brush-off by both of them didn't improve my mood any.

"I saw Dorian at the office," she told Dad over lunch. "He thought we should bring the girls in."

"For testing?" He spoke round a mouthful of sandwich, but for once Mum didn't tell him off. "Don't need to. I've got everything here."

"I think he was more concerned about publicity. He felt it might be better to go into hiding for a while."

That sounded promising. Maybe we'd finally find out what the hell was going on.

CJ's ears pricked up too, though not for the same reason. She had other priorities. "For how long? It's the Year 12 formal on Friday night. We can't miss that."

"I told him we'd think about it," Mum said. "Don't worry, I'm sure we can still get you to the formal."

"Who's this Dorian guy anyway? Is he your boss?"

"No. We don't actually have a boss. He's a warder, like us." She took a deep breath, as if handing out a few crumbs of information was some big scary deal. "There are seven of us, and we all have an equal say in the affairs of the Council."

"Only seven of you?" I pushed for more. Crumbs weren't going to be enough to satisfy my appetite. Not when their secret magic crap was screwing up my life. "No wonder we have to keep moving so often."

"Oh, there's lots more people in the organisation. I think we have a couple of hundred now. But only the seven warders—it's a hereditary position. We're the descendants of the original seven who trapped the Sidhe."

"Why's it hereditary?" CJ asked.

"And how come you and Dad are both warders then?"

"The original seven were the greatest mages of their time— possibly of all time, which is why they succeeded where others had failed," Dad said. "Since magic is passed down in family lines, it only made sense to ensure that the subsequent warders were from those same families, to keep the power strong."

Mum had an odd look on her face, but I was too focused on what Dad was saying to pay her much attention.

"You mean you can do magic?" CJ looked openly sceptical.

It was hard not to be. Dad was great with gadgets, but he

could barely boil an egg, or put together an outfit on his own that didn't make your eyeballs bleed. The idea that he might be a powerful mage was kind of hard to swallow.

"No." Well, that was a relief. At least I wouldn't have to rethink my whole worldview. "The great irony of it was that, in locking the Sidhe away from the human world to protect it from their magic, the Founders also locked their own powers away."

"How did they do that?" My brain was racing, trying to keep up with all this new information.

"They drained all the aether from the world, sucking it into the Sidhe realms, and created a force to hold it there. Magic can't be worked without aether. In a nutshell, the magic's all in Fairyland, and we're out here. We can't get in, and they can't get out, and no one on the outside can work magic any more."

"But now something's leaking out, right?"

"Right." He looked troubled. "Well, I won't find any answers sitting here. Best get back to work."

Mum and Dad disappeared into the study, and I tried to focus on the Ancient History essay I had due on Friday, to take my mind off all the crap that was going on. It was a pretty half-hearted effort, though. I mean, it's not every day you find out that magic is real and your own parents seem to know all about it. Crazy stuff. But in between my visions of mages and fairies, a certain dark-eyed boy kept popping up. How could I ever face Zac again? What if Dad couldn't figure out a way to get rid of these stupid frogs?

CJ didn't seem too fussed. She spent most of the afternoon texting back and forth with someone on her phone, but I ignored all my incoming messages, and ended up turning my phone off.

Most of them were from Sona, and what could I say to her? *Yeah, apparently I have a magic curse, but it's okay, my parents run Alcatraz for fairies, and they're working on a way to fix it.* The only thing I was sure of was that Sona's reaction would be loud.

Mum's phone rang just after three, and then Dad's, and there was a hurried discussion before Mum appeared, car keys in hand again.

"I've got to dash back to the office," she said. "Another crisis."

"To do with us?"

"No, no. I'm sure it's nothing. Some crazy readings on the activity monitor. I'll probably get there and find it's just a malfunction. Everyone's just a bit jumpy lately, so I have to go in and soothe a few people." She rolled her eyes. "There's a lot of that in this job."

Wondering what the hell she was talking about sure made it hard to focus on Ancient Greek politics.

"Apparently Dad's descended from someone called Maeve the Red," CJ said, when Mum had been gone a while.

"Really? Sounds like a pirate."

"Yeah, he was telling me when you were in the bathroom. The greatest witch in Ireland, according to him."

"Our great-great-whatever-grandmother was a *witch*?"

"Well, he might have said 'mage', but whatever. Same thing. Bet they called her a witch in those days."

"What about Mum? Who's her famous great-great?"

"Edmund Anderson." She paused. "Or maybe it was Andrew Edmunsen. Whatever. He was English."

"Hmm. Not as cool as being Maeve the Red."

CJ shrugged. "It probably just meant she had red hair."

Like me. Bet she had the glow-in-the-dark skin too.

"I guess. Who are you texting?"

She tilted the phone away from me. "No one."

That was just an invitation for me to pry but, luckily for her, the doorbell rang. She shoved the phone in her pocket. "Come on."

I hung back. "What if it's someone from the press?"

She leered at me. "What if it's the man of your dreams?"

"I don't think Hollywood actors do house calls."

She flung the door open, and for a moment I was too blinded by flashes going off to see who stood there. The one van from the morning had turned into five or six, plus assorted photographers who'd arrived in cars. The street was as parked out as Josh's place had been on Saturday night.

"Girls, over here!"

"Violet, say something!"

"CJ, are those diamonds real? What are you going to do with all the money?"

"Violet, what's it like having frogs come out of your mouth?"

We fell back, open-mouthed, as the whole pack surged up the driveway. Zac stood on the doorstep with shoulders hunched like someone who'd been sent to the principal's office. I was so surprised to see him I just froze, but CJ grabbed his arm and hauled him inside, slamming the door on the crowd.

We were going to look pretty stupid in some of those photos, like two fish gasping for air on the doorstep. Even CJ looked shaken.

"There's so *many* of them," she said.

We huddled by the front door, staring at each other in shock.

"You guys are big news," Zac said. "Have you been on the internet today? That video of you in class yesterday has gone viral. I heard it was on the news, too. People are wondering if it's connected to that thing with the girl in the glass coffin."

"But how'd they find out where we live?"

"All they had to do was turn up at school. Half a dozen reporters were hanging around this morning until the teachers chased them off. But they found plenty of kids happy to talk."

"And what are you doing here?" CJ asked, with unusual bluntness. She bristled like a dog standing guard, as if she suspected Zac of trying to cash in on our fame by turning up here and digging for goss. I pressed against her side, hoping Zac wouldn't notice the silk scarf that tied our wrists together. I didn't want him thinking we were into some weird kind of bondage.

He flushed at the sharpness in her tone. "I came to return Vi's calculator."

I'd forgotten all about lending him my calculator. "You didn't have to do that. You could have given it to me at school."

"I was kind of worried about you." He grinned, and the dimple peeped out. "And so was Sona."

"I'm surprised she didn't come herself." He was worried? That was so sweet.

"Oh, she wanted to, believe me, but she has tutoring on Tuesday afternoons. She said she'd sent you a million texts but you hadn't replied to any of them and she was starting to worry." He gave me a quizzical look. "I guess you got over the laryngitis?"

Heat flooded my cheeks. He may as well have said *So, you were lying about having laryngitis, huh?*

'Yeah. Just in time for the holidays.'

'Oh, and speaking of holidays: don't worry about that essay for Ancient History for Friday. We've got all holidays to do it now.'

'How come?'

'Mr Chadwick fell down the stairs yesterday afternoon and broke his leg. We've got this new teacher, Miss Moore, for a few weeks. She said we can hand it in next term.'

'Cool. Guess she didn't feel like doing any marking in the holidays.'

'Guess not.'

Dad cleared his throat behind us.

'I heard the doorbell …' He frowned at Zac. 'Who's this?'

'My friend, Zac. He dropped in on the way home from school to return my calculator.' Maybe more than a friend. He'd said he was worried about me. The thought warmed me, but it made it kind of hard to look at him. Plus I was still blushing. Stupid pale skin. 'Zac, this is my Dad.'

'Nice to meet you, Mr Reilly.'

'Pleased to meet you, too.' He didn't look pleased, though. 'I'm sorry, but I'm going to have to ask you to leave. We're in the middle of something rather important.'

'Oh. Okay, then.' God, this was awkward. Zac looked back at me. 'Will you be at school tomorrow?'

'Maybe. I don't know.'

'Okay.' He hesitated, as if he would have liked to have stayed longer, but Dad stood there, all stern and impatient. 'Well, see you round.'

He slipped outside and disappeared into a roar of shouted questions and an explosion of flashes.

Chapter Nine

"What the hell is that racket?" Grumpy as a bear waking up from hibernation, Dad glared at the front door as if he was holding it personally to blame.

"It's the press. They're still camped outside."

"The press?" He strode into the lounge room and peeked through the slats of the venetians. "Bloody hell!"

He wasn't always the world's best listener. It was quite possible he'd been so caught up in whatever he was doing that he hadn't even heard Mum mention the first TV van. Even if he had, he'd probably dismissed it as something Mum would deal with, and not given it another thought.

"Bloody hell," he said again. "Have you seen how many of them are out there? It's a circus. We can't have this kind of attention! Where's your mother?"

"She went into the office, remember? Something about a malfunction."

He looked at his watch. "That was an hour ago. Okay, let me make a phone call. Get your shoes on, girls, we're going out."

'Where to?" CJ asked, but he headed back to the study without answering. "I can't go yet, I haven't done my makeup!"

"Better hurry, then," I said.

She dashed upstairs, but as it turned out, she needn't have rushed. Dad didn't reappear for another half-hour.

'Ready?" he asked, as if we'd been keeping him waiting, instead of the other way around. "Let's go."

"Where are we going?" I asked as we got into the car.

"To the office." He paused with his finger on the button to open the garage door. "Better keep your heads down."

I slumped down in my seat, feeling like a criminal on the way to trial, as he backed the car out. At the bottom of the driveway the media swarmed the car, thrusting cameras and microphones our way. So many shouting faces! I shrank back in alarm as they buffeted the car. Dad continued to reverse slowly, so they had to get out of the way or be run over.

The whole pack of them spilled onto the street, still shouting, but some of them broke away, heading for their vehicles. Dad roared up the street, and three vans pulled out straight away, determined to give chase. I looked back and saw car doors slamming as others prepared to follow.

"How are we going to shake them off?" I asked.

Dad actually grinned. "Watch this."

He took a fast right at the end of the street. Behind us, two big black cars pulled smoothly away from the gutter where they'd been waiting and parked end to end across the intersection, blocking the end of our street. The row of vans pulled up, unable to follow us. The driver of the first van leaned on his horn and yelled out his window, but the black cars didn't budge. The glass of their windows was tinted so dark I couldn't see who was in them.

"Friends of yours?"

"Just a couple of boys from the office."

"Won't they get into trouble? What if those idiots take their registration numbers and report them?"

"I don't think the police would be all that sympathetic in the circumstances. Don't worry about it, honey." He gave me a lopsided grin. "Haven't you got plenty of better things to worry about?"

True enough. I sat back and watched the world go past. It occurred to me I didn't actually know where Mum and Dad's office was—not that it would have meant anything to me if they'd told me. We hadn't been in Sydney long enough for me to know my way around.

We swept up the huge hump of a multi-lane bridge, and off to the left I saw the city laid out, pretty as a postcard. The waterways snaking towards the distant Harbour Bridge shone a vivid blue in the sunshine and the buildings stood tall and shining. The strange top-heavy silhouette of Centrepoint Tower was the only one I recognised.

Closer in, the city lost its sunny sparkle. Down on street level there was the usual grime and graffiti you find in every big city, and the roads were choked with traffic. In amongst them, the height of the buildings wasn't such a great thing. They leaned over the narrow roads, blocking the sun and creating shadowy canyons.

"Where are we going?" I asked as we stopped at yet another set of lights to let crowds of pedestrians stream across the road.

Now some of the skyscrapers had been replaced by smaller, older buildings. Most of them glowed a honey gold in the sunshine, and some had intricate scrollwork and other decorations carved into the stone.

Dad noticed me looking. "A lot of the older buildings in Sydney are made from the local sandstone. Headquarters is in a part of the city called The Rocks. Very old, full of lots of historic buildings."

Up ahead a huge sandstone arch soared over the road, and I realised that the Harbour Bridge loomed to one side.

"That's the Argyle Cut," Dad said, indicating the archway. "It's so old part of the work on it was done by convicts. The harbour's just over there."

We turned off after the Cut, running through narrow streets barely wide enough for two cars to pass, lined with rows of tiny narrow houses on either side. Suddenly the view opened up and there was the harbour, laid out in a spectacular vista. Ferries crisscrossed the blue water, churning up a white wake behind them.

"Wow," said CJ. "I didn't realise Sydney Harbour was that big. Where's the Opera House?"

"Over there," Dad said. "You can't see it from here. Our building's down this way."

We turned away from the view and took another narrow street, then turned abruptly down a driveway to an underground carpark. I'd barely had time to notice the building itself. I had a brief impression of dark bricks and arched windows, maybe two storeys tall, and then we were pulling into an empty spot in a rather cramped garage.

Mum's car was right in front of the lift.

"Which floor?" I asked when we stepped in, my finger hovering over the buttons. There were only four to choose from: P, B, G and 1. Not a very big place, then.

"Ground," Dad said.

Up we went, the lift making a rather unnerving clanking as we started off. Hopefully it wasn't as old as the building appeared to be. But when the lift doors opened, I discovered that, however old the exterior looked, the inside was reassuringly modern. A large reception desk made of a polished red wood faced us, and thick, expensive-looking carpet muffled our footsteps as we approached. The place smelled faintly of paint, as if they'd redecorated recently.

The woman behind the desk smiled at Dad. "Good afternoon, Warder Reilly."

"Hello, Katie. Any messages for me?"

"No, sir."

"Is Dorian in?"

"I think he's in the monitor room with Warder Winters."

Winters was Mum's maiden name. Did she mean Mum? I guess having two "Warder Reillys" would get confusing.

"Thanks." Dad headed off down the corridor and we hurried after him.

"Things seem very formal here," said CJ. "Warder Reilly?"

"I'd be just as happy if they called me Doug," said Dad, "but Dorian insists on formality. He's very big on tradition."

We came to an intersection, and a man in the cross-corridor called out.

"Douglas! There you are—just the man we need."

He strode down the corridor and Dad stopped to wait for

him He wasn't particularly tall, though taller than Dad—but everyone was taller than Dad. He looked a little older too; the hair at his temples was greying, though it was still dark everywhere else. He was good-looking for an older guy, with a strong, square jaw and a straight nose just the right size for the rest of his face. He wore a dark blue business suit with the ease of a man accustomed to nice clothing. Next to him, Dad looked rather rumpled in his grey trousers and faded polo shirt.

"Hi, Dorian. These are my daughters, Crystal and Violet. Girls, this is Dorian Kincumber, one of the warders."

Dorian smiled, showing even white teeth. "Pleased to meet you. I've heard all about your little problem. Make yourselves at home. There's a kitchen behind reception, and Katie can get you anything we don't have in stock."

Little problem? I bet he wouldn't be saying that if *he* was the one spitting frogs. And there was no way I was going to sit in the kitchen like a good little girl. I wanted to be where the action was.

"Hopefully we won't be here long," Dad said. "The press are crawling all over our place. Thought we might come in and let the excitement die down a while."

"Just what I was suggesting to Jane earlier," Dorian said. "Forgive me for asking, but why the scarf?"

He caught at the loop hanging between our wrists and ran the silk between his fingers.

"The curse is negated when they're touching each other," Dad said. "The silk is the only conductor I've found that maintains that effect while allowing them some distance."

"Interesting," said Dorian.

"I hope I can find a more workable solution while we're here."

"I'm sure the young ladies would appreciate that." He flashed that picture-perfect smile again. The man could have gotten a job in a toothpaste commercial. "Are you heading for the monitor room? I'll come with you."

He turned and walked with us.

"Any developments today?" Dad asked.

"Well, we sent a crew over to the Johnson house. No one was home, but they told the neighbour they were checking for gas leaks and she let them in. Full of complaints about the party, apparently. Said she didn't get a wink of sleep."

CJ and I exchanged a look. They weaselled their way into Josh Johnson's house? How did they get away with stuff like that?

"Did they find anything?"

"Nothing unexpected. Strong traces of a Sidhe presence, but no sign of anything now. Whoever it was probably left as soon as the job was done."

He glanced at us as he spoke. Did he mean the toads and diamonds spell, or whatever it was?

"Any ideas on who it was?"

Dorian shrugged. "We're just stabbing in the dark here. There hasn't been anything this big since the Cottingley affair."

"What about the Johnson boy himself?"

"I've sent Simon over to the school this morning. He's not back yet."

We arrived at a set of double doors. Dorian opened the right-hand one and gestured us into the room.

"Wow," CJ said.

I nodded. We both stopped just inside the door and stared. The room looked like something from a movie—maybe a space mission, or one of those ones where there's a terrorist threat or some huge military disaster, and the president and all his advisors are gathered around a huge table, or in front of an enormous screen—you could take your pick, this room had both—while around them a hundred busy people do busy things on a hundred computers.

After a shocked moment I realised that there weren't that many people here. Probably more like forty or fifty—but the impact was still enormous. Dad and Dorian hadn't noticed we'd stopped, and kept going, still chatting. A couple of people looked up from their screens, but whatever they were doing was too serious to take much notice of two girls, however pretty one of them was.

An enormous screen filled the wall at the far end of the room. It was easily as big as the screens you get at the movies, maybe bigger, and even though this room was large, it dominated the space. On it was displayed a map of the world, with the continents glowing a soft green. All except Australia. It had little pinpoints of red light coming and going in a big clump right over Sydney.

"Hey, there's Mum," CJ said, and dragged me forward.

I hadn't even noticed her standing in front of the screen until then. She turned as Dad and Dorian reached her, and waved to us. Everyone looked very serious and businesslike. It made me look at Mum and Dad in a new light. If I'd thought of them at work at all, I'd imagined them at a desk in some little cubicle, reporting to someone higher up the food chain. Now it seemed there was a lot more to the picture than that. Maybe there *was* no one higher up the food chain than Warder Winters and Warder Reilly.

"—definitely not a glitch," Mum was saying. "Hi, darlings! Gretel's run diagnostics on the whole system and Ronnie's had the mainframe in pieces. Nothing. Isn't that right, Ron?"

She called over her shoulder to a woman bent over the innards of a computer, who looked up and blinked like someone waking from a dream. "Sorry, Warder? Did you say something?"

"She asked about the mainframe," said another woman, coming forward, and now it was my turn to blink. Just as well Ronnie had short hair and this one had a ponytail, because otherwise I wouldn't have been able to tell them apart. "There's nothing wrong with the monitors, Warders. The system's running like a dream. Everything you see up there is happening in real time."

She waved a hand at the giant screen and for a moment we all contemplated the slowly multiplying dots. Sydney looked like it was coming down with a bad case of chickenpox.

CJ was studying the twins with undisguised interest. They only looked a few years older than us. She'd always wished we were identical. It seemed so much sexier somehow, being an exact copy of another person, instead of just a random sibling who happened to have been born at the same time. I'd pointed out numerous times that her fantasy of having someone just like her was all well and good, but what if we'd both looked just like me instead? Bet she wouldn't find that such an appealing idea. Yet it was still a disappointment to her, just as she longed for hair like Sona's, that fell past her butt. It was hard for CJ, with all her physical advantages, to accept that there were some things she wanted that she just couldn't have.

Ronnie's twin noticed her stare. "Hi, I'm Gretel," she said. "This is my sister Veronica. I'm guessing you must be Warder Winters' daughters?"

"That's right."

We drifted closer, ignored by the three warders, who were discussing the map with worried frowns.

"I heard you had a little problem with a Sidhe curse."

I hadn't heard it called that before, but it was obvious what she meant.

"Yeah." I held up my wrist, showing her the silk scarf. "If it wasn't for this there'd be frogs jumping all over the place by now."

"That's terrible! Still, I bet if anyone can get it sorted your Dad can. He's a whiz with the machines, Warder Reilly."

"What do you do?" CJ asked, eyes bright with twin worship.

"Oh, Ron and I are in IT. Neither of us had the latency to be a seeker, and someone's got to keep all these computers running."

"What's a seeker?"

She frowned. "You know, the ones who go out hunting for Sidhe artefacts and get them safely under lock and key before anyone does anything stupid with them."

Artefacts? When we talked about artefacts in Ancient History, we usually meant everyday things like pots or bowls, jewellery or little statues. Basically remnants of lost civilisations that helped us piece together a picture of life in those times.

"Sidhe artefacts?" I repeated. Did she mean magical objects? What other kind of artefact would a race of fairies leave lying around?

"Mirrors," she said. "Jewellery, lamps—the usual. Most of them are useless now the aether's gone, of course, but sometimes the seekers find a live one, even after all these years. We can't leave objects of power lying around for any idiot to play with, can we? Much safer locked up here in the vault."

I nodded as if I knew what she was talking about, but I was completely lost. The vault? What, like a bank vault? Maybe I should ask a question where I had more chance of understanding the answer.

"What are all those red dots?" I gestured at the screen. "Everyone seems pretty concerned about something."

Her expression clouded over. "Yeah. That's measuring aether. Suddenly we're leaking aether like a sieve, when there hasn't been any to speak of for centuries. Everyone was hoping it was just the monitors going haywire, but we've double-checked and triple-checked, and it's nothing that simple."

"Where's it coming from?"

"Only place it can be—the other side of the wall. The Sidhe side. But how the hell it's doing that, I don't know. And neither does anyone else. That's why they all look so worried."

Before I could ask any more, two police officers came in. Even though I hadn't done anything wrong, I felt a reflexive twinge of guilt. Was this about those black cars blocking the end of our street?

Dad turned around and saw them. "Simon! You're back. How did it go?"

"The Johnson boy's clean, sir."

CJ and I exchanged a confused look. The guy *looked* like a policeman, but …

"Did you have any trouble getting access to him?" Dorian asked.

"No, sir. We told the principal we wanted to discuss reports of underage drinking at his party and she couldn't have been more helpful. Even let us use her office for the interview." He smiled. "That's one kid who'll think twice before breaking the law again."

Gretel was staring at him as hungrily as if he were made of chocolate. I blinked. He didn't seem that special: mid-brown hair, average height. Nice blue eyes, but that smile hadn't been very pleasant.

"And you're sure he's who he says he is?" Mum asked.

"Absolutely, Warder. One hundred per cent human teenager. He doesn't know anything about the Sidhe. Whoever impersonated him did so without his knowledge."

"Good. Thank you, Simon."

The two "policemen" left the room. Gretel sighed, a wistful look on her face.

"Those guys aren't really cops, are they?" CJ asked her.

"No, that's Simon and Kyle. They're two of our seekers. They go out and get their hands dirty while people like me and Ron stay here and play computers." She sighed again, still staring at the door the seekers had left through. "Still, we can't all do the glamorous jobs. Someone's got to keep the home fires burning."

"Do you like him?" CJ must have noticed the way Gretel looked at him too, and she'd never learned not to ask personal questions. Usually she got away with it. There were advantages to being pretty.

"Who, Simon? He's all right. Some of the seekers get big heads, think they're something special. He's okay." Was her face a little redder than it had been?

"Ah—Warder Winters?" called a voice. One of the computer operators had popped up from her station like a meerkat. "We're getting some unusual activity locally."

"Put it on the screen, Angie."

The picture on the screen zoomed in so fast it was like falling down a well. We zeroed in on Sydney with dizzying speed, closer and closer, until The Rocks and Circular Quay filled the wall. The building where we stood was marked HQ, and the hodgepodge of streets around it were neatly labelled.

I swayed to the right as the view shifted over to show the Botanical Gardens, the Opera House on its point, and the Domain. Some of these names were only vaguely familiar. The Domain looked like a big park—was that part of the Botanical Gardens? A big building in the middle of it was marked "Art Gallery".

Then a huge splotch of red came into view, moving fast.

"College Street!" said Dorian, a note of panic in his voice. "Get a containment team down there *now*."

"No!" said Mum. "I'll go with them. Let's see if we can catch them this time. We need some answers."

Dorian opened his mouth to object, but she was already out the door, running like Usain Bolt going for gold.

Chapter Ten

The room exploded into action. Half of them suddenly had urgent places to be, including Dad.

"I'll have to rig something up in the vault," he said. "You three, come with me."

Three rather startled technicians obediently followed him to the door. I thought he was just going to leave us there, but at the last minute he stopped.

"Gretel, can you set up a video feed from the vault back to Jane's office? No sense all of us being exposed."

She nodded, so she must have understood what he was talking about. Then his eye fell on us and he frowned, as if he'd only just remembered we existed.

"Take the girls to the library on your way, would you? I'll see you later, girls. Just try to stay out of everyone's way for now. There's plenty to keep you occupied in the library."

"Bet they don't have wi-fi," CJ muttered as we followed Gretel out.

"Or TV."

Not that I didn't like reading. I did. But there probably weren't going to be any of my kind of books in an office library, even if it was a very peculiar kind of office.

"What was all that about?" I asked as Gretel hurried us out into the corridor. "Where's Mum rushing off to in such a hurry?"

"That big red spot on the map," she said. "It was moving. Aether doesn't move in big clumps like that—unless it's contained in something. Or someone."

I frowned. "People can have aether inside them?"

"No." She looked worried. "Not normally. Only Sidhe. Looks like we have an escapee out there."

CJ was frowning too, but it turned out her mind was running down a different track altogether.

"I've never met any identical twins before," she said, as if she hadn't even heard that there was an escaped fairy loose on the streets. Possibly she hadn't. She was like Dad in that way, very single-minded.

"Really?" Gretel seemed eager to change the subject to safer ground. Bet she wished someone else had scored babysitting duties. "There's another set working for the Council, but they're stationed in Perth. We have quite a lot of twins, of course."

"Why 'of course'?"

Gretel looked a little surprised. "Well, because twins tend to run in magical families."

It took me a minute to follow that to its logical conclusion. "Do you mean that everyone here is from a magical family? Not just the warders?"

Now she looked almost shocked. "Didn't you know that?"

"Until yesterday we didn't know any of this existed," CJ said.

"Mum and Dad never told us anything about their jobs. I bet they still wouldn't have if we hadn't managed to get cursed somehow."

She sounded sulky, like a child who'd just discovered a wonderful playground that everyone else had been playing in for years.

"I'm sure they had their reasons." Gretel seemed uneasy now, and she picked up the pace. With my shorter legs I had trouble keeping up.

CJ looked like she wanted to argue, but all she said was: "Who else is a twin here?"

"Umm … who have you met? There's Katie, on reception. She has a twin brother in operations. Darrell and Hamish—they were the two guys sitting next to Ronnie. Oh, and Simon—but don't tell him I told you that."

"Why not?"

"His twin didn't make it. He doesn't like to talk about it."

"You mean he's dead?"

"No! God, no. He just can't work for us." She looked uncomfortable. "You should ask your parents. I probably shouldn't be telling you this stuff."

Not if they hadn't told us themselves. She didn't need to add it; I could tell that was what she was thinking. I guess no one wants to get into trouble with their bosses.

"Here's the library!" She smiled brightly. "Make yourselves at home."

She opened the door to a large, comfortable room and waved us in. It felt reassuringly familiar after the strangeness of the monitor room, just like the library at school. Books were still books, whatever the subject, and they had that wonderful, slightly musty smell of old paper that promised hours of wonder lost in other lands and strange stories.

There were comfy chairs scattered about, and big arched windows on one wall that let the sunshine stream in. Opposite the door was a glassed-in room.

"That's the restricted section." Gretel indicated the glass room. "It's locked, though. You can read anything you like out here."

"Are there spell books?" CJ asked, with visions of Hogwarts dancing before her eyes, no doubt. She'd been a big Harry Potter fan when she was younger.

Gretel smiled. "No. Most of this is more of a historical collection—the works of regular humans concerning the Sidhe world. Some of them are surprisingly accurate. We even have Shakespeare."

"Shakespeare?" CJ looked like she'd swallowed something nasty.

"You bet. He had quite a lot to say about witches and fairies in his works. Ever read *A Midsummer Night's Dream*?"

CJ groaned. "Yeah, we're studying it at school. Are you saying that stuff is true?"

"Not gospel truth, no. But a lot of the basics are there."

My opinion of fairies went way down. "But all they seem to care about is sex and wife-swapping and messing around with love potions."

"The High Sidhe are often very focused on affairs of the heart." Obviously this information wasn't classified; she'd lost that harried look. "Or at least the body. I'm not sure they have hearts, the way we understand them.

"Anyway—" She checked her watch. "I'd better run. It's been so long since anyone's had dealings with the Sidhe we have to rely on our records to get a feel for what they were like. And I've got to tell you, some of those old mages were dry old sticks. At least with Shakespeare and people like that, you get more than just lists of attributes and known haunts. I'll see you a bit later!"

She headed back out, shutting the door behind her in a rush, as if she was relieved to escape. Shame she'd realised we knew nothing and clammed up; she'd dropped some interesting info before that. Seekers and magical artefacts; twins in magical families.

CJ looked at me. "I don't know about you, but *I* sure ain't reading Shakespeare to pass the time, whatever she says."

She flopped into the nearest chair and pulled out her phone.

"Who are you texting? Ashleigh? I'm surprised your thumbs aren't bleeding yet, you've been texting so much today."

I leaned over, trying to see the screen, but once again she tilted it away from me.

"Get off. Go find a picture book that won't strain your intellect too much."

"Be anti-social then. See if I care."

I slipped out of our scarf and wandered off, but I wasn't letting go that easily. I had more than a sneaking suspicion that there was a boy involved. With CJ, there usually was. But who? The only guy she'd shown any interest in at all was Josh Johnson, but I refused to contemplate the horror of my sister going out with that waste of space.

I pulled a book off the shelves at random. Ironically enough, it was a picture book, though not intended for children. More like a field sketchbook, full of whimsical drawings of "the fae and other ungodly sprytes", with notes on their behaviours. Some of the pictures were quite striking, but I pretended to be more engrossed than I was as I circled back to CJ's chair.

I needn't have worried; she was so caught up in what she was doing I could have stood behind her blowing The Last Post on the trumpet and she mightn't have noticed. I peered over her shoulder and my heart sank.

When u coming back 2 skl babe?

Y? U miss me? CJ texted back.

Ill show u how much …

I stood there for a couple of minutes, watching them flirt, until I was certain. It had to be Josh. I was going to have to disown my sister.

She giggled at his latest attempt at flattery—or maybe she was just laughing at his spelling, who knows?—and then she finally realised I was standing behind her.

"What are you doing?" she snapped, spilling diamonds on the floor. "Spying on me?"

"What are *you* doing? Why are you encouraging that jerk?" At least I had the sense to grab the scarf before I opened my mouth.

She tossed her beautiful black hair over one shoulder. "Who says he's a jerk?"

"Ah—*you* did, the first day we met him."

"He's not so bad once you get to know him."

"I don't think I have a strong enough stomach for that."

"Nobody's asking *you* to go out with him."

"Oh, but *you* are? Since when? This has come on pretty fast, hasn't it? You hardly ever spoke to him on Saturday night, and you haven't seen him since."

She clasped her phone protectively against her chest. "We've been texting a lot, and we skyped last night for hours." Her face glowed with the memory. "He's actually quite a sweetie."

I dropped into the chair beside hers and gave her a stern look. "So basically, ever since he found out you've got diamonds coming out of your mouth he's been hot to trot. You don't see anything suspicious about that?"

She gave me a glare that could peel paint. "If you do, it's because you've got a nasty mind. We have a lot in common."

"Right. He likes diamonds, you've got diamonds …"

Couldn't she see he was just like the prince in the stupid fairy tale? *Oh, look, this girl is a walking diamond vending machine. Let's get together!*

"Oh, for God's sake. Is it so impossible he might like me for myself?"

Of course not. There was a lot to like in that pretty package, and she knew it. What else could I say? I didn't trust him, and she was determined to ignore me. I guess time would tell who was the better judge of character.

"You just don't like him because of that whole scene in the bedroom with the absinthe." She leaned forward, intent. "But *that wasn't him*, remember?"

True. There had been something very unsettling about that guy, but if that hadn't really been Josh … Maybe I was being too harsh. If Mum and Dad were right, that had been a Sidhe pretending to be Josh, presumably so he could get close enough to dump this stupid curse on us. Was that what he'd meant when he said he had a gift for us? Creepy bastard.

A swell of noise in the corridor distracted us both. Raised voices were coming closer. Footsteps ran past the library door.

Quarrel forgotten, we looked at each other. "Do you think that's Mum back?"

We hurried to the door. I paused with my hand on the door handle. What would we see when I opened the door? A real live fairy?

"Come *on*." When I didn't move, CJ yanked the door open and stepped into the corridor.

Six big guys in dark clothes escorted two people towards us. One was Mum. The other was a short, very ordinary-looking young guy in a scruffy T-shirt and faded blue jeans with a hole in one knee. If *he* was a fairy I wanted my money back. What a let-down.

He looked up and his bright green eyes flashed when he saw CJ.

"Hi there, babe. Fancy another drink?"

⁓✢⁓

Gretel looked up from the computer as we came into Mum's office. "Are they back already?"

"Uh-huh." CJ slumped on to a couch, looking surly, as well she might. Mum hadn't been amused, to put it mildly. She paused only long enough to send one of the men to show us to her office, then stormed off with a face like thunder. The scruffy guy had winked at CJ as he was hustled away.

"And? Did they find anything?"

I shrugged, perched uncomfortably on the arm of the couch next to CJ. "Just some guy."

114

"A guy?" She shook her head in wonder. "They really did it. They captured a Sidhe."

She turned back to the computer. Her hand on the mouse was shaking. "I've got to see this."

CJ had her phone out again, pretending she wasn't interested. From where I stood I could see over Gretel's shoulder. She'd set up a video link, and the screen showed part of a room where Dorian Kincumber paced back and forth past the camera. Dad stood in the background, leaning against the wall.

"Where's that?" I asked.

"The vault," she said.

"As in, where they keep the money?"

She grinned. "No."

"That's right, you said that's for the artefacts the seekers find." I couldn't see anything that looked like a magical object, just desks and computers and typical office-type stuff, but the camera didn't show a very big slice of the room.

"Among other things. It seemed like the obvious place to take a Sidhe prisoner."

"Sorry, you've lost me. Obvious how?"

"The Sidhe have an aversion to iron," said Mum, closing the office door behind her. "And the vault is lined with it—walls, floor, ceiling, even the doors. To contain the aether."

Gretel sprang up from the chair and held it out for her.

"All ready for you, Warder Winters."

"Thanks, Gretel." Mum glanced at CJ, who carefully didn't look up from her phone, but clearly she had more important things on her mind now than ferreting out what the Sidhe had meant by his comment. Not that she would forget. That look promised a thorough interrogation to come—once the interrogation on screen was done.

Gretel left the room. On screen Dorian stopped pacing and looked up like a bloodhound quivering on point. The group we'd met in the corridor came in. Two of them handcuffed the prisoner to a chair, while the others took up stations around the room. Were those handcuffs made of iron too?

An odd boxy contraption stood on a tripod next to Dorian. There was no lense, so it wasn't a camera. It looked a little like those things surveyors use. I could see the leg of another one on the other side of the screen. The way Dorian rested his hand on it and stared at the Sidhe man, it looked almost threatening. I wanted to ask Mum what the thing did, but Dorian had started speaking.

"What is your name?"

The Sidhe laid a hand on his chest, pretending shock. "Why, don't you know me, Warder Kincumber? I'm hurt."

"How should I know you? Your kind hasn't been seen in the world since the incursion of 1920."

"By reputation, then. I flatter myself I was quite well known at one time. Even your great Shakespeare wrote of me."

"I'm afraid my memory of Shakespeare's a little rusty. Tell me your name."

He shrugged. "I've been called many things. Call me Robin, if you wish."

Mum leaned forward and spoke into the microphone on her desk. "Robin Goodfellow?"

The Sidhe looked up, directly into the camera, and performed a mocking half-bow. "The very same."

"Otherwise known as Puck," said Dad.

Puck? I'd heard that name before—he was one of the fairies in *A Midsummer Night's Dream*. The one who spent all his time playing tricks on people.

Dad was still leaning against the wall, arms folded. If he'd been about forty kilos heavier that might have looked intimidating, but when you're shorter than nearly everyone else, it's hard to be taken seriously. I should know. Puck only glanced at him, then turned his attention back to the more imposing Dorian.

"What were you doing near the Cathedral?" Dorian asked.

Puck leaned back in his chair and crossed one leg over the other. There was a hole in the knee of his jeans. "Just going for a stroll. Working on my tan, you know."

"How did you escape the Sunlit Land?" Dad asked.

Puck glanced over at him again. I sensed he was enjoying himself, despite the presence of the threatening contraption. He seemed perfectly at ease. Maybe he didn't know what it did either. "Ah, well—you have your internet to thank for that. It's a wonderful thing, you know. Brings the world closer together."

"What are you talking about?" Dorian sounded exasperated, but Dad was looking thoughtful, and Mum leaned on her intercom, one step ahead of both of them.

"Katie, get Gretel in here, would you?"

Gretel appeared in the doorway so quickly she must have been lurking outside. "What's up, ma'am?"

"Get me an analysis as fast as you can on the spread of that YouTube video. Who's watching, how many, where they're located, where's the heaviest traffic, everything you can."

Gretel nodded and ducked out again. She didn't ask which

YouTube video Mum meant. They'd probably all watched it multiple times already, seeing those frogs explode out of my mouth, and the mad scramble for diamonds when CJ spoke. In this place there was only one YouTube video worth mentioning.

"I'm talking about the connectedness of the world these days," Puck was saying on screen. "We could have done a lot with a reach like that. We still could, in fact. They say it's never too late, don't they?"

Dorian's face grew red. The Sidhe man was a hard person to get a straight answer out of. Dad laid a hand on his fellow warder's arm just in time to stop an angry outburst.

"Tell me this, then. Why did you curse my daughters?"

"Your daughters?" He looked at the ceiling and tapped one long finger on his lips, pretending to think. "Oh, you mean the pretty girls I saw in the corridor. That dark one does like a tipple, doesn't she?"

Mum stiffened. Oops. CJ was going to cop it.

"Are they *your* daughters? What a coincidence."

Dad's lips tightened. He rarely lost his temper any more, but when he did it was like fireworks going off. It was the red hair. Something else I'd inherited from him.

"Don't play games with me, Sidhe."

"But that's like telling a fish not to swim, mortal. Playing games is what we *do*."

"Which is why we want you out of our world! Humans are not your playthings."

"Poor helpless warder. You don't even know what game we're playing yet, do you?" He smiled, that same unpleasant smile he'd worn as Josh Johnson. "Such a shame. It's a *very* good game. And this time, we're playing for keeps."

Chapter Eleven

"What did that creature mean by another drink, Crystal?"

There'd been a lot more to the interview, but the men never got any straight answers out of Puck, and in the end they gave up and left the vault. With the interview over, Mum took the opportunity for a little quality time with her eldest daughter.

CJ tried playing dumb. "I don't know. I've never seen him before."

Mum wasn't having any of it. "Crystal Jane, don't act any stupider than you have to. How many Sidhe do you think are walking around out there? He was wearing the appearance of Josh Johnson last time you saw him. Now cut the crap and tell me what really happened."

So the whole sorry absinthe-soaked story came out, and Mum's face grew blacker by the moment.

"Well," she said as Dad and Dorian entered the room, "it looks like Violet will be going to the Year 12 formal on her own."

"Mum, no!" we cried together.

"I've already got the dress!" CJ said. "And you've paid for the tickets."

"I don't even want to go!" I added.

"This is not open to negotiation," she hissed. "Now sit there and be quiet."

Dorian paced, while Mum sat behind her desk scowling and Dad slouched in a visitor's chair, apparently at ease. Only the jiggling of his leg as he tapped his foot double-time on the carpet gave away his true feelings.

"We may as well condense him," Dad said, breaking the long silence. "He's obviously not going to tell us anything. Leaving him loose in the world is just asking for trouble."

"He's hardly loose," Mum said. "He's surrounded by iron, under constant watch—what is he going to do?"

"I don't trust him," Dad said.

"Of course," she said. "Nobody trusts him—he's a pookah. They live to cause trouble. But let's not do anything rash because we're *afraid* of him. He's contained as well as he can be for now. I think we should call a full Council meeting and let the others have a chance to see him before we decide."

"Jane's right." Dorian stopped his pacing. He'd literally worn a track in the carpet—the nap of the carpet where he'd paced was laying in the opposite direction to the rest. "We need as much information as we can get. What are the Sidhe doing?"

"More importantly, how are they doing it?" Dad rubbed tiredly at his stubble. "I think *what* they're doing is fairly clear. They're attacking warders. First Bryan's sister with the Snow White thing, now our girls."

Three pairs of worried eyes rested briefly on us, still parked on the couch in the corner of Mum's office.

"And what did he mean about the internet?" Dorian looked as if he were about to start pacing again, but Dad nudged a spare chair toward him and he sank into it instead. "What does technology have to do with magic?"

"It's not the technology so much as what it can do," Mum said. "I've got Gretel compiling a report for me now. I'm afraid he was referring to the spread of belief. You know they thrive on it. Because of that one YouTube video, belief in magic is spreading again, and there's nothing we can do to call it back. The genie is out of the bottle."

"But that's got nothing to do with it," Dad objected. "Yes, lack of belief weakened them to the point where our ancestors could trap them, but that doesn't mean that restoring belief is enough to free them. As long as the anchors hold, those walls are not coming down."

"That's right." Dorian nodded in relief. "Look at how much belief there was around the Cottingley affair—and that made no difference. The walls were still rock solid."

That was about the third time I'd heard somebody mention this Cottingley affair. It must have been big, whatever it was. I would have to find out soon.

"I don't know." Mum still looked worried. "The reach of the internet is vast. Maybe now it's enough?"

Dorian shook his head. "No, there's got to be more to it than that. Some extra step. What was that creature doing in College Street, so near to the Cathedral?"

"It couldn't be the spear. How could he get in?" Dad sounded like a man who was trying to convince himself and failing badly.

"Maybe he's just trying to fake you out," I said. *Playing games is what we do*, he'd said. If this was the same Puck guy that Shakespeare had written about, he'd shown a fine talent for misdirection, impersonating other people and tricking half the cast into falling in love with someone else.

They all jumped, as if they'd forgotten we were there.

"Fake us out?" Dorian repeated, as if I were speaking some weird foreign language.

"Yeah, you know—pretending to go after this spear to distract you from whatever he's really doing. What's the big deal with the spear?"

Mum frowned, but before she could say anything there was a knock at the door and Gretel poked her head in. "I've got that report you wanted, ma'am."

"Excellent. Bring it in. Girls, go with Gretel. We'll be here a while."

Okay, so no one wanted to tell me about this spear. Gretel held open the door and we filed out. Well, I filed. CJ more stalked. The door was barely shut before she whirled on me.

"How could she do that to me?" she demanded. "The Year 12 formal! I've been looking forward to it all *year*."

I said nothing. I was crankier about getting kicked out like little kids as soon as things started to get interesting, but CJ had different priorities. The way she was glaring at me, you'd think it was all my fault. I'd been looking forward to the formal too— back when we lived in Townsville. Then it would have meant something, going with our friends. Now I truly wasn't interested. And if I went and CJ missed out, I'd never hear the end of it.

"I won't go," I offered. "I'll stay home with you."

"I am *not* staying home," she said through gritted teeth.

"Uh ... girls?" Poor Gretel looked uncomfortable. "Why don't we head down to the kitchen and I'll get you something from the snack machine?"

"No thanks. I think I want to go back to the library."

The lift pinged as we walked past it, and Simon stepped out.

"Hi, Simon!" Gretel said brightly.

He nodded and strode off. She watched him until he turned the corner. She must have it *bad*.

"Gee, would it have killed him to say hello?" CJ said.

Gretel flushed a dull crimson. "When you get to know us a bit better you'll see what a traditional focus this place has. It's all built on who's got the most status, and latency is the currency we trade in. It's not exactly a meritocracy. Seekers don't tend to have much to do with us lowly technicians."

Wow. Bitter, much? We both stared at her, and she laughed self-consciously. "Umm ... you were saying? The library?"

"I just want to check a few things."

"Oh? Like what?" She led the way, following in Simon's footsteps.

"Like what's this Cottingley affair everyone keeps mentioning?"

"You haven't heard of it? It's pretty well known, even in the non-magic world."

I shook my head.

"It was a big deal, back when photography was first getting started. Two girls in Cottingley, in England, produced some photos of themselves playing with fairies in the garden."

CJ snorted. "And people believed them?"

"Oh, it was true, all right. A photographic expert examined the photos and declared them genuine. A lot of people were convinced—including Sir Arthur Conan Doyle."

I stared. "The guy who wrote *Sherlock Holmes*?"

"Yep. It caused big problems for us when he went public on it. See, it was only when the Industrial Revolution started that we managed to get the upper hand over the Sidhe. The age of science and machinery—and the huge rush to the cities that went with it—turned people away from them. Things that had seemed real when you lived in a cottage in your little village in the countryside, with nature all around you, started to seem more like dreams, or stories for children, when you worked in a factory and lived surrounded by bricks and steel. That weakened their power."

"Is that why Mum and Dad are so worried about that stupid video going viral?" I'd felt guilty enough before, but now I felt a hundred times worse. What if the Sidhe got back into the world all because I couldn't keep my mouth shut?

She nodded. "They feed on people's belief. It makes them stronger. We were lucky; the Industrial Revolution not only weakened belief in them at a time when some of our greatest mages were alive, it provided the means for us to chase them from the world forever." She frowned. "Or so we thought. And then to have belief surging again, only a century or so later—it was a great worry. Would the spells hold? Or would the Sidhe break through again?"

"So what happened?" I asked. Gretel seemed perfectly happy to talk about history, so I was going to find out as much as I could. We'd reached the library door, but even CJ looked interested now, though she still had a scowl on her face.

"Our technicians managed to replace the original photographic plates with ones that had been altered ever so slightly to make the fairies look less real. That was huge! They invented three new photographic techniques in the process. These days, with Photoshop, it would have taken someone five minutes, but it was a big deal back then. And then we had to get those photos into circulation, and get rid of the original ones. It was a big operation."

"Didn't anyone notice the change in the photos?"

"They were very subtle changes—and reproduction techniques were pretty primitive. Most people had only seen a grainy print in the first place. And of course we had people in the newspapers saying it was all a load of rubbish, but we couldn't get the girls to budge. It wasn't until one of them was an old lady that we finally pressured her into saying it was all a fake. Anyway, here's the library. I've got to run."

Wow. I felt kind of sorry for the old lady. Fancy seeing real fairies, and even getting photographic proof, and then having to tell the world it was all a scam. No wonder she stuck to her guns so long. I wondered how they'd managed to persuade her in the end, but Gretel was already gone, so I couldn't ask.

We went inside and sat in the same chairs. We had the place to ourselves again; the quiet had a relaxing weight to it. Not just a temporary absence of noise, it was a purposeful silence, a place to get lost in study and contemplation.

Well, at least it was if you weren't tied to a thoroughly peeved sister.

"They treat us like children," she complained. "Go here, stay there; Gretel, take them away and wipe their butts for them."

"They *are* kind of busy. Crisis, you know?"

"Not too busy to ground me, though. Can you believe that? *It looks like Violet will be going to the formal on her own.*" She mimicked Mum's voice, her face twisted into a bitter rage. She was good at accents in general, but her Mum imitation was so perfect it usually reduced me to helpless giggles. Not today, though. "And then she just shoves us out so we don't interrupt their precious grown-up chats."

"What do you care? You weren't listening anyway. Too busy sending texts to your caveman."

"I heard. All that stuff about Cottingley, and some panic about a cathedral. Nothing about us, though. I thought Dad was going to try and do something to help *us*. Isn't that why we came in here? Nobody seems to give a toss any more that we're walking around tied together so we don't spew diamonds every time we open our mouths. And frogs," she added, in what was clearly an afterthought.

"Well, it could be worse. At least we're not in a coma in a glass coffin like that other poor girl."

Although … I don't know, the idea held a certain appeal. I could catch up on some sleep and not have to deal with an irate twin. An irate twin who was *tied* to me.

"I mean, who cares if some Sidhe is walking around near their precious cathedral. Dad said he couldn't get in, right? They should be focusing on what he's already done—to their own children—not where he chooses to go wandering now. He's probably just enjoying being *able* to walk around, if they've had him locked up in this magic prison thing they keep going on about."

'Yeah, but it sounds like there's a spear in the cathedral they don't want him getting his hands on."

"Well, don't bother asking why, because they won't tell a little kid like you anything." CJ pulled out her phone, going back to a full-on sulk.

Poor Princess CJ. I bet what was really getting up her nose, more than the diamonds thing, or even being grounded, was the fact that no one was taking any notice of her. Maybe it was easier to keep things in perspective when you weren't used to star treatment.

I shrugged. Dad had mentioned a spear, though a cathedral seemed a funny place to keep one. What would you do with it? Poke people who fell asleep in the sermon and started snoring?

I slipped my silken leash and wandered the bookshelves again, looking for something that might give me answers. I pulled books at random, sampling their pages: *The Encyclopaedia of World Myth*, *A Dictionary of Mythology*, *Legends of the Celts*, *The Book of Magic*.

The Book of Magic was full of weird things like "A Potion to Turne a Mayden's Thoughtes to You" and "Posset for the Relief of the Ague", with long lists of ingredients, most of which I'd never heard of. What was St John's Wort? Or feverfew?

I put that one back and took *The Dictionary of Mythology* back to my chair. There were several pages on the Sidhe. At least it gave me somewhere to start.

> *The Daoine Sidhe, the people of the fairy hills, are the remnants of the once-great Tuatha de Danaan, the pre-Christian gods of the Celts, supposedly driven into their hills by the arrival of the Milesians in Ireland. They are*

a capricious and often cruel people, roughly divided into the "trooping fairies", the beautiful riders who tempt mortals away into Fairyland, and their less attractive kin, who range in temperament from mischievous to deadly.

They were ruled by a king and queen, who seemed to change quite a lot, and a host of unpronounceable names sprawled across the pages. Their great father god—kind of like a Celtic Zeus—was called the Dagda and, just like Zeus, he seemed to marry and/or carry on with most of the others, so they were all interrelated.

I ran my eye down the page. Four great festivals to honour the gods … that one, Samhain, seemed to ring a bell. It was their new year, marking the start of winter, on the first of November. That wasn't far off, though of course it wasn't winter in November on this side of the world. It involved various ordeals, often including human sacrifice. I wrinkled my nose. Glad we didn't do *that* any more. November the first was also the day the Dagda married the Morrigan, one of his wives. What was it with these people? Why couldn't they have normal names that didn't have "the" in front of them?

Four seemed to be a favourite number. The Sidhe also had four great treasures. Oh, *hello*.

"CJ, listen to this. The Sidhe have four magical treasures: the Dagda's cauldron, the spear of Lugh, the sword of Nuada, and the stone of destiny."

"So?"

"The spear of Lugh! Maybe that's the one Dad was talking about."

"What does it do?"

"Don't know." I scanned the page. "Umm … kills with a single scratch, never misses, battle-type stuff. It doesn't say much."

"But if it's a Sidhe treasure, why would it be in a human cathedral?"

"How should I know? Why don't you make yourself useful for a change and Google College Street—find out what this cathedral is that they're talking about."

"St Mary's," she said after a moment. "It's a Catholic church. You still think they're going to have a Sidhe spear lying around? It's more likely to be Roman."

"A lot of Irish people are Catholics." I didn't want to let go of the idea that it might be this spear of Lugh, though I had to admit, it seemed unlikely.

"Besides, why would it be such a big deal if it was this Lugh guy's spear? It's hardly going to be the end of the world if the Sidhe take back one of their own treasures, is it? How is that going to help them break out of prison?"

"I don't know."

There was too much I didn't know. There was probably something, somewhere among all these books, that could answer all my questions. The problem would be finding it. I could read for years and never get through all the books in this room—and that wasn't even counting the restricted section.

And ten to one, whatever I needed was going to be locked away in there.

CJ was right. No one was going to tell us this stuff. Mum and Dad hadn't even told us we belonged to a magical family, with all this going on under our noses, until Puck had cursed us and forced their hand. And sure, the Sidhe might be going to all this trouble just to regain a lost treasure, but that seemed pretty unlikely.

One thing was for sure: if I wanted to find out, I was going to have to get sneaky.

Chapter Twelve

"**O**kay," said Dad. "Try that."

"Blah blah blah." My voice came out muffled by the contraption strapped to my face. It looked a lot like one of those gas masks they used in World War I. CJ wore one too, and we both looked ridiculous, like two weird mechanical anteaters.

"Hey, no frogs!" Dad clapped his hands like a little kid at a magic show—which was kind of odd, since he *was* the magic show.

We'd been in his lab since breakfast, after bunking down at Magic HQ for the night. Dad had run some experiments before we went to bed, but their success could be measured in the sheer number of frogs still hopping round the place this morning. Now it looked like he might have succeeded after all.

There was just one problem.

"I hate to burst your bubble there, Dad," said CJ, "but I am *not* walking around in public wearing this thing on my head.

"Aw, come on. Where's your sense of adventure?"

He grinned, but CJ had no sense of humour where her appearance was concerned, and she refused to even crack a smile.

"Not funny, Dad."

"Okay, okay, take them off." He still looked pleased with himself. "At least we know it's do-able. I just have to find a way to get the dampener close enough to the source of the aether so that it's still effective without offending the fashion police."

Yeah, whatever. As long as he knew what he was talking about, I didn't have to understand.

"Dad?"

"Hmmm?"

"How come Simon's twin doesn't work here?"

"Didn't have high enough latency." He sighed. "There are never enough people who do."

"You mean he failed that test you told us about?" He was still fiddling with the setting on his gas mask, only half paying attention to the conversation. "But why does it matter? Your powers are latent because there's no aether in the world, right? So if you can't do magic anyway what difference does it make if you've got magic potential or not?"

"A lot of what we do here requires latency," he replied absentmindedly. "Seekers need the most, of course, but even technicians need a certain affinity with magic to operate some of the tools we use. And we have enough aether in the vault for those. It's no kindness to wave the world of magic in the face of people who can never be a part of it."

It took me a minute to grasp his meaning. "You mean he doesn't even know about you guys? Aether and the Sidhe and stuff? He doesn't know what his twin brother does?"

That seemed … hard. No wonder Simon didn't like talking about his twin.

"The best way of keeping a secret is not to tell anyone. Or at least, no one who doesn't absolutely need to know."

I tried to imagine keeping such an enormous secret from CJ. Nup. I couldn't do it.

"Must get back to work," Dad said. "I don't suppose you'd consider something like a surgical face mask?"

CJ gave him The Look. "No. Way."

"Just asking. No need to get tetchy."

We left him to it and wandered back to the library via a brief stop in the kitchen for donuts. No one seemed to use the library except us, and CJ was pretty keen to stay out of Mum's way. Maybe she thought Mum would somehow forget she'd said CJ couldn't go to the formal if she didn't see her for a while. If so, she was kidding herself. There wasn't enough magic in the *universe* for that.

"How long do you think we'll have to stay here?" CJ asked, moodily contemplating the silk scarf that still tied us together. "I want to go home. This place is boring."

I didn't see how anyone could find this boring—there was a whole new world to discover. That was just the grumpiness talking. But I did miss my laptop—I wished I'd thought to bring it with me. And I wouldn't have minded catching up with Sona. Plus there'd be schoolwork piling up. Just as well the holidays started the next week. Starting a new school was hard enough without falling behind.

Who do you think you're fooling? You don't care about any of that. You just want to see Zac again.

Okay, so maybe I'd thought of Zac a few times. A few hundred times, tops. I couldn't get that almost-kiss out of my mind. Those dark eyes of his were haunting me.

"It shouldn't be too long." Hopefully that wasn't just wishful thinking. I had to see him again so I could figure out if it was all my imagination, or if there really was something there. "As soon as the next big news story comes along, the press will forget all about us. Especially if Dad manages to stop us spitting frogs and diamonds. We'll be old news."

"Do you think we could go back to school if he does?"

"Why? You pining for Maths and English?"

She snorted. "As if."

"You want to see the caveman, don't you?"

"And what if I do?" She curled herself into a tight, defensive ball on her chair, knees pulled up to her chin. "There's nothing wrong with having a love life. You should try it some time."

Maybe I would. I sighed and went back to reading *Legends of the Celts*. There was no point talking to her when she was in this sort of mood.

A couple of hours later I closed the book, my head full of larger-than-life heroes and ridiculous quests and battles. CJ had her eyes shut. Not asleep, but I was happy to ignore her if she was still grumpy.

The door opened with a soft click and I looked up, expecting to see Gretel, come to summon us to lunch or another experiment. She seemed to have become our unofficial minder. But it was Dad, swinging two dog collars in his hand.

"So this is where you're hiding out."

As if we had somewhere better to be. He looked mighty pleased with himself. I eyed the things he was holding nervously. Seriously, Dad?

"What are those?"

"Your ticket to freedom, I hope."

That's what I was afraid of. Did he really expect us to wear *those*? He held one out to each of us. Up close, they looked like something a punk rocker might have worn in the eighties, with random bits of metal sticking out at odd angles from a thick base of leather and chain links. All we needed was a safety pin through the eyebrow to complete the look. Oh, and a radical haircut, preferably in hot pink.

"Put them on," he urged. "I want to see if they work."

CJ looked as dubious as I felt, but she obediently took one and held it round her neck. Then she turned her back to me so I could do it up.

"Go on," said Dad.

"Umm ... is it working?" she asked.

"Take the scarf off, idiot," I said.

"Right." She slipped her wrist free. "Well? Any change?"

The drops flew from her mouth and I sighed ... but then I realised there were no diamonds sparkling on the carpet. I grabbed the other collar and urged Dad to fasten it at the back.

"Is it working?"

I hardly dared to hope. I felt the droplets leave my lips, but no frogs appeared. The magic seemed to fizz out as soon as it had begun.

"Eureka!" Dad punched the air.

"That's amazing!" I held my hand up to catch the drops, but they just disappeared into thin air. "How did you do it?"

"Sheer genius." He grinned. "But I don't know how long the effect will last. It should hold indefinitely, but we'd need to run some more tests to be sure."

"Oh, no more tests," CJ begged. "Can't we just go back to school?"

"Good Lord," Dad said. "It's more serious than I thought. The Sidhe have actually stolen my daughter and left this changeling in her place."

"Ha ha. I'm just sick of all this weird stuff. I want to go to school and do normal things like everyone else. Is that so much to ask?"

Yeah, right. She wanted to go to school and suck Josh Johnson's face. Normally she'd take any excuse to skip school.

"Actually, that could be very helpful." His face settled into an unusually serious expression. "We need to stop the spread of belief in magic if we can. If any more Sidhe escape, belief will only strengthen them."

"Do you think they will?"

"Well, I hope not. But since we don't know how this one managed it, we can't be a hundred per cent sure."

Well, that was comforting. We could have more of these troublemakers running around spreading curses?

"How does us going back to school help?"

"You can talk to the press." Beside me CJ stood a little straighter at the thought. Photos! TV! Attention! "Show them there's nothing magical going on."

CJ's eyes were shining, but I wasn't so thrilled with the idea.

"You mean you want us to lie? And say what? That we pulled some stupid prank?"

"Essentially, yes."

Great. Go on national television and make myself look like an idiot. What an outstanding idea.

"Don't make a big deal out of it, Vi." CJ wasn't going to let anything stand in the way of her getting back to school. "It'll be easy. You can just stand there and nod, if you like. I'll do all the talking."

"Fine. Whatever." I knew from experience that I wasn't going to win an argument against CJ, and I had my own reason for wanting to get back to school. He was tall, with floppy brown hair and gorgeous dark eyes, and had the world's cutest dimple. "But what if more Sidhe escape? Will they come after us, too?"

Dad looked thoughtful. "I don't want you worrying about it. We'll deal with the Sidhe. But if it makes you feel better perhaps we could spare a couple of seekers to keep an eye on you. I'll ring the school and talk to the principal. I'll tell her you've had threats on the internet."

That could even be true, for all I knew. Obviously she said yes, because half an hour later a familiar guy who looked like he never smiled came into the kitchen in search of us. It was Simon, the seeker whose twin had failed the test.

"Warder Reilly has asked me to escort you ladies to school this afternoon."

I guess babysitting duty wasn't as sexy as scouring the world for magical treasures, or whatever he usually did, but his face was carefully expressionless. I couldn't tell what he thought of his new assignment. I wasn't too sure I liked the idea myself. Surely if there was no danger, Dad wouldn't have given us a bodyguard? It made me a little uneasy. Spitting frogs was bad enough. I had no desire to meet any more Sidhe. Who knew what else they might do? And what could this guy do about it if they tried something?

"Thank *God*." CJ leapt up, ready to rock and roll. I was still eating a sandwich, but what was my nutrition compared to the chance to see Josh Johnson again? "Hurry up, Vi."

"No rush," said Simon. "I'll just wait outside until you're ready."

"She's ready." CJ made furious *hurry up* faces at me, so I shoved the rest in my mouth and stood up. And promptly choked.

I coughed so hard I thought I was going to bring up my whole lunch. My eyes watered furiously. CJ thumped me hard on the back, which did nothing to help, but eventually I managed to catch my breath.

"You okay?" Simon offered me a glass of water, a look of concern on his face. Probably wouldn't look good on his resume if I died in the first five minutes he was responsible for me.

"Much—better, thanks," I gasped, still struggling to breathe normally.

Out in the hall we found Kyle, the other fake policeman. Apparently he was also part of our new security detail.

"Won't people at school recognise you?" I asked doubtfully. After all, they'd spent the morning there yesterday pretending to be policemen. Surely Josh at least, and probably the principal, Mrs Crawley, wouldn't have forgotten their faces already.

Simon pulled out a pair of sunnies and put them on. With his dark suit it made him look like a bouncer. "We look different now."

"No. You look like the same guy wearing a pair of sunglasses and a suit. Not the world's greatest disguise."

"You'll see." There was a certain smugness to his smile.

"Uniforms are amazing. When you're wearing one, no one ever remembers your face. You're just a policeman, or a fireman, or whatever. Anyway, I doubt we'll run into Mrs Crawley."

And Josh would be too busy oozing all over CJ to notice what anyone else looked like.

We passed the library and were nearly at the lift when I had a Brilliant Idea.

"Oh, hey, I nearly forgot. Dad wanted me to take one of the library books with me. Read up on magic history and stuff."

"Okay," said Simon. "We'll wait."

"Great." I walked to the library door and paused as if trying to remember something. "Damn. What was the name of it again?"

Simon raised an eyebrow, though I couldn't see his eyes behind the glasses he still wore. I swallowed hard and brazened my way on.

"He said to read the really famous one about the original seven warders and how they imprisoned the Sidhe. You know the one?" My heart beat faster, but I tried to look calm. It was a pretty safe bet that there'd be such a book. As long as it wasn't in the restricted section I was probably all right.

There was a long pause. I struggled to keep staring at him expectantly, fighting the urge to look away guiltily.

"You mean *The Gilded Cage*?"

"Yeah, I think that was it. Do you know where to find it?"

"Sure. May I?"

He gestured at the door and I stepped back politely to let him pass. He went straight to a shelf at the back of the room—not in the restricted section, thank goodness—and ran his finger along the spines until he found the book he wanted. It wasn't very big.

"Thanks." I took it and followed him out. In the mirrored walls of the lift, CJ caught my eye and raised a curious eyebrow. She could tell I was up to something, but the habit of backing each other up was strong. Twins first, always. She was smart enough not to ask questions. I clutched my prize as we rode down in the lift to the parking garage. Somewhere in here, I hoped, would be a clue as to why the Sidhe were after the spear of Lugh, if that was really what was hidden in St Mary's Cathedral.

I remembered how assured Puck had seemed, how he'd laughed at his so-called interrogators. *You don't even know what game we're playing yet.* Somebody had to find out. I had a feeling we were running out of time.

Chapter Thirteen

We took one of the big black cars with the tinted windows. Simon drove and Kyle sat in the front passenger seat, both looking very official. I had an urge to call them "Agent Simon" and "Agent Kyle", but I wasn't sure if they'd find that funny. It probably wasn't the right time for *Men in Black* jokes.

We sat in the back, being chauffeured like ladies, and I flipped open *The Gilded Cage* and scanned the contents page. The Origins of the Council didn't sound too interesting. Maybe the chapter The Rise to Prominence of Maeve Reilly? She was our ancestor on Dad's side.

It wasn't a thick book, so I should be able to read the whole thing in a few hours. I was just so impatient to *know*. Shame I couldn't ask Simon instead of sneaking around like this, but I felt sure he wouldn't tell me. Gretel had told us plenty about the Cottingley affair and some basic history, but she always seemed to develop urgent business elsewhere whenever I asked something she thought I shouldn't know. Was it because Mum and Dad hadn't told us anything before the curse struck? Were we supposedly too young to be trusted with the truth? We weren't exactly five years old. It wasn't as if we were going to blab about magic's existence the first chance we got. I glanced up and saw Simon watching me in the rear vision mirror. Maybe that was why we had babysitters—they thought we couldn't be trusted to keep our mouths shut. Would he mention the book to anyone? Probably. I'd just have to read fast before someone took it off me.

I saw there was a chapter on The Cottingley Disaster, so I turned to that one. Gretel had given us the basics, but there was a lot more detail about the testimony of the various experts, the public speeches and presentations. Apparently Conan Doyle had even written a book on the subject, he believed so strongly in the girls and their photos. I couldn't help feeling sorry for him, being made to look like an idiot by the technicians of the Council when he was right all along. A bit like us, really. I was *not* looking forward to talking to the press.

> *The Cottingley Disaster was a turning point for the Council. It became clear to the seven warders that as long as the Sidhe remained pent anywhere in the Northern Hemisphere, so close to their places of origin and associated belief systems, such outbreaks would continue. Accordingly, at the historic Council of 1920, the warders resolved to move the Cage to the Southern Hemisphere and relocate it in the arid heart of the newly federated country of Australia, far from the population centres of the Old World.*
>
> *To this end the four treasures of the Sidhe, which had been used as anchor points for the original condensing,*

had to be regathered from their hiding places and sent to Australia, where work was begun at the four points of the compass in Sydney, Perth, Broome and Townsville, to build the anchors anew. The work was completed in 1921 and the relocation accomplished without mishap.

It was considered safest to remove the treasures once more when the relocation was complete, and accordingly three were returned to the care of their guardians in the Old World. Only the Spear remained in Australia to permanently anchor the Cage there.

That was the end of the chapter. So there was a spear in Australia, though it didn't say where. I bet it was in Sydney, though, since that was where Magic HQ was located. I wished the book would tell me more about the four treasures—it seemed to assume anyone reading would know all about them.

I knew what they were from my reading in the library: the Dagda's cauldron; the Spear of Lugh, who was some kind of Apollo-type sun god; a Sword belonging to one of the Sidhe kings called Nuada; and something called the Stone of Fal or sometimes the Stone of Destiny. The Stone of Destiny didn't seem all that useful—it cried out in a human voice when touched by the true king of Ireland. Maybe that had come in handy when the Sidhe's ancestors had strode the world as the gods of Celtic Britain but it was pretty obsolete now. The others were two weapons for hand-to-hand combat and a cooking pot—also a little outmoded, or so it seemed to me, anyway.

Not that I was an expert in magic, of course, so maybe I was missing something here. The mention of the treasures being used in "the original condensing", whatever that was, sounded important. I sighed and settled in to read the whole book from the beginning. Knowledge is power, so they say. I wasn't going to be caught napping by any more Sidhe troublemakers.

I was only a few chapters into it when I noticed we were in familiar territory.

"We'll have you home in a couple of minutes, ladies," Simon said.

I wished he wouldn't call us that. It made me feel forty years old.

"We'll just make a brief stop here so you can change into your school uniforms and gather any books you need. Your father's given me the remote controller for the garage door, so we'll drive straight in. Let's not mess around with the press until we get to school. Might as well only do this once."

I closed the book and sat a little straighter, a small knot of anxiety beginning to form in my stomach. The press of bodies around the car, the shouting and thumping as we'd left home, had been a little unnerving. I wasn't looking forward to going through that again.

But the street was relatively clear when we turned into it. There were no TV vans, and only a couple of parked cars outside our house. When the people in them realised the big black car was turning into our driveway, they got out, thrilled to see some action after sitting around waiting. Stakeouts must be so boring. But Simon followed his plan and none of them caught so much as a glimpse of us through the car's tinted windows, and we were soon inside out of the sight of prying eyes and camera lenses.

We dashed upstairs and got changed in record time. Even CJ only paused long enough in the bathroom to apply a quick coat of mascara and some lip gloss, which was unheard of. She must be desperate to get to school to see Josh.

Quick as we were, Simon was still checking his watch when we came back downstairs. Kyle was in the front room, discreetly keeping an eye on the handful of photographers waiting on the footpath outside the house.

"Let's go," Simon called, and we all piled back into the car and headed out again. The photographers seemed to have realised they weren't going to get any photos. Instead of surging toward us when the car reappeared, they all ran for their own cars, determined to follow and find a better opportunity.

So we drove to school at the head of our own little convoy, three cars tailing us. I slipped *The Gilded Cage* into my backpack, unable to concentrate on reading any more. It was only a ten-minute ride to school.

"When we arrive you can say a few words before we go inside, then Kyle will accompany Crystal to her classes, and I'll go with Violet. We have copies of your timetables and will be escorting you to each class."

"Really?" CJ didn't look too pleased with that idea. "You don't need to do that—the press aren't allowed onto the school grounds, are they?"

Kyle turned to look over his shoulder at her. "The press aren't the only concern here. Every student in that school has a phone and is a potential source of leaks—of information or video footage. Our role is to discourage them from taking liberties, and also to ensure no one tries to incite another incident like the other day. We'll be as discreet as we can, but I'm afraid we'll have to stay close."

But surely our new collars would prevent any more "incidents". That didn't seem to have occurred to her; she was more concerned with how she was going to sneak some alone time with the caveman with Kyle looking over her shoulder every moment. "Are you going to come into class with me too?"

"No, I'll wait outside unless I hear a need for me to come in."

"Damn." She gave him a lazy smile. "I thought you might be able to do my maths homework for me."

He laughed. "Trust me, you wouldn't want me doing your maths homework. You'd end up with a D."

"Don't answer any questions you don't want to," Simon added. "Just smile a lot and tell them it was just a prank. Understood?"

Of course. We weren't stupid. The guy couldn't seem to open his mouth without patronising us. Frankly, I wondered what Gretel saw in him. CJ threw him a mock salute and I saw his lips tighten. Naturally she got Kyle, who at least knew how to crack a smile, while I was stuck with Simon.

Then the car turned into the school's street and I clutched my backpack tighter, scanning the street for suspicious cars. Everything seemed quiet enough—looked like the only photographers around were the ones trailing after us like baby ducklings following their mama. I swivelled in my seat to watch them make the turn too—there were four of them now. That wouldn't be so bad. I forced myself to release my deathgrip on the straps of the backpack before my hands started to cramp.

I was just turning back to face front again when I caught a flash of red and Simon slammed on the brakes. As we lurched forward against our seatbelts a little red convertible turned straight across the front of us. If Simon hadn't stopped when he did we would have slammed right into the side of it. I caught a glimpse of the driver as the car roared down the driveway to the teachers' car park: a woman with long black hair streaming behind her in the wind of the zippy little sports car's passage. I didn't know her, but then I wasn't familiar with many of the teachers yet.

"Bloody woman!" Simon snarled. "What does she think she's doing, driving like that around a school?"

He pulled in to the kerb outside the main entrance, still shaking his head. I got out and stuck close to him as instructed. He had a ferocious scowl on his face, though whether that was for the woman or the photographers sprinting toward us I wasn't sure.

"This way, ladies." He put an arm around my shoulder and began herding me toward the gate.

"Violet, how are you feeling?" one man shouted, raising a microphone. The girl next to him had a massive zoom lens on her camera, and was shooting furiously. I ducked my head, suddenly self-conscious.

"Crystal, can you tell us how the last two days have been for you?" someone else called, while flashes went off all around.

We stopped in the gateway and turned to face them.

"It's been a bit crazy," she said with a bright smile. "I can't believe everyone's making such a fuss about a little prank."

"So those frogs weren't real, Violet?" The man asking sounded disappointed.

I glanced at CJ, horribly conscious of the strange collar digging into my neck underneath my uniform. What if it stopped working now? I'd be an international laughing stock before the day was over.

CJ grabbed my hand and squeezed, then stepped in smoothly to fill the gap. Times like these her self-confidence came in handy.

"Of course they were real. We can't make frogs appear out of thin air. We're not magicians, you know."

Someone laughed. In a minute they'd be eating out of her hand.

"Say something, Violet!"

I scowled at the speaker. "Like what?"

"My sister's the strong, silent type," CJ said.

More laughter, and someone asked us to pose for a picture, so she smooshed her face against mine and we both smiled until our cheeks ached. Then she cut smoothly through the questions by saying we were late for class and had to go, and then we were through the gate at last. No one followed us.

"Well done," said Kyle, and CJ rewarded him with a dazzling smile.

As we hurried past the hideous statue out the front of admin, I noticed that Year 7 had finished cleaning up the toilet paper. Now the only thing decorating it was a large crow perched on its head. It cawed mournfully and flapped away as we entered admin.

"Won't be a minute," Kyle said. "We just have to sign in."

The office ladies gawked at the two large official-looking security types invading their foyer, but the formalities were soon completed and we were on our way to class. I had Physics in E block.

"There's that stupid woman," Simon said as we cut through C block past the canteen.

Up ahead, mounting the stairs, was the woman from the sports car. She wore a tight-fitting red dress that hugged some rather impressive curves. Her long hair rippled down her back past her waist, but she was soon out of sight round the bend in the stairs, so I didn't see her face.

"Is she one of your teachers?" Simon's expression made it clear what he thought of teachers who drove like maniacs.

"I don't know her," I said. "We're new here."

"She must have got her licence out of a cereal box."

It was a relief to arrive at the lab. As if it wasn't bad enough having a grumpy sister, now I had a grumpy bodyguard too. I hoped he didn't cross paths with the woman in the red dress again. I could just see him having a go at her, which wouldn't earn me any brownie points with the teachers at my new school.

As it turned out, the universe had other plans.

Chapter Fourteen

After Physics I had Ancient History, my one subject that was just for fun. CJ's electives were all like that—arty-farty things like Visual Arts and Drama, but most of mine were focused on a career in science: useful subjects like Physics and Chemistry. But I'd always loved history, the older the better. At our last school we'd been studying ancient Egypt, which fascinated me, but here they'd spent the whole year on Greek history. The first semester had covered the Peloponnesian Wars and the city-states of Athens and Sparta. Now they were on to the Persian Wars, where the empire of Persia was trying to invade Greece, a mighty Goliath against a puny little David.

Having missed all the background, I'd been wading through the writings of Herodotus trying to catch up, but today Herodotus and how much work I had to do was the last thing on my mind. I was going to see Zac again.

I was a little surprised to find the whole class already here, seated and waiting. Usually most of the boys straggled in right on the bell, but here they were, looking as keen as if someone had offered free beer. Zac was over by the windows, next to a boy I didn't know. He smiled at me and I gave him a little wave, then immediately felt like an idiot. I dropped into the seat next to Sona, the heat of another blush creeping up my cheeks. Nice one, Vi. Very smooth.

"What on *earth* are you wearing around your neck?" Sona asked.

Before I could answer, the woman in the red dress walked in, and the reason for the boys' eagerness became clear. If the word "sexy" hadn't existed, they would have had to invent it just for her. I'd forgotten Zac had said we had a relief teacher for history. Miss Moore, or something like that. Somehow he'd forgotten to mention she looked like a supermodel. I cast him a reproachful look, but he was oblivious, staring at Miss Moore like a kid on Christmas morning just longing to unwrap his present.

Great. Now I had to compete for his attention with Miss Sex Kitten Australia? And how was Simon going to react to my new teacher? He was waiting outside, out of sight. I hoped he'd keep his opinion of her driving to himself, but nothing I hoped for lately seemed to be working out. Why should this be any different?

"Good afternoon, Year 11. I have permission notes for you to take home to your parents, and I will need them returned by Friday, as the excursion is planned for the second day back next term. Don't forget! You won't want to miss out. We'll be going to the Art Gallery to see the exhibition 'Treasures of the Ancient Hellenic World', which will be a marvellous opportunity to see some artefacts that rarely leave the Louvre in Paris."

Her voice was so deep and husky it even made *me* think about sex. The guys had no chance.

She passed a bundle of notes to the front row, who then passed them back to the rest of the class. Her movements were fluid and graceful like a dancer's. I barely looked at the note before shoving it into my backpack. Like everyone else, I was mesmerised by Miss Moore.

She perched on the edge of the teacher's desk and surveyed the room with eyes that were such a dark brown they appeared black, matching her raven hair. Her skin was as pale as mine, but she made it look good, as if she was a goddess carved from marble. Her dress wasn't low cut or even particularly short, skimming just above her knees, but the way she filled it out made it the sexiest garment I'd ever seen.

"Now, on to Thermopylae. Last week with Mr Chadwick I believe you looked at the Persian advance and the Greek preparations for battle. Did everyone read the passage from Herodotus?"

Most people nodded, though in a kind of dreamy way.

"And what did you think?"

Hands shot into the air. Even the boys in the back row, who usually chatted to each other and refused to participate in class discussion, were straining to answer her. She chose one. "Miss, I thought Leonidas was a bit of an idiot."

"Oh?" Her dark eyes glittered, but her face showed only polite attention. "Why is that?"

The boy shifted uncomfortably. His desire to impress the glorious Miss Moore warred with his natural inclination not to draw the teacher's attention. "Well, he only had three hundred men."

"Three hundred *Spartans*," she corrected. "There were also the Thespian and Theban contingents."

"Yeah, but it still wasn't very many, was it?" someone else piped up. "Not compared to the thousands of Persians they were facing."

"So you think he should have run away like the rest of the Greeks and let the Persians take the pass without contest?"

The first boy shrugged. "He got defeated anyway, didn't he? And he must have known he couldn't win. What was the point of throwing away their lives for nothing?"

Miss Moore rose and prowled across the room, more panther now than sex kitten. Something about her had changed: a hardness in the eyes? A slight tightening of those full lips? Whatever it was, it had us sinking lower in our seats, hoping to avoid her notice. I bet that kid was wishing he'd kept his mouth shut.

"You're forgetting the prophecy. Herodotus, Book 7, verse 220, everyone. Herodotus has already told us Leonidas is descended from Herakles, or Hercules, as you may know him. Here the prophecy tells us that either Sparta will be sacked, or a king descended from Herakles must die. So Leonidas faces a choice—either give up his own life, or see Sparta itself fall to the enemy. Leonidas makes the noble choice, the only acceptable choice for a king of Sparta, and chooses to die in glorious battle."

True, the Spartans seemed a bloodthirsty lot. In my reading I'd found they trained their young men from a very early age in the arts of war, and Spartan women considered it better for their menfolk to come back from battle dead than return defeated. So three hundred Spartans were worth a hell of a lot more than three hundred regular soldiers. But still …

"It was only a prophecy," I said. "Anything could have happened to change things afterwards."

"Only a prophecy," Miss Moore repeated. Her lips were a slash of red in her still, pale face. "You're the new girl, aren't you? Violet, isn't it?"

I nodded. Her gaze rested for a moment on the hideous thing around my neck, but she didn't comment. I waited as the silence lengthened ominously. Why hadn't I kept my mouth shut?

"Well, Violet, in those days there was no 'only' about it." There was ice in that husky voice now. "Men paid attention to such things. They lived much closer to their gods, and they knew better than to tempt fate. The Oracle at Delphi had spoken, and Leonidas was doomed. His only choice was the manner of his death, and so he chose the route of glory.

"The Spartans were the greatest warriors the world has ever seen." She moistened those blood-red lips, and her dark eyes took on a dreamy quality. "What if the numbers of Persian arrows were so great they blotted out the sun? To a Spartan, that only meant they should enjoy fighting in the shade.

"The Persians whipped their men into the pass, but the Spartans leapt forward to embrace battle and waded through oceans of Persian blood. The screams of the dying meant nothing to them. They were merciless killing machines. They fought until their spears shattered in their hands, and then they fought with swords. When their swords broke they used their hands and even their teeth, ripping their enemy's lives from them in whatever manner they could till the last of them fell, covered in glory.

"The fighting lasted until nightfall, and thousands of Persians bled their lifeblood onto the ground of that narrow pass. The ravens feasted that day. Such a battle has never been seen since."

You could have heard a pin drop in the classroom, and nobody dared move. My skin crawled. She spoke as if she'd seen it. Worse, seen it and loved it. Her face was alight. Something was seriously wrong with this woman, however beautiful she was.

Her eyes refocused on the class and she smiled. It was as if a cloud had passed and now the sun shone again. "So, the Spartans lost the pass and the battle—but did the Persians really win? Thermopylae inflicted a terrible blow on Persian morale. When victory feels like a defeat, there are no winners. How do you think this affected the outcome of the battle that followed at Salamis?"

Zac put up his hand and the class resumed along more normal lines, but it took a moment for my heart rate to return to normal. I couldn't shake the memory of her face as she described the blood and death. Not a pleasant expression. I hoped Mr Chadwick's leg got better real soon.

When the bell went for the end of the period, I packed up and got outside as fast as I could. The boys all lingered, taking their time to pack away their gear, as if they couldn't bear to part from the beautiful Miss Moore. My reunion with Zac would just have to wait.

'Is she *crazy*?" I muttered to Sona.

"Who? Miss Moore? What do you mean?"

"All that bloodthirsty stuff. She sounded like she was right into it."

She shrugged. "She's just a history nut. She likes bringing it alive for her students." She glanced at Simon, leaning against the railing with his arms folded across his broad chest. "Who's your friend?"

"Ahh … security. Because of the … you know. CJ's got one too."

Simon moved closer in a meaningful way. Obviously he thought we'd spent long enough chatting.

Sona took the hint, though her dark eyes were alive with curiosity. "I'll see you later, then. You can tell me *everything*."

Miss Moore came out carrying her books. Simon frowned and dropped the casual pose. Oh, no. *Here we go.*

"I want a word with you."

"Yes?" She tossed her long black hair and smiled. Sex kitten was back.

"You nearly caused an accident outside the school."

"Oh, that was you?" She laid a hand on his arm and leaned closer. "I'm so sorry! I had the sun in my eyes and I just didn't see you. Are you all right?"

"Yes, we're fine …" She'd sucked the wind right out of his sails. Even grumpy Simon had trouble staying mad with someone who was smiling at him like that. "No harm done, I guess," he finished lamely.

"Wonderful! I must run, I have another class."

Her high heels tapped their way down the walkway while we stared after her, the sun catching blue highlights in her raven hair. The sway of her hips was mesmerising. A crow swooped down and picked a half sandwich off the walkway mere feet away, hopping under the railing to snatch it up. Not until Miss Moore rounded the corner and disappeared from sight did Simon stir, disturbing the crow. It flapped lazily into the branches of a tree in the courtyard below and watched us leave. The piece of ham dangling from its mouth made me think of ravens feasting on the battlefield and I shuddered.

Sona was loitering by her locker, not far from mine. Other students swirled all around us in the passageway, the air full of the metallic slamming of locker doors and the hubbub of voices. When she saw me she gave up all pretence of fiddling with her key and came over.

"Where'd you get the bodyguard?" she asked in a low voice.

"Mum and Dad insisted," I said, opening my locker and shoving Herodotus and the other two big heavy history texts I'd been lugging back into it with relief. I looked around for Zac, but there was no sign of him. Damn. "There's been some crazy talk on the internet. People saying we're witches. Death threats and stuff. They have to stay with us all day."

"But who *are* they?" Sona was a woman on a mission. "Where do you get a bodyguard from? Bodyguards 'R' Us?"

"Oh, they work with Mum and Dad," I said, trying to keep it vague. I should have known that wouldn't work with Sona.

'Come *on*, Vi, spill! What's going on with you? I haven't seen you since Monday. I didn't even get to see the big frog-spitting scene. Well, I saw it on YouTube … but that's not the same!"

"Yeah, you and fifty billion other people."

I sighed. She hadn't seen me since Monday? It was only Wednesday, but so much had changed. If only I could tell her.

It was kind of strange that I wanted to. Usually I was a pretty private sort of person. When you have a twin, you have a built-in confidante. They're always there to vent to and share secrets with. Sure, I'd had *friends* apart from CJ; I wasn't some weird loner. But no one as close. When I thought about it, I'd only really known Sona since Monday, but already I felt comfortable enough with her that it felt much longer than that. Some people were just like that.

She was still waiting, her big brown eyes hopeful. I wondered if she'd believe me if I did tell her. Maybe.

"You sure you couldn't make a frog appear?" She leaned against the bank of lockers and eyed me expectantly, as if frogs might come spewing out of my mouth if only she asked nicely.

"Sona."

"Just checking. It looked pretty realistic in that video. How'd you do that?"

I slammed my locker shut, maybe a little more forcefully than necessary.

"I really don't want to talk about it."

She twirled one long strand of hair around her finger, considering my surly bodyguard. "And is Mr Happy here to protect you or to make sure no more frogs appear?"

Hmmm. Keeping secrets from her could be trickier than I'd thought.

"Everyone's seen the frogs," she continued. "You can deny it until you're blue in the face, but half the world is now convinced magic is real and happening right here at Fernleigh High."

"And the other half?"

"Thinks it's all a scam and you and CJ are devious little bitches."

Now I knew what those Cottingley girls had felt like.

"Nice. And which half do you belong to?"

"I'm not deciding until I get the inside goss. Although, you know, either way I'm cool."

CJ appeared out of the rush of students heading for the next class. The lockers were on the ground floor of E block, outside the science labs, and a little too close to the main entrance into the block, which was the largest in the school. Apart from all the people actually using the lockers, we were competing for space with students lining up for science classes and others streaming in or pushing their way out of E block. The noise of slamming locker doors competing with the tramp of feet and loud chatter meant Sona and I had to stand close just to hear each other.

CJ's locker was on the other side of the passage from mine. She didn't appear to notice me among all the bodies, though Kyle nodded to Simon. He looked rather harried, as if trailing CJ around school was proving more of a challenge than he'd expected.

"You can't blame me for being interested," Sona said. "This is the most exciting thing that's ever happened. Everyone wants to know!"

As if the universe wanted to prove her right, a younger kid stepped out of the flow of bodies and stood looking expectantly at me.

"Hi, Violet." He looked like he might be in Year 7 or 8. "I was wondering if I could interview you for the school newspaper."

I stared at him, horrified. "No!"

"I like frogs," he offered.

"Good for you. The answer's still no."

He shrugged and cut through the crowd toward CJ, obviously hoping for a better reception there.

"See?" Sona's expression was all *I told you so*. "You guys are big news."

I leaned against my locker and stared across the crowd at CJ. I couldn't hear what she said, but the little newspaper guy looked disappointed as he left. A group of Year 7s hurried past. When they saw me they all started giggling and whispering to each other behind their hands. I looked away, then realised others were doing it too. One guy was actually pointing at me, and another had his phone out. Simon headed purposefully toward that one.

Looking around, I realised everyone that walked past was looking at me. Everyone, even the teachers who passed, were staring as if I was the prize exhibit at the zoo. Or maybe the best freak in sideshow alley. It was like I wasn't even a person to them, just something weird to look at.

I started to breathe faster. "Everyone's staring at me."

"Of course they are," said Sona. "Don't let it get to you. Hey, is that Josh Johnson?"

I followed her gaze and my heart sank. Yep, that was Josh Johnson all right, standing so close to my sister he was practically inhaling her. The crowd was starting to thin out now, but I still couldn't hear what he said to her. She laughed and looked up at him, and the expression in those blue eyes made me groan.

I'd seen that look before, several times, in fact. It never ended well. CJ expected a lot from a boyfriend, but the ones she picked never seemed able to deliver. Shame she had such crappy taste in guys. Josh was another one in the same disappointing pattern. Maybe she ought to consider using some other criteria apart from looks. The good-looking guys she went for always seemed to love themselves more than they loved her.

They were standing so close together, utterly absorbed in each other. Josh's perfect blonde head bent close to her dark one.

"Oh, my God, he's going to kiss her," Sona breathed, frogs forgotten.

Of course he was going to kiss her. He was the best-looking guy in the school. This kiss had been inevitable from the moment CJ enrolled. His lips touched hers and I sighed. *Here we go again.*

A cheer went up from Josh's mates and they broke apart. CJ's lovely face was more beautiful than ever, aglow with happiness. Josh looked insufferably pleased with himself.

"Wow," said Sona. "They look so good together. They're going to be, like, the hottest couple at the formal."

That cheered me a little. Josh was leaving, so I wouldn't have to watch the inevitable rise and fall of the relationship played out every day at school. If I were really lucky, he'd lose interest once he left and the big wide world beckoned. Having a schoolgirl for a girlfriend wasn't so cool when you were a man of the world.

"What are you wearing?" Sona asked.

It took me a minute to realise she was still talking about the Year 12 formal on Friday night. At least it beat discussing frogs and magic.

"Oh, we're not going," I said.

"Not going?" she shrieked.

Josh glanced over, but as soon as he realised the noise was coming from his new love's ugly sister and her geeky friend he looked away, supremely uninterested.

"What do you mean, you're not going?"

"Mum grounded us. Well, she grounded CJ actually, but I don't want to go without her."

"What is your *problem*? You can't miss the formal."

"Why not? I've never heard of Year 11 going to the Year 12 formal anyway." And I'd been to a lot of schools.

"It's a small school," she said. "They need to make up numbers to get a good venue. And it'll be awesome. There's all this crying and hugging and kissing and then everyone goes to the after party and promises to be best friends forever and there's so much *goss*. You have to come!"

"Sounds boring."

"How can it be boring? *I'm* going to be there—and I'm counting on you."

"I haven't even got a dress."

It was nearly time for the next bell. I should really have been in class by now. The crowds round the lockers had thinned out—only the lovebirds and a few stragglers remained. Simon and Kyle stood to one side, looking bored, but then Josh pulled out his phone and snapped a selfie of him and CJ, smiling faces smooshed together. Simon sprang to life and marched over.

"You don't have time to go shopping now," Sona said. "You must have something you could wear? Why don't I come over and we'll go through your wardrobe? I've got a couple of things I could lend you."

"Look, I've got to run," I said as the bell boomed over the speakers. "I'm late for Chemistry."

Simon was ordering Josh to delete the photo he'd just taken. I lingered, not sure if I should wait for him or not.

"I'll call you," Sona said. "We can get together tonight."

"Whatever." I waved as she walked off, but my mind was on other things. Josh was facing off against Simon, a mulish look on his face.

"I'm just taking a photo of my girlfriend, mate," said Josh, a challenge in his tone. Prince Josh was used to getting his own way. "There's no law against that."

"There's been enough publicity already," Simon said. "Crystal's parents want me to ensure there's no more. Please delete that photo."

"It's just a photo. I'm not going to publish it. And who are you, anyway?"

"A friend." Simon looked anything but friendly, but what could he do? The caveman was right, there was no law against taking photos. Simon really didn't have a leg to stand on. He obviously knew that, and the knowledge did nothing to improve his temper. Poor Simon wasn't having a very good day.

"Well, I'm her friend too, and she doesn't mind, do you, Ceej? So I don't see what business it is of yours."

And with that he swaggered off, CJ's hand clasped in his paw. After a moment Kyle gave a helpless little shrug and followed them. Simon turned to me, frustration written large on his face.

"What time does school finish?"

"Another hour," I said.

"Thank *God*."

Chapter Fifteen

He was waiting when I came out of my last class—my own personal thundercloud. Not that I cared. I had no plans to become his best buddy. Was he always like this, or did he just not like babysitting duty? Or maybe he didn't like me.

We headed for the car, meeting up with CJ and Kyle on the way. Kids poured past to the waiting buses, shouting and talking and laughing, like every other day—but there were no photographers lying in wait at the gates for us. Even when we got into the car and pulled out from the kerb, no one else pulled out in pursuit. Kyle and Simon looked at each other, but said nothing.

"No press," I said at last. "That's good. They must have bought our story this morning."

CJ hadn't even noticed, too busy texting the caveman. It had only been an hour since she saw him. What did they find to talk about?

"No," said Kyle. "There's been … a development."

The odd phrase caught CJ's attention. "What do you mean?"

"Google Sydney Airport," he said.

She did, and I leaned over to read the results with her.

Sydney Airport magic attack, Sydney Morning Herald, 2 hours ago

Ogre at Sydney International Airport, abc.net.au, 1 hour ago

Latest on the ogre at Sydney Airport, updated 1 hour ago

… and on and on down the page.

"Bloody *hell*," said CJ, clicking on the first link that promised video footage. Like our moment of YouTube fame, it looked like it had been taken by someone with a phone camera, probably someone waiting to greet a visitor at the airport. The scene showed a gate lounge at Sydney airport. A few people stood around, watching the trickle of passengers coming through the gate. Others sat in the rows of uncomfortable chairs reading or eating junk food. A mother with a little bald baby stepped forward eagerly as a man with a briefcase came through the gate, but most people headed off on their own, with no one to meet them. There were a lot of guys in suits, so they were probably mainly business travellers.

As the little family of three hugged on the edge of the frame, a roar cut through the background noise of announcements and people talking. You could see people stopping in their tracks. Heads swivelled toward the gate, and the roar came again. The staff member who was farewelling the departing passengers at the gate stepped forward and peered down the corridor that led to the plane.

The little bald baby began to cry, and the family hurried away. Some joined them, but most moved toward the noise, rather than away, overcome with curiosity. It wasn't the roar of a jet engine, which wouldn't have turned a hair at the airport. It sounded more like an animal. People looked at each other uncertainly.

The roar sounded again, closer this time, and a small Asian man darted out of the gate, his face contorted in fear. He dropped his jacket as he bolted through the gate lounge, but he didn't stop to pick it up. Others began to leave too; his fear was catching. The gate staff backed away, uncertain what to do.

Then an enormous figure burst from the gate. It had been bent nearly double to get through the tunnel from the plane. Now it rose to its full horrifying height. The picture wobbled as whoever held the camera backed away. Screams filled the air, then suddenly the view tilted dizzily and all we could see was the floor swinging backwards and forwards as the person filming bolted for safety. We could still hear the roars though, and the terrified screaming.

"What was *that*?" I asked as the clip finished.

The creature had been man-shaped, but twice the height of any man, and its face was so hideous it could have got a job as an orc extra on *The Lord of the Rings*. Its arms were massive, and hung low like a gorilla's.

"An ogre," said Kyle.

Thanks, Captain Obvious. I'd actually got that part from all the screaming headlines on Google.

"I mean, where did it come from? How does a thing like that get on a plane?"

Kyle sighed. "As far as we can tell from the passenger lists, that thing used to be Warder Nabukov."

Whoa. The poor guy.

"So it's another fairytale attack?" CJ asked.

"But how?" It didn't make sense. "Puck hasn't escaped, has he?"

"No. He's still locked in the vault."

Then how had the Sidhe managed to strike again? Why hadn't anybody seen magical activity on the monitors?

"We have seekers all over the airport," said Simon. "Maybe they'll find something."

He looked even grumpier than ever—he was probably longing to be there with the others instead of babysitting two teenage girls.

"What fairy tale is he from?" CJ asked.

Kyle shrugged. "Take your pick—there's plenty of ogres in fairy tales. I just hope to God it isn't *Puss in Boots*, or we could find one of the other passengers has turned into a cat."

"Where is he now?" I asked, afraid that some enthusiastic policeman may have put a bullet through him.

"They had to call in a vet from Taronga Zoo to tranquillise him. As far as I know he's still at the airport. Last I heard they were holding him in one of the hangars. I think your Dad's gone down there with Warder Kincumber to see what they can do."

Wow. It sure put things in perspective. I fingered my ugly dog collar. Frogs and diamonds were pretty tame in comparison to being turned into an ogre.

"Does it seem to you that the curses are getting stronger?"

Simon met my eyes in the rear vision mirror, a thoughtful expression replacing his usual frown. "How so?"

"First was Snow White—they just put her to sleep."

"It's a bit more than that," CJ pointed out. "She can't wake up."

"True, but sleep is natural. It's just the not-waking-up part that's odd. Then there was us, with our frogs and diamonds—unnatural, but we're not changed. We're still ourselves. And now there's this. Poor Warder Nabukov is completely transformed into something that's not even human."

Silence fell in the car. What would the next progression be? Simon got onto the expressway before I realised we weren't heading home.

"Where are we going?"

"Warder Winters is concerned about security. She's called everyone into HQ."

Poor Mum. This wasn't a great time to be a warder. Ever since our YouTube video had gone viral, the current affairs shows had been full of talking heads discussing magic and whether it was real or not. After today's little episode it was going to be pretty challenging to argue that it wasn't. Puck must be sitting back laughing as all the little humans scurried around like a kicked ants' nest. No matter how they tried, the ants were never going to be able to put their world back the way it had been.

We pulled into the underground garage at HQ. How long until the press discovered this place?

As we got out of the car, an ambulance came down the ramp and stopped by the lift. The driver hopped out and opened the back doors wide. His partner jumped down and together they pulled out the trolley inside, pulling its wheeled legs down with a metallic crunch.

The person on the trolley was jostled by the movement, and her head rolled toward us.

"That's her," CJ said. "The Snow White girl."

We stood back while the ambulance guys wheeled her into the lift. She was very pale; even her lips were bloodless, only the faintest pink colour showing now the bright red lipstick was gone. Up close, she looked somewhere in her mid-twenties.

"Don't call her that," Simon said. "Her name's Kerrie."

"She a friend of yours?" The anger in his tone set all CJ's antennae quivering. We could both sense there was a story here.

"We worked together a couple of years ago in Perth," he said.

"And?"

He gave her a cold look. "And nothing. She's a real person with a real name, that's all. I don't like it when people treat her like an object or a puzzle to be solved."

The lift came back and the doors opened with a cheerful *ding*. Simon strode in and punched the button for Level 1 with a little more force than he really needed. I carefully didn't meet CJ's eyes, knowing what I'd see there. CJ smelled a secret romance. Given Simon's general grumpiness, I was more inclined to suspect unrequited love—I had a hard time imagining anyone actually fancying him. Though there was Gretel, I guess, as proof that at least one woman found Mr Happy appealing.

"Have they thought of finding a prince to kiss her?" CJ asked. "Even if you don't like people calling her Snow White, you have to admit that's the fairy tale the Sidhe are working with; and in the story it was the prince's kiss that brought her back to life."

"Princes aren't exactly thick on the ground in Sydney," Kyle said. "And most of the European ones are married, even if we could persuade one to visit."

"A boyfriend, then?" CJ cast a sidelong glance at Simon, who resolutely stared straight ahead at the closed doors. "Maybe it's more a 'one true love' thing, not a prince thing."

"We thought of that too," Kyle said, seeing that Simon had no intention of joining the conversation, "but she's not in a relationship at the moment, and ex-boyfriends don't really meet the criteria."

I wondered if Simon was one of those exes, but he was clearly not interested in pursuing the topic. Gretel would know.

The lift doors slid open on the quiet carpeted corridors of Level 1. Simon strode off without waiting to see if we were following.

"You can wait in your Mum's office," Kyle said, leading us after Simon. "She shouldn't be too long."

I could have found my way there on my own by now, but I allowed Kyle to deliver us like so much unwanted baggage on the doorstep. He and Simon were gone before the door had even shut behind us, obviously relieved to be rid of us for a while. Probably gone to get the low-down on what was happening with the ogre.

CJ flopped onto the couch in the corner, but I prowled around, picking up things and putting them down again, unsettled by the new developments. My collar was feeling uncomfortable after wearing it all day—all those protrusions had a way of poking into you—but I was afraid to take it off in case it somehow stopped working if I did.

Or maybe something worse would happen. I picked up a heavy glass paperweight shaped like a dolphin. Who knew what could happen? What if another curse struck us? We could be ogres, or cats, or even frogs. There was the tale of the frog prince, after all. Bad enough to be spitting frogs, but to be one—!

I set the dolphin back down on the desk with a heavy thunk. What if we became dolphins, or something else that couldn't even live on land? I had a vague memory of a fairy tale about a magical wish-granting fish.

These thoughts were making me crazy. Distracted, I ran my finger uneasily under my collar, trying to make it more comfortable. There was a door to my right I hadn't noticed before. Maybe a bathroom? Mum was a kind of executive after all—why shouldn't she have an executive bathroom?

Sadly, it was nothing that glam—only a very small walk-in cupboard with shelving floor-to-ceiling. It looked like the wall behind reception at the doctor's we used to go to in Townsville, with all the patients' files ordered alphabetically. Were they employee files? That didn't seem right. I was pretty sure someone had said Magic HQ had about 200 employees. There were a lot more than that here.

I pulled one out at random, vaguely aware that I probably shouldn't be looking. *Curiosity killed the cat* got mentioned a lot in our house. CJ and I were both stickybeaks.

It seemed to be a personnel file, for a guy called Emmet Branson. It had test results, work assignments, assessments from various supervisors: "Emmet is an original thinker but does not take direction well." Emmet also made more than $150,000 a year. Nice work.

I pulled out another, wondering if I'd stumble across someone I knew. I didn't actually know anyone's surname except Warder Kincumber, and his wasn't there—I checked. I checked Reilly too, though I figured if Warder Kincumber wasn't there, Dad wouldn't be either.

But there was a Reilly file.

"CJ! Get in here." She looked up, caught by the note of excitement in my voice. "I've found our file."

Chapter Sixteen

We huddled together between the shelves. The cupboard was so tiny there was barely enough room for both of us. We had to shut the door so we could both fit, jammed up against cold metal shelves. The space smelled of old paper and dust.

"Give me that," CJ said. "I don't believe you. Why should there be a file on us?"

"It's test results. Remember Dad said everyone from magical families was tested as children?"

He'd also mentioned the importance of latency. *The Gilded Cage* had given me a bit more information on that too. Apparently bloodlines were a big deal: no one could be a warder unless they were descended from the Founders, the seven mages who'd trapped the Sidhe originally. No one could be a seeker unless their latency score was higher than seventy-five per cent, and people like that mostly came from the same small group of families. I hadn't yet discovered *why* these rules were so important; the book seemed to assume that any reader would already know.

There were several pages of graphs, and scores for all sorts of things I didn't recognise. I handed her the bundle labelled *Crystal Jane Reilly*.

"What's perception?" CJ asked, tilting the pages toward the light of the dim bulb above us. "I got 38% in that when I was five. And 34 in projection."

My own five-year-old attempts were no better. "I've got 35 in projection and 52 in resonance." I flipped through the sheets. "I can't find one for perception."

"I don't remember any of this," CJ said, frowning at the pages as she turned them. "Look, it says here we were retested at puberty. That's only a few years ago. *I* don't remember any magical testing."

"Me neither. They must have ways of doing it that aren't obvious." Considering how many weird and wonderful gadgets Dad usually had in the house, he could have been up to anything. I flipped over until I found my own most recent results. "Hey, look at that. My projection's up to 86, and resonance is through the roof."

CJ said nothing.

"How's yours?" I leaned over to see, but she flipped the pages closed.

"Never mind."

"Come on—tell me."

"Fine. It says 'no latency detected'."

Her tone was flat and final. The message was clear: *I don't want to discuss this any further.* I tried to get her to look at me, but she turned away. Was that a tear?

"Hey, don't be upset." I took the pages from her, shoved

everything back in the folder and put it away on the shelf. "It doesn't matter—there's no magic in the world any more anyway. So what difference does it make if you're latent or not?"

Then why are you so pleased your scores are so high? I had to admit, it felt good to know that in another place and time I might have been a mage. It was a pretty cool kind of secret to have. What might I have been able to do? Cast illusions? Spin straw into gold? And maybe—just maybe—it felt good to finally be better than CJ at something. It's not like I was going to rub her face in it, but I was only human. I couldn't help a little buzz of pleasure.

CJ shrugged off my hand as if she knew what I was thinking. I guess it was a new experience for her, not being better than me at everything. She was taller, prettier, more popular. More of a people person. She was always the one that people gushed over, while I hovered in the background. Not that I was complaining; I *preferred* the background. But she'd grown used to the limelight.

"It doesn't make *any* difference," she said, but she still wouldn't look at me.

She had the door half-open when we heard the click of the office door opening, and voices in the corridor outside. There was no time to dash back to the couch and pretend we hadn't been snooping; there was no time for anything but what CJ did—shut the door as quickly and quietly as possible, leaving us hidden in the dark of the filing cupboard.

We heard a number of people enter the room and shuffle around finding chairs. Mum offered drinks, followed by the clink of glass on glass as she poured.

"What's the latest on Sergei?" Mum asked.

"Dena's with him," Dad replied. "Fortunately she arrived this morning. We have him heavily sedated, and a crew posing as police have secured the hangar. I'm afraid I have no idea where to go from here."

There was a long pause, then someone sighed heavily.

"How can these attacks keep coming?" That sounded like Dorian.

"And getting worse?" another asked, a woman's voice I didn't recognise. "I thought we had the Sidhe responsible in custody."

"We have Puck," said Mum, "but clearly there are others, though for some reason the monitors aren't showing activity."

"This makes no sense," the other woman replied in obvious frustration. "They shouldn't be able to get out at all! How can there be multiple escapees?"

"As to that, it seems they've had outside help." This was a new voice, another man.

"What do you mean?" Dorian asked sharply.

"My team has found evidence of tampering with the seals."

There was a collective intake of breath.

"*What?*"

"I expected something of the sort," Dad said. "It stands to reason. They've been locked up in there for two centuries— they're not going to suddenly come up with a way to break out after so long. Someone must have helped them."

"But who would do such a thing?" the unknown woman asked, horror quavering in her voice.

"And who would have the power?" Mum added, which caused another uncomfortable silence.

"It must be one of the seekers," Dorian said at last. He sounded reluctant to believe such a thing. "They're the ones with the security clearance and the highest latency."

"I suppose so," said Mum.

She sounded exhausted, and I suddenly felt horribly guilty for overhearing this conversation. She had so much on her plate already—if she knew we were in here listening it would only make more trouble for her.

"I wish they'd hurry up," CJ whispered. "I have to pee."

"Sshh!"

We could hear them clearly through the closed door; I had to assume they'd be able to hear us too.

"Well," said Dad, "we'll have to look into that. Bryan, I assume your team has checked out clean?"

"Yes."

"Then you can give them the task of going through the other seekers' records. See if we can turn up anything in their history, any motive for betrayal—money, health, love. Anything."

I shifted nervously. That better not mean he had to come in here right now and grab people's records. That would be one hell of an awkward conversation.

"Doug, what about my sister? Can you do anything for her?"

Right. Bryan must be the warder who was Kerrie's brother.

"Ah ..." Dad shifted in his chair. "I had some success with my girls, but I don't want to get your hopes up. Kerrie's case is quite different. There's no aether physically emanating from her that I can pinpoint with dampener, and I'm hesitant to go too deep in case I cause some damage. But I'll certainly do my best."

"I appreciate anything you can do."

"And I assume we have the same problem with Sergei?" Dorian asked. "The aether must be buried quite deep in his case, to have that effect on his whole body."

"I'm afraid so," Dad replied. "The initial assessment isn't promising. Dena's very good, though, and she may see something I've missed."

"Let's hope so. We now have four warders affected by these attacks, directly or indirectly."

The other three must be wondering if they were next.

"And what of this Puck?" the other woman asked. "What do you propose doing with him?"

"We should condense him," Bryan said immediately. "What's the sense in leaving loose ends? If there are traitors among us, they'll try to free him. Hasn't he done enough damage already?"

"We have guards watching him night and day."

"And who's watching the guards? Send him back, and get rid of the problem."

"I understand you feel strongly about this," Dorian said. "We're all worried about Kerrie—"

"It's not just Kerrie!"

"—but it may not be the best idea to send him back. If he's escaped once before, he can do so again. At least at the moment we know where he is."

"I think Dorian's right, Bryan," said Mum. "While we have him in the vault he's not out causing more mischief."

"Do we have any idea yet what he was doing when he was captured?"

"He was within spitting distance of the cathedral," said Dorian. "I think we have to assume the spear was his target."

"But that's not possible," the other woman said. "The Sidhe can't enter holy ground. And the spear is well-protected."

"Frida, if he had human assistance to escape in the first place, it seems likely his human allies would have a plan to access the spear—if that was indeed his target. The question we have to answer is why he would be going after the spear."

"Perhaps they simply want it back," Dorian said. "More likely, they have a plan to use it against us in some way. It seems clear that Puck's ability to break out isn't widespread, or we'd be inundated with Sidhe by now. Perhaps they think the spear can help them widen the gateway, as it were."

"What of the other treasures?" the other woman asked—this must be Frida, the warder who'd just flown in. "Are we sure it's only the spear they need?"

"We're not sure of anything," Mum said. The frustration in her voice was clear. "I've checked with the guardians of the other three, and there is no suspicious activity."

"That doesn't mean they're safe, though, does it? The four of them were used to anchor the very foundation of the Sidhe prison. What if the Sidhe have found a way to use them to reverse the process?"

"Perhaps we're jumping at shadows," Dorian said, "but I must confess, I share Frida's unease. For the last century we've assumed that because the cauldron, the sword and the stone are in the Northern Hemisphere, they are out of the Sidhe's reach. But we've also assumed that the Sidhe were unable to break out of their prison. Can we afford to rely on any of our assumptions any more?"

"What would you have us do?" Bryan asked.

"I think we need to consider strengthening the anchors."

Talk about dropping a bombshell. Whatever "strengthening the anchors" meant, it wasn't a popular idea, judging by the shouting that broke out. It sounded like a playground brawl out there. Any minute someone was going to start chanting "fight, fight, fight".

Eventually Mum managed to calm everyone down enough that we could make out what they were saying again.

"Obviously that would be a last resort," she said. "In the meantime, we need to put everyone on high alert, particularly at the other sanctuaries. But I at least would sleep better if one of us were at each site."

"I can go to Stockholm," Frida said. "I have family business there anyway."

"I don't like to leave Kerrie," Bryan said, "but there's nothing I can do for her by staying. Perhaps I could be more use elsewhere."

"I could make a quick trip to Paris," Dad said. "I want to consult with Luthor anyway. Emmet can run the trials for a couple of days without me."

"Good!" Dorian clapped his hands, and we both jumped. "That's settled, then. But I want you all to think about the other option."

CJ bumped a folder on a lower shelf. I caught it just before it thumped on its side, then we froze, waiting to see if anyone in the outer room had heard our quick, furtive movements.

Apparently not. The meeting broke up soon after, and we waited, listening for the last of the warders to leave. The outer door closed, cutting off Dad and Bryan mid-conversation about Kerrie. I shut my eyes and let out a long, relieved breath.

Then the cupboard door opened. Mum stood there, hands on her hips, that terrible *I am so disappointed in you* look on her face again.

"How much of that did you overhear?"

Chapter Seventeen

"**I** wish we were back in Townsville." I stared at the back of Kyle's head as he drove us home in disgrace. Mum hadn't been that angry since the time we played hairdressers when we were seven, and CJ hacked off most of my hair. "So far Sydney really sucks."

"I don't know," said CJ. "I think it has its compensations."

She'd already texted the caveman, asking him to come over. She was so caught up in her new romance it hardly seemed to bother her that Mum was furious, Dad was too preoccupied to see us as anything other than a problem to be solved, and we were being ferried around like unwanted baggage. Plus we had to wear atrocities round our necks that made us look like Frankenstein's monster, to ward off the curse some fairy had placed on us. Oh yeah, and magic was real and apparently trying to take over the world.

Townsville had been *much* quieter.

"How many Sidhe do you think have escaped?" I asked Kyle.

He gave me a brief, troubled glance in the rear vision mirror.

"According to the monitors, there's not enough aether showing for anyone to have escaped except Puck."

"But someone cursed Sergei, didn't they?"

Maybe the monitors had been tampered with, if there was a human traitor involved. But Gretel and Ronnie had been all over the hardware, and they said nothing was wrong with it.

Unless Gretel and Ronnie were the traitors. That wasn't a happy thought. I *liked* Gretel and Ron. But Bryan had said someone had tampered with the seals, so *someone* was playing for the other team. I hated having to suspect everyone I knew.

"Yes. Someone did. Maybe Puck did it before we caught him, but the curse didn't take effect for a while."

Well, that was another possibility, I guess. Or maybe Kyle was the traitor, and he was making up crap to throw me off the scent. What did I know about how magic worked? He could tell me anything.

"What will you do if more Sidhe turn up while we're at home?"

Mum had said we'd be safe there, but I couldn't see how one guy on his own could protect us from a curse like the one that had hit poor Sergei. Even if he wasn't a traitor. I fingered my collar nervously. I would almost rather have stayed at HQ, but Mum said it was more important than ever to keep up normal appearances, and had shoved us out the door as fast as possible. Guess she didn't want us poking our noses into anything else we weren't supposed to know.

"The house is protected by iron boundaries," Kyle said. "No Sidhe could even set foot on the property. Warders' homes have always been protected, just in case."

Okay, then. There were no press lying in wait to protect us from, either. Kyle set himself up in the dining room with his laptop and proceeded to ignore us. That was fine with me. I could do with a quiet night.

Sadly, that only lasted until Josh turned up on the doorstep. CJ dragged him inside like a starving woman who sees food and they snuggled up on the couch in the family room, supposedly watching TV, but really just exchanging spit.

Eww. I retreated to my room and texted Sona. She reminded me that she was supposed to be helping me find something to wear to the formal, and announced she was coming over. I pointed out that I wasn't going, but she wasn't having any of that.

I came downstairs when I heard the doorbell, and CJ and the caveman quickly rearranged themselves on the couch into a more upright position.

"Hi, Sona."

She was dressed in jeans and a T-shirt that said "Geek girls rock", and lugging a bulging shopping bag. I'd never seen her out of uniform before; it made her look older.

"Hi! Did you miss me?" She stepped inside and threw a kiss at the air beside my cheek. "Of course you did! How are you?"

"Yeah, okay, I guess."

"That's what I like about you, Vi, always so positive. Come on, why so serious?" She was a terrible Joker impersonator.

I led the way back through the family room. "My sister is sucking Josh Johnson's face in my own house."

"Hey, I heard that!" CJ said.

I gave her a deadpan look. "Whoops."

'Hi, Sona," she said, ignoring me. "What's in the bag?"

'Dresses for the formal. I'm helping Vi find something to wear."

'Cool."

"Except we're not going, remember?" I gazed at both of them in exasperation.

CJ smiled sweetly up at me. Her dark hair straggling over Josh's shoulder reminded me of Kerrie, her long hair neatly arranged in that glass coffin. "You can stay home if you like, but I'm not missing the biggest event of the year."

I glanced through the door into the dining room, but Kyle had a set of headphones on and was working away, oblivious of our conversation.

"You can't go. Mum grounded us."

She shrugged and pretended to be fascinated by the TV.

"Is your sister always so straight?" Josh asked.

Jerk. I ignored him. "Remember last time you went out without permission? Remember how well that turned out?"

"So? You think Puck's going to show up at the formal? That was a one-off, Vile, so get out of my face."

"Who's Puck?" Sona asked, looking confused.

I wasn't going to enlighten her. "God, you are such a *jerk* sometimes, CJ. Come on, Sona, let's leave these two alone. They deserve each other."

Fists clenched, I marched upstairs and slammed the bedroom door behind us.

Sona regarded me seriously. "Your mum grounded you too? But I *need* you. What did you do?"

And that was another question I couldn't answer. This was getting tricky.

"You don't need me. You didn't even know me a couple of weeks ago." I threw myself on the bed and put one of my pillows in a headlock. "God, she makes me so mad. She always has to get her own way! Never mind what *I* want, or what anyone else says to her. I don't know why Mum even bothers grounding her. She doesn't take the slightest notice."

Sona sat down next to me, kicking off her shoes and curling her long legs underneath her. She dropped her bag on the floor and gave me an anxious look.

"Maybe your mum will change her mind. After all, she's already paid for it. You do *want* to go to the formal, don't you?"

"Honestly? Not really. The only people I really know are you and Zac, and I'd rather hang out with you somewhere quieter where I didn't have to dress up and listen to some crap DJ play bad music."

"But I'd like to go," she said, "and it wouldn't be as much fun without you."

"You won't even notice I'm not there," I said. I really couldn't see why she was making such a big deal about it. "You've known everyone else for years, and you've only known me for a few days. If I hadn't come you'd still have gone and had a fabulous time."

She tipped her head to one side and stared at me with those big brown eyes, like a little lost puppy.

"I would have gone," she agreed. "I've been working on my parents all year for this. You know what they're like about parties, and mixing with people they think aren't a good influence— which basically means everyone who's not Indian. It's only because there'll be teachers there that they'd even consider it. But as for having a fabulous time—you know before you came most of my friends were guys, right?"

"Yeah?" I couldn't quite see where she was going with this, but I let go my deathgrip on the pillow and sat up. She fiddled with the end of her long plait, not meeting my eyes as she spoke.

"Yeah. The cool girls think I'm weird because I like things like robotics and Star Trek, and the uncool girls are mainly Asian, with even stricter parents than mine, and tutoring up the wazoo after school, so they've got no time for friends. You know I used to be best friends with Julie Lee in primary school? Now she goes to Mandarin school all day Saturdays and has tutoring every afternoon. Even at school she's always in the library at lunchtimes studying. What's the point of a friend if you never get to just hang out together?" She turned those huge puppy-dog eyes on me. "Zac and the other guys are great, but it's nice to have a friend who's a girl. As much as I like geek stuff, there's more to life than that, but guys don't get that. And I don't want to spend the whole Year 12 formal talking robotics and watching other people dance and have fun."

Wow. That was quite a speech.

"So I guess you'd hit me if I said I'd rather talk robotics than dance?" Actually I'd rather stay home and out of trouble than do either, but my new friend had just turned out to be the queen of the guilt trip. And if CJ was going whatever I said, then I probably had to go too to keep an eye on her.

"You bet." She smiled, a little uncertain. I hadn't realised how important this was to her. "So you'll talk to your mum?"

"Okay," I lied. Mum was just as stubborn as CJ. There was no way she would change her mind. We'd just have to work around it somehow. I had a bad feeling I was going to regret this.

"Fantastic!" She threw her arms around me and squealed in

my ear. Then she bounced up off the bed, dark eyes sparking with excitement again. "Let's have a look at your wardrobe then."

She threw open the doors and frowned. There were a lot of jeans and shirts hanging there, and only a handful of dresses. Her hand went straight to a sapphire-blue maxi dress that was probably the pick of the bunch. The fabric was nice and slinky, and a row of fake gemstones decorated the neckline. She held it up, glancing from me to it appraisingly.

"Could work."

"Don't you think it's a bit casual?"

She laid it on the bed and went back to the wardrobe. "What else have you got here? What's this?"

It was a short black dress I'd worn to my cousin's twenty-first a couple of years ago.

"I'm not sure I can even get that one done up anymore."

"Try it on. You can never go wrong with a black dress. We could dress it up with some nice jewellery."

I struggled into the dress to please her, but it was too tight. Sona managed to get the zipper done up after a heroic struggle, but then I couldn't breathe.

"Get it off before I pass out," I gasped.

If I had to be hit with a fairytale curse, why couldn't it have been Cinderella? I could do with a fairy godmother to provide the perfect ball gown right about now—then I could dance the night away with my handsome prince. I bet Zac would look hot in a suit. I still hadn't really had a chance to talk to him—there always seemed to be other people around—but I'd done a lot of looking.

"CJ and Ashleigh and all of those girls are wearing short

dresses." I contemplated the blue maxi doubtfully. This was why I liked jeans and T-shirts. It was so much simpler. I'd had enough of people staring at me for all the wrong reasons. I wanted to wow Zac. "I'd feel like an idiot if I was the only one in a long dress. What are you wearing?"

"Mine's short too. It's gold. Wait until you see it! My mum wanted me to wear a sari—can you believe that?"

"I bet you'd look great in a sari. Like something out of a Bollywood movie."

She rolled her eyes but didn't comment, returning to the problem of the blue dress. "Maybe we could shorten it?"

"Maybe." The length was what I'd liked about it in the first place, the graceful sweep of fabric making me look taller. I tried to picture it shorter.

"Has CJ got something you could borrow? Or your Mum?"

"No and God no. They're both bloody Amazons. Everything they've got is too big for me. I'd look like a little kid playing dress-ups with Mummy's clothes."

"Okay. Well, in that case ..." She sat down on the bed again and picked up her bulging shopping bag. "I hope you won't be offended—promise you won't get mad at me! I brought a couple of dresses with me."

"Why should I be offended?"

She upended the bag, and two piles of gorgeous satin slithered on to the bedspread. One was a rich chocolate brown, the other a deep emerald green. I was drawn immediately to the green one. Such a beautiful colour. I held it against myself and checked the mirror. It had a ruched bodice, and a shortish skirt with an uneven hemline that swayed around my knees. The colour was amazing against my hair, making the orange glow like fire.

"Wow! Where did you get this?"

"I was bridesmaid for a family friend when I was thirteen." She gave me an anxious look. "But it doesn't look kiddie, does it?"

It certainly didn't. I slipped into the dress, hoping it would fit. "Is that why you thought I'd be offended? Because you wore this when you were a kid?"

She stepped up behind me to do up the zipper and met my eyes in the mirror. "I didn't know how sensitive you were about … you know … being short."

I laughed and gestured at our reflections. Sona was nearly a head taller than me. "Look at us! There's no chance I'd fit into your clothes now. You're as bad as CJ. Sure, it used to bug me when I was younger, being short, but what can you do? You can get a nose job if you don't like your nose, or have implants if your boobs are too small, but height? You get what you get, and that's that. It's a waste of energy being upset about something you can't change. We can't all have legs like supermodels."

I smoothed the fabric over my hips and turned to admire the back view. It was a lovely dress, even if it had been made for a thirteen-year-old.

"Besides, even the supermodels don't have legs like supermodels, by the time all their photos have been Photoshopped to death."

"So you like it?"

"It's beautiful." I grinned at her in the mirror. "I feel like a million dollars in it."

"You don't think the straps are too babyish? The older bridesmaids had strapless versions, but Mum wouldn't let me. We could cut the straps off, if you like."

"You can't do that!" I was horrified she'd even suggest hacking at her beautiful dress.

She shrugged. "Well, it's not as if I'm going to wear it again. It doesn't fit me any more. You may as well keep it."

"Seriously?" The thought of Zac seeing me in this dress set my heart pounding with excitement. I turned and grabbed her in a bear hug. "Thank you! It's perfect—and I like the straps."

I also liked the fact that she hadn't mentioned she'd grown out of it in more than just height. Her cup size was easily two or even three sizes bigger than mine. Which made thirteen-year-old Sona's dress just about a perfect fit for seventeen-year-old me. Oh, well. At least the ruching made me look like I had *something* up top.

I twirled in front of the mirror, watching the skirt flare out around me. Now I was excited about going to the formal. Grounded? Who cared?

"Why don't you take that collar thing off and try it with a nice necklace?"

I met Sona's eyes in the mirror. "I—I can't." My stupid face started turning red as I scrambled for an excuse. "It's a ... bet. With CJ. Whoever takes it off first loses."

"But surely you won't wear it to the formal?"

I shrugged. "I will if she will."

Sona shook her head. "You guys are crazy. But I guess I knew that already."

"What do you mean?"

"You know—the frogs and diamonds stunt at school. How did you do that? It sure looked like you were spitting those frogs out. You didn't really put them in your mouth, did you?"

"Of course not. It was probably just the camera angle."

"But what was the point of it?"

"I don't know. It just seemed like a bit of fun, you know?" God, this was awful. I hated lying to her. She stood there nodding, her big brown eyes trusting. How could I call myself her friend when every word out of my mouth was a lie? "We never expected to get so much publicity."

"Where'd you get the frogs?"

"There's a whole bunch in our backyard. You can come and see them, if you're that interested."

I changed back into my regular clothes and hung the beautiful dress in the wardrobe. We went downstairs and I took Sona out the back past the paved outdoor dining area to the garden where the fishpond was. It was after seven, but there was still plenty of daylight, and I didn't expect to have any trouble finding the usual gaggle of bug-eyed little critters scattered around the pond and hiding in among the surrounding maidenhair.

But there were only two little guys enjoying the last of the sunlight on the rocks at the edge of the pond.

"There they are," I said, frowning. "There's usually more of them, though."

I hunted around under the maidenhair, carefully pushing fronds aside, in search of their buddies.

"They're so cute!" said Sona. "They looked bigger on the video."

She sat on the edge of the raised garden bed and stared at the two little frogs, who stared back without blinking. A cockatoo screeched overhead, and I looked up to watch a flock of them pass. Had they been eating my little frogs? No, I had a feeling they were seed-eaters. Kookaburras ate meat, though. Or were the frogs just dissolving back into the aether, the way Dad said the diamonds would? The earliest ones had been around for five days now, so it was possible. I certainly wasn't sorry to see the last of those horrible toads. I'd have to ask CJ if she still had all her original gems.

Sona looked at her watch. "I guess I'd better head off. Mum said to be home by 7:30 for dinner."

"My Dad'll be at the airport now, getting ready to take off." A crow hopped down from the back fence and started pecking in the grass for something. "He's going to Paris."

"Lucky him! Still, at least we've got the formal."

"I'd rather see Paris," I said.

"Yeah, me too. We should go together when we finish school."

"That'd be fun! Better than schoolies on the Gold Coast." The annual booze-fest in Queensland was the pinnacle of the year for many Year 12s. In fact, I bet that's where the caveman and his mates were headed as soon as they finished their exams. I could hardly think of anything I'd rather do less. Paris sounded way better. "We'd have to save up like crazy. Do you think your parents would let you do something like that?"

"Probably not," she admitted cheerfully. "We might have to leave it a year or two—but that gives us more time to save up, right?"

"Right."

We headed for the door. Sona squealed and ducked as something black flashed past her head. We turned in time to see the crow taking off from the fishpond, something small and green dangling from its beak.

"Get away from there!" I stamped and waved my hands, but it was too late. The crow landed in the lower branches of our neighbour's big gum tree and tipped its head back. The little green legs disappeared. "Bastard."

"Oh, the poor little thing!" Sona ran back to the pond. "Where's the other one gone?"

"Hiding somewhere if he knows what's good for him." I glared at the crow. Knowing the little frogs weren't truly real didn't make it any easier to watch one get eaten alive. I hoped the stupid bird got magical indigestion. "Bloody bird. I hate crows."

The crow stared back, its beady eye cold and unblinking.

Simon and Kyle were both on deck again next morning, with no mention of our disgrace yesterday. Maybe they didn't know. I felt sure Simon would have said something snarky if he did. His mood certainly hadn't improved any. Was he always this bad, or was it concern for Kerrie making him so dour? CJ was convinced there was a doomed romance there. I would have asked Gretel, except she seemed to fancy him too, so that might not be the most tactful move.

Maybe it was just all the fairytale attacks getting him down.

"How's Warder Nabukov?" I asked. On the radio this

morning they'd started calling him Shrek, even though he wasn't green—and his situation wasn't a joke.

"No change," said Kyle.

They accompanied us to the senior study and took up their posts outside while we went in. Despite the name, there was rarely any studying done here. It was more of a common room where the senior years could hang out.

CJ and Ashleigh dumped their bags in a corner and started a conversation about hairstyles. The formal and the after party the next night was all anyone could talk about lately. I drifted away, wondering where Sona had disappeared to. I was sick of hearing about the formal.

"I'm *so* sorry about the limo," Ashleigh was saying to CJ, "but we booked it weeks ago, and it will only take the ten of us. If only you'd been here we could have got a bigger one."

"That's okay," CJ said. "I'm going with Josh in his limo."

"Really?" Ashleigh's eyes narrowed. "I thought that was just for Year 12s?"

"Well, I *am* his girlfriend."

"Whatever." Ashleigh shrugged and the conversation moved on. I watched her closely for a moment. *Be careful, CJ.* That superior tone didn't seem to sit too well with the other girl. Ashleigh had seemed pretty keen on Josh herself, come to think of it. I remembered the way she'd said his name, that day on the bus, as if it was something so delicious she wanted to eat it. Maybe the green-eyed monster was rearing its ugly head.

Sona came in with an armful of library books, so I stopped listening. Zac was with her, and they were chatting animatedly— for once, about something other than robotics. Well, Sona was chatting at least. Zac was more listening.

For a moment I felt hurt that he'd gone to the library with Sona instead of walking with me to the study. *Don't be an idiot, Vi. He's known Sona forever. He's not going to stop being friends with her just because he likes you.* Not that I would want him to. And it wasn't as if we were even going out.

"We just ran into Miss Moore," said Sona, dumping her books next to my bag with a thud that rocked the table. "You should see the heels she's wearing today. They are to *die* for."

"Beats me how she walks in those things," Zac said.

"Walk shmalk," said Sona. "Who cares about walking when you look so fabulous? And guess what?"

"What?" I asked, trying my best to look interested in Miss Moore's footwear. I didn't do a great job, but Sona didn't seem to care.

"We asked her if she was coming tomorrow night and she said yes, so we asked her to sit at our table!"

"Really?" I could see how Zac might find that exciting—the woman was a bombshell, after all, and I hadn't forgotten how weird the boys had all acted in Ancient History yesterday—but Sona's enthusiasm was a little strange. "But we hardly know her."

"So? I bet she wears something amaaazing. She'll be the coolest teacher there. Did you want to get stuck on a table with Mr Ormond?"

"I guess when you put it like that …" Sitting through three courses with Mr Ormond would be an ordeal. Or my physics teacher—that would be worse. Lovely man, but duller than watching paint dry. Miss Moore might be a tad on the bloodthirsty side but at least she had personality. I just wasn't sure I liked that personality. Something about her made me feel uncomfortable. She was too intense, too fierce, too … something.

"How are you and CJ getting there? Are your bodyguards taking you?"

"They're not bodyguards." I don't know why I bothered— she insisted on calling them that whatever I said, seemed to think it was a great joke. "And no, they're not. We're not supposed to be going at all, remember? CJ's going with Josh and his mates."

I wasn't entirely sure how we were going to shake the "bodyguards". CJ reckoned she had it under control, but I didn't find that as comforting as she obviously meant it to be.

"What about you?" Zac asked. "Do you need a lift?"

"You could come with me but my parents would grill you on your entire life history the whole way there," Sona said. "They're pretty keen to check you out."

"Gosh, sign me up."

"I can give you a ride if you like," Zac said.

"Ooh! Are you asking her to the formal with you?"

"Shut up, Sona!" I could feel my cheeks heating, the traitors. If only I had skin like Sona's it wouldn't be so horrendously obvious every time I blushed. "He didn't mean it like that."

He was sitting on the desk top next to me, feet on a chair. I could smell his deodorant, something pine-scented and manly. Or maybe it was aftershave. His cheeks were a little pink too.

"Look at you two—you're blushing! That's so cute." Sona looked from one to the other of us, grinning, and started to sing. "Zac and Viiii, sitting in a tree, K-I-S-S-I-N-G."

I turned my back on her, aware that my face was blazing red, trying to act as if this wasn't the most awkward thing that had happened to me since frogs started falling out of my mouth—which is harder than you'd think when your face is lit up like Rudolph's nose on Christmas Eve.

"Ignore the madwoman in the corner," I said to Zac. He smiled and the dimple peeped out. For some reason that made me flush even redder. Bloody Sona. "I'd love a lift."

"Okay. I'll pick you up around quarter to seven."

He didn't say that he *had* meant it like that—but then he didn't say he hadn't, either. Thank *God* the bell rang then, because I didn't know where to look and I could cheerfully have throttled Sona, who was still humming that stupid song. We all funneled out into the courtyard amid the usual roar of voices and noisy feet on the stairs.

Mr Ormond and Miss Moore came out of the English staffroom and saw us. Mr Ormond called CJ over so I hung around, wondering what he wanted.

"Crystal! I have a job for you."

CJ smiled politely. "What's that, sir?"

"It's customary for a Year 11 student to make a toast to the outgoing prefect body at the formal. Miss Moore suggested it might be nice this year to have one of our newest students make the toast to our oldest."

Miss Moore smiled as if she'd done CJ a great favour. Today she wore a red silk top and tailored black pants. The heels were as impressive as Sona had said—towering strappy things with a touch of bling.

"Vi's a good public speaker."

Nice one, CJ. Trying to drop me in it. I melted back behind a pillar, but Mr Ormond didn't even look my way.

"I'm sure you'll do a great job. We only want something short. Besides, I hear you have a special connection with a certain member of the prefect body."

He gave her an arch smile, and I nearly gagged. If even Mr Ormond had heard about CJ and the caveman, the whole school must know.

"Glad he didn't ask me," Sona said as she dragged me up the stairs. "I hate public speaking."

I grinned. "So does CJ."

Chapter Eighteen

I came out of my bedroom and nearly choked on the clouds of hairspray and perfume coming from CJ's.

"What are you *doing* in there? Should I call for toxic waste disposal?"

"Bite me."

She was leaning in close to the mirror, making that weird stretchy face that women everywhere do when they put on mascara. Her long black hair rippled down her back in mega curls, but she made it look hot instead of cutesy. It had a tousled kind of *I've just got out of the sack in my skimpy nightwear* vibe, an impression that the smoky eye shadow only added to. Her dress was a simple strapless cream sheath that made her tanned skin glow golden. She looked fantastic.

"Nice dress."

"Thanks." She finished with the mascara and turned to check me out. "You look good too. Is that Sona's dress?"

"Yeah."

She assessed me with a critical sisterly eye. "The colour's good on you. Pity it wasn't strapless."

I rolled my eyes. Why did everyone go on about the straps? "Well, we don't all have your assets to hold our dresses up."

She grinned and adjusted those assets in the mirror, letting even more cleavage show. Josh was going to have a heart attack when he saw her. Outside a car pulled up and I peeked out the window.

"It's okay. It was someone next door."

"You're not still worried about Kyle, are you? Relax. He's not coming back."

Poor Kyle. He'd received a phone call half an hour ago from Warder Winters giving him the rest of the night off. She'd said she was on the way home and there was no need for him to stay with the girls any longer.

Only of course it wasn't Warder Winters at all, but CJ doing her Mum impression. He hadn't suspected a thing, and two minutes later we had the house to ourselves and were racing upstairs to get ready. I was torn between guilt and excitement, though for now the excitement was winning. Zac would be here soon, and I was wearing that gorgeous green dress.

"I hope he doesn't get into trouble. What if Mum really does ring him? Or if he mentions something about having the night off to someone tomorrow?"

CJ snorted. Tomorrow was a problem for Future CJ. Present CJ rarely let consequences get in the way of a good time.

"What if you stopped worrying about things that might never happen and just focused on enjoying yourself?"

Before I could think of a smart answer the doorbell rang and she pushed past me. I heard Josh's voice then the slam of the front door as she yelled goodbye. I eased a finger under my collar as I followed her downstairs more slowly. CJ had partially camoufluaged hers with a chunky gold necklace, but I hadn't bothered trying. It was so in-your-face there was no real way to disguise it. I was grateful for its powers, but tonight more than ever I wished it was just a teensy bit more attractive. And maybe had slightly fewer pointy bits.

In a few moments the doorbell rang again. I checked the clock: 6:45 exactly. Zac was right on time.

"Hi!" My heart did a little flip at the sight of him. It was like my perfect man had stepped out of my dreams and landed on my doorstop. "Wow, you look … different."

In a suit he looked about five years older and ten times hotter. I could hardly believe the transformation. He'd even gelled his hair so it didn't flop into his face the way it usually did.

"Different in a good way, I hope. You look amazing, by the way."

"Thanks." I did a little twirl to show him the whole effect. "You like the dress? Sona gave it to me."

"It's beautiful. You look really pretty." He bowed and offered his arm. "May I escort madam to her chariot?"

I smiled up at him, dazzled by that sweet dimpled smile and the admiration in his eyes. I laid my hand on his arm and we paraded down the path like royalty. He was taller than me—hell, everyone was taller than me—but in high heels the difference wasn't too ridiculous, and I felt very grown-up and glamorous. My heart danced a quick little cha-cha inside my chest.

He held the car door open for me, then came around and got behind the wheel.

"Not that I'm not grateful for the ride, but the chariot seems to have shrunk since last time." He was driving a little red Mazda, not the big sedan he'd driven us home from the party in.

"Yeah, this is Mum's car. Mum and Dad are using the Commodore tonight." He smiled across at me as he pulled out from the kerb. "It gets tricky sometimes, with three of us driving and two cars. I'm saving up for my own—hopefully I'll have enough to get something early next year."

"Cool. What do you do for a job?"

"I teach guitar. It pays a hell of a lot better than working at Maccas, and I can more or less set my own hours."

"I didn't know you played guitar! You must be pretty good if you're teaching it."

"I'm not too bad. I've been playing since I was a kid. Most of my students are beginners, though, so it's not all that challenging."

"Electric guitar or classical?"

"Classical mainly. I play electric sometimes, but I prefer classical."

"Wow. I never would have picked you for the musical type. You don't even do music as a subject, do you?"

"Nah. I get enough of it outside of school." He grinned. "I guess there's lots of things you don't know about me."

"Okay," I said, taking that as a challenge, "what's your favourite food?"

"Aaah … nachos? I don't know. My mum's corned beef pie? I can't pick just one. What's yours?"

"Chocolate."

"Oh, I thought we were talking real food, not junk."

"Chocolate's a real food. It's one of the five essential food groups."

He laughed. "They must do things differently in Townsville."

I loved that I could make him laugh. It was kind of cozy, just the two of us in the car. "What about sports? What do you like?"

"To watch or play?"

"Play."

"Well, I used to like basketball, but they only take the really tall guys for the team these days. Cricket's all right, but baseball's better."

"What about winter sports? Soccer or footie?"

He pulled a face. "I'm crap at both. All right, my turn. What's your favourite book?"

"Oh, that's a hard one. Maybe *The Lord of the Rings*?"

"Seriously? I tried to read that but I couldn't stand all the poetry. The movies were better."

"Well, they did have Viggo Mortenson. And no Tom Bombadil. Do you read much fantasy?"

"Sometimes. I'm more of a science fiction guy. Space battles and alien planets and stuff."

The little Mazda turned in at the gates of a reception centre that looked more like a small castle.

"Oh, wow, this is beautiful."

"I know. Can you believe this used to be someone's home?"

I shook my head. "It'd be nice to be rich, huh?"

"Maybe some day I'll know. I'll have to invent something that makes me millions."

"Good plan. Keep working on the demented chicken."

He found a spot and parked the car. We'd talked all the way here, about all sorts of trivial things, but never mentioned the one thing everyone else in the world was discussing. Magic. He didn't even ask about the infamous video. He had a way of focusing on what I was saying that made me feel as if I was the most interesting person he'd ever met, unlike most guys, who listened as if they were waiting for you to stop talking so they could talk about themselves. Cough, cough, Josh Johnson. I felt absurdly grateful for the chance to laugh and chat and act as if everything was normal, as if my life hadn't been overtaken by magic and weirdness.

I could easily fall in love with a guy like that.

He came around and opened my door, still playing the gentleman. I got out, smoothing the emerald folds of my dress, and admired the building and its lovely gardens. Even from the carpark, at the back, it was impressive. People in formal dress were chatting on a large terrace, and music wafted across the carpark. It sounded like Vivaldi. Pretty upmarket for a school formal. Hopefully there'd be dance music later.

We crunched together across the gravel and around to the front of the building, where a long white limousine was sweeping in around the circular driveway. More partygoers arriving in style.

"What's your favourite colour?" I asked, watching girls in all the colours of the rainbow spilling from the car.

"Normally I'd say red." He looked down at me, something serious in his eyes. "But tonight … it's green."

My heart started to race.

"Very smooth!" I joked, to cover my sudden nerves. "I like your style. Dance with me later?"

He laughed, and the moment passed. "I thought you knew about my dancing."

"I'm prepared to take the risk. Maybe I could ask the DJ to play YMCA."

"You are never going to let me forget that, are you?"

Laughing, I grabbed his hand and pulled him inside, suddenly reckless. He seemed happy to let himself be tugged through the bright chattering swirl of people in the foyer. A grand staircase swept up to the first floor, and a photographer was using it as his backdrop for group photos. A giggling group of Year 12 girls were arrayed on the stairs, hugging each other and posing for the camera. Other students milled about, waiting for their turn. Through the archway at the back I could see the terrace, where others were enjoying pre-dinner drinks, presumably non-alcoholic.

Sona appeared in the archway as we wove our way through the press of people.

"Vi! Zac!" She waved madly and shoved her way through the crowd to us. "Let's get our photo taken."

I gave her a quick hug. "Love the dress!"

"Thanks."

She looked gorgeous, in a gold dress with the most beautiful beaded bodice. The colour was perfect against her dark skin, and her hair was piled high in an elaborate braided style. She looked impossibly exotic.

"You scrubbed up all right, too," she said to Zac, who laughed. "It's not fair. Boys have it so easy—all they have to do to look great is put on a tux. We have to stuff around for hours with hair and makeup and shopping for the right dress …"

"Oh, you poor thing. I bet you hated every minute of it, didn't you?"

She grinned. "Maybe not *every* minute."

We worked our way toward the front of the queue, but it took a while. On the staircase now CJ posed on Josh's lap for one shot, then all Josh's friends piled in around them, filling the width of the grand staircase.

"I see you won the bet," Sona said.

"What?"

"The bet with CJ. She's not wearing that hideous thing around her neck any more."

What? I'd been so focused on the warmth of Zac's hand still in mine, the nervous happiness fizzing away inside me, that I hadn't even noticed CJ wasn't wearing her collar. What the hell was she doing?

I started pushing my way to the front of the line.

There was lots of laughter and good-natured teasing among the group posing on the stairs. CJ was grinning, but at least she had the sense to keep quiet. Where was her collar? It must be in her handbag; I couldn't even see it.

I hovered helplessly at the foot of the stairs, just out of the shot, and tried to get her attention. But of course she was completely focused on Josh, still perched on his lap like a queen on her throne.

Next thing Josh started tickling her. Oh, God, no. I darted forward, but it was too late. She giggled, then the giggles turned into a full-on laughing fit, and diamonds started spraying everywhere. A roar went up as if the home team had just scored the winning try at a football game, and the photo shoot devolved into chaos. People surged forward, jostling for diamonds. Girls fell to their knees, squealing, searching the carpeted steps. One boy tried snatching them out of the air as they fell. I was afraid CJ was going to be mobbed.

"Free diamonds!" Josh roared over the noise. "Come and get your free diamonds."

Someone bumped the tripod and the photographer just caught his camera in time. I snatched at CJ's arm, trying to drag her away, and she stumbled and nearly knocked me down the stairs.

That was when I got a good whiff of her breath and realised she'd been drinking. Already? They must have hit it hard in the limo on the way here.

"What the hell are you doing?" I yelled over the uproar. "Where's your collar? For God's sake, put it on. If you get your face plastered all over the internet again, Mum and Dad will go apeshit."

"What difference does it make, Vi?" Her face was flushed with alcohol and bravado. "The secret's out, the whole world already knows. Magic is real! Once a guy turns into an ogre in a public place, there's no hiding it any more. Why go on pretending?"

"Because that's what Mum and Dad want, and they know more about this shit than we do."

I was horribly conscious of phones being raised, of the photographer still shooting behind us. Mum and Dad were going to *kill* us.

"I don't care. It's not as if diamonds are *ugly*."

But frogs were. She didn't have to say it; I knew exactly what she meant. Why shouldn't she flaunt her diamonds? She was *special*; she always had been. The centre of attention was exactly where she was meant to be.

Maybe Mum and Dad wouldn't get a chance. I was going to kill her myself.

"Chillax, Vi." Josh emerged from the crowd and draped a proprietary arm around CJ's bare shoulders. He had a fistful of diamonds and the world's most infuriating smirk on his stupid face. "It's no biggie. It's not like you took *your* collar off."

Oh, my God. Killing was too good for her. "You *told* him?"

She shrugged, then pulled her collar out of her bag and clipped it back on. "Whatever. I just wanted a nice photo. Is that such a crime?"

I turned my back on her. It was either that or punch her in the face. Zac and Sona stood at the bottom of the stairs, staring at us in shock. Oh, damn. How was I going to explain this?

Mr Ormond came in from the terrace to see what the noise was.

"Ladies and gentlemen! A little quiet please!"

Gradually he managed to restore order. I walked the last few steps down to my friends. Damn CJ. I'd been having such a nice time, and now she'd gone and turned us into a freak show again. The photographer set his tripod up again, and I noticed his lens was pointing our way. I bet some of his photos weren't going to be in the official snaps. He was probably already planning how to spend the money some gossip column would pay him for shots of the mad scramble for diamonds.

Mr Ormond shooed CJ and her group toward the terrace. "Please remember this is a formal, not a wrestling match."

"You'd better keep quiet, Frogface," Ashleigh said as she went past. "We don't want any of those nasty things jumping around here."

"Ribbit," said the boy with her, and they both cracked up.

Sona glared at them. "Idiots."

"You want to tell us what that was all about?" Zac asked, his dark eyes wide.

"Isn't it obvious?" Sona turned back to us with a brave attempt at her usual grin back in place. "I was right, wasn't I? Magic is real."

"Sona …" All at once I felt exhausted. I was sick of lying and pretending. Why was I even bothering, with CJ putting on displays like that? It wasn't as if I could singlehandedly convince the world magic didn't exist when all around me the evidence was piling up.

"What? Oh, come on, you're not going to give me that line about it being a prank again, are you? I was standing right here! I saw those diamonds come out of her mouth."

"Are you okay, Vi?" Zac asked.

Well, at least he wasn't running in the other direction yet.

"I don't think I want to have my photo taken now."

"Sure." He stooped and picked up a diamond that had been missed in the frenzy. "Want this?"

I shook my head. I was sick of the sight of the things. "It's worthless anyway. In a few days it'll disappear." I took a deep breath. "You can't trust a fairy gift—they're never what they seem."

He shrugged and flicked it to Sona.

She caught it and held it up to the light. "Shame. I've never seen such a big one. Maybe I'll take it home and give Mum a thrill."

"Suit yourself."

Zac put an arm around my shoulders and drew me gently against him. I leaned into him gratefully. "Let's go out onto the terrace."

Sona trailed along behind us. "So let me guess … those hideous collars of yours have something to do with it, right? As soon as CJ put hers on she stopped spraying diamonds everywhere."

She was sharp. How many other people had noticed that?

"And I bet if you took yours off we might see some frogs. Am I getting warm?"

"Red hot."

"I knew it!" She punched the air in triumph. "But how do you do it?"

I sighed. "It's not something I *do*. We just woke up one day like this."

A few people noticed us the minute we stepped out onto the terrace. Others turned to stare as word spread. Great. *And tonight the part of resident freak will be played by Violet Reilly.* I shrank a little closer to Zac's side.

"So tell me all about it! When did it start? How does it feel? Is it gross? Why do you think it happened to you two and not somebody else?"

"Sona—"

"Oh, and where did you get the collars?"

"Sona!" Zac interrupted more forcefully. "I don't think Vi really wants to talk about it."

Oh, my God, I could have kissed him.

"Oh, come on! This is the biggest story this century. Maybe ever! Don't leave me hanging."

Tears pricked at my eyes, and I blinked furiously. "I don't *know* anything to tell you. I don't know how it works, or what caused it, or why it happened to me. I just wish it hadn't. I just want to be normal again."

Zac and Sona exchanged a quick look.

"I'm sorry." Her tone changed to something more sympathetic. "It must be awful for you. We can talk about something else if you'd like."

I almost burst into tears on the spot. Coming from Sona, that was a big deal. She was obviously still bursting with curiosity, but she was prepared to put that aside for my sake.

"But, you know, if you ever do want to talk about it," said Zac, "I love frogs."

What a sweetheart. I gave him a shaky smile. "Thanks."

Sona looked over my shoulder and let out a little squeak. "Hey, there's Miss Moore."

Miss Moore looked stunning tonight, in a floor-length gown that wouldn't have looked out of place at the Oscars. A deep blood-red, it sat perfectly against her creamy skin. Her hair was swept back in a classical chignon.

"Wow," Zac said, gazing after her. "Looking that good should be illegal."

I followed his gaze, trying not to feel jealous. I could never look as good as her, not in a million years. Her height, her elegance, her sleek dark hair—my wild curls were up in a messy bun tonight, with a couple of ringlets trailing down past my ears. It didn't look too bad, and that was about as good as it ever got with my hair. Plus of course she didn't have the added bonus of occasionally spitting frogs when she spoke.

Was Zac's favourite colour still green, or was red making a comeback? But he *had* said he liked frogs.

His warm hand closed around mine and he gave me that cute dimpled smile. "Ready? Let's get this party started."

Chapter Nineteen

Dinner was nothing exciting—prawn cocktails to start, then a choice of chicken or lamb. They probably figured there was no point wasting cordon bleu cooking on a bunch of schoolkids. It didn't matter; the night wasn't about the food, but about the dancing to come, the tears and vows of eternal friendship and, most of all—the after party.

Ashleigh was hosting one for most of Year 11, which she'd half-heartedly invited me to just because I was CJ's sister. As it turned out, CJ wasn't going to it anyway, because now she was invited to the Year 12 one at Josh's place. But Ashleigh didn't need to worry; I wouldn't have gone to her stupid party if she'd begged me, after her earlier crack. I was going to tag along with CJ. With a bit of luck I could persuade Zac to come too. I felt a growing certainty that that might just make my night.

He was sitting next to me at dinner. Our table was pretty quiet, as we had a few of the robotics club guys with us. They were clustered together down one end with Mr Dunkley, my physics teacher. At the other end were me and Zac, Sona and Julie Lee, and the fabulous Miss Moore.

Between the two of them, Sona and Miss Moore kept the conversation flowing through the first two courses. Just as well, since I didn't feel like chatting now. I was too conscious of people looking, people whispering about me.

Miss Moore seemed to have travelled over half the world, and had a lot of stories to tell. None of them were bloodthirsty, but there was still something about her that made me uneasy. Once or twice I caught her looking at me, a thoughtful, almost amused look, as if she knew a secret about me that I wasn't going to like. Maybe it was just all the publicity about the stupid frogs and diamonds, or the fuss in the foyer before dinner, but it made me uncomfortable. I was sick of people staring at me.

Another time it would have bothered me a lot more, but Zac's leg was pressed against mine under the table and I was devoting a lot of brainpower to the vital question of whether this was merely accidental or more accidental-on-purpose. That whole side of my body felt warm and tingly, and as a result I was having a little trouble following the conversation. Zac wasn't saying much either. I couldn't tell if that was a good thing or a bad thing. Or just, you know, a thing. He was often quiet.

Julie Lee, of course, was even quieter, and barely spoke, though she followed the conversation with all the appearance of enjoyment. She was wearing a black halterneck dress and looked very nice, if a little sedate. Seeing her next to the flamboyant Sona made me wonder how these two had ever been best friends.

I ran my finger nervously under my collar, pulling it out from my throat. Was it my imagination, or did it feel hotter than usual? I must be more flustered by Zac than I'd thought. *Get a grip, girl. It's not like you've never had a boyfriend before.*

I'd gone steady with Matthew for six months in Year 9, and in Year 9, six months was practically a lifetime. We'd been the old married couple of our group—until suddenly we weren't. But never in that six months had I felt such nervous excitement over Matt as I felt now sitting next to Zac. And I'd only known him a week! What was wrong with me?

I sneaked a sideways glance at him. He looked so cute tonight I could hardly believe I'd thought he wasn't anything special that first day on the bus. Though in my defence, I *had* noticed the dimple straight away. But it was more than looks that had my heart going skippety-skip. He'd driven us home from that dreadful party; he'd come around to see how I was. And tonight he'd said he liked frogs. He was someone I could count on, and in this messed-up magic-infested world, that meant something.

Plus he'd said green was his favourite colour. Just thinking about it gave me goosebumps.

I loosened the collar again. No, it definitely felt hotter. The ends of the pointy bits felt as if they'd been out in the sun. Weird. I glanced over at CJ at the next table, but she was laughing and talking as if nothing was wrong.

"I'm going to the ladies'." I pushed my chair back, suddenly worried. I needed to check the stupid thing.

"I'll come with you," said Sona.

Julie looked vaguely alarmed at being left alone next to Miss Moore.

"Don't be too long," Miss Moore said. "They've started bringing out dessert, which means the speeches will be soon."

As we passed CJ I noticed a pile of diamonds on the table next to her. Josh was arranging them in patterns as they chatted. At least she looked sober now.

In the bathroom I leaned in to the mirror, scrutinising my collar. It was definitely getting hot; the skin underneath was a little pinker than normal.

"What's the matter?" Sona reapplied her lipstick and blew a kiss at her reflection, then frowned at me in the mirror. "Is it sticking into you?"

"It's getting really warm—but it doesn't look any different. I hope there's nothing wrong."

"Let me see." She moved closer and poked a tentative finger at the back of my neck. "Were these bits always a funny colour?"

"What do you mean, funny?"

"This part here near the clasp is all black and dull. Was it always like that?"

"I'm not sure." I'd never really looked that closely. "I don't think so."

I turned the collar around so I could see what she was talking about. Three of the big links were much darker than the rest. The clasp itself still gleamed silver in the middle of the dull section. That didn't look right.

While I stood there, twisting the collar this way and that, a fourth link turned black in my hands.

"Oh, shit."

Automatically I looked down, more than half expecting to see a toad materialise in the sink. But the drop that fell from my mouth wasn't even coloured. It shimmered faintly before disappearing in mid air. So the collar was still working.

But for how much longer?

Of all the times for Dad to go to Paris, why did it have to be now? Was there anyone else at Magic HQ who might know how to fix this?

"What's wrong?" asked Sona. "What's happening?"

"I don't know, but it doesn't look good. I think it might be about to start raining frogs again."

"Oh, no. Poor you." Her dark eyes were full of sympathy.

"Why now?" I clenched my fists in frustration. Couldn't it have held off for just a little longer? So much for my plans for the after party. Who was going to want to kiss a girl with frogs coming out of her mouth? Zac was a great guy, but even someone who liked frogs might draw the line at that.

"It might last the night," she said, trying to be positive, but even as she spoke another link died.

"Yeah, it might." And pigs might fly. I sighed. "I guess we'd better go. That sounds like the speeches starting."

We got back to the table as Mrs Crawley started her speech. The principal was a good speaker, not one of these people that likes the sound of their own voice. Her speeches were short and to the point, and usually entertaining. But tonight I didn't hear a word, too busy obsessing about the collar and its imminent failure. It was like having an exam hanging over your head, only worse, because at least with exams you know when they're going to be. But any moment now I could find myself spitting frogs again, even in the middle of saying something. Just as well *I* wasn't giving any speeches tonight.

Miss Moore was staring at me, watching my fingers fiddle with the damn collar. I forced myself to fold my hands in my lap and tried to at least look like I was paying attention to the speeches. The collar was growing uncomfortably warm.

Mrs Crawley finished her address to a round of applause, then introduced CJ to come up and propose the toast to the outgoing school leadership team. CJ rose, her collar firmly in place, and walked up to the microphone. From where I was sitting I couldn't tell if there was anything wrong with hers. Maybe I could borrow it if it was still working properly, since she didn't seem to care whether she wore it or not.

"Mrs Crawley, teachers, and fellow students," she began. "It's my honour and privilege tonight to propose a toast of appreciation to all the prefects and school leaders who've done such a fantastic job this year. You may wonder why a newcomer like me was chosen for this role, but I can tell you, even in the short time I've been at Fernleigh High, I've come to know some of the leadership team *quite well* ..."

She grinned and paused until the laughter died down. While she was waiting she ran her finger around under her collar in a gesture I knew all too well. Damn. Looked like I wouldn't be borrowing hers after all.

"... and I can truthfully say that already I can see what an asset they've been for our school." She paused again and cleared her throat. "On behalf of the whole student body, I'd ... ahem ... I'd like to—"

She lifted a hand to her throat, a strange look on her face. She whispered to someone at the front table, and they handed her a glass of water.

"Sorry, everyone, just a little frog in my throat."

There was laughter at this too, and many glances my way.

Gee, thanks, CJ, just what I needed to make this night super special, more people laughing at me.

Zac reached over without a word and took my hand.

"As I was saying, on behalf of everyone here tonight, I'd like to … propose … a toast OH MY GOD."

Right there, with the eyes of the whole room on her, a frog materialised from CJ's mouth and dropped into the glass of water with a resounding *plop*. She screamed and hurled the glass. It smashed in the middle of the dance floor, spraying the two front tables with water and broken glass.

Everyone scrambled up with screams and shouts of surprise. CJ kept screaming too, spewing a constant stream of frogs from her mouth.

I jumped up too. "CJ!"

A single perfect diamond dropped from my lips. Oh, *no*. This couldn't be happening. I stared at it, more horrified than I'd ever been by the damn frogs, then looked at Zac.

"We have to help her!"

Someone, thank God, had at least taken the microphone from her, so her amplified screams weren't ripping through the room like fingernails on a chalkboard. As Zac and I pushed through the crowd toward her she ran for the safety of Josh's arms, her eyes streaming tears and mascara.

He stepped back, putting a table between them. His handsome face was twisted into a grimace of disgust, his blue eyes cold. "That's close enough. Sorry, babe, but I don't do reptiles."

Her face crumpled. Rejection was a new experience for CJ. I wanted to punch his face in. The guy was a complete jerk.

"They're amphibians, arsehole." I shoved him out of the way. He didn't deserve my beautiful sister anyway. We stood in the centre of a circle of accusing faces, though what they accused us of I didn't know. Being unlucky? It wasn't as if CJ was pulling some stupid stunt to ruin the formal on purpose. "Come on, Ceej, let's get out of here."

Like bodyguards, Zac and I took an arm each and hurried her away.

Chapter Twenty

She was still crying when we got to the car, little hiccupping sobs that left a trail of frogs behind us. Like Hansel and Gretel dropping breadcrumbs—except their breadcrumbs didn't hop away. It was dark outside, but the building blazed like a Christmas tree, all lit up, its glow sending dark shadows staggering ahead of us.

"It's all right, Ceej, calm down."

I tried to put my arm around her but she only cried harder at the sight of diamonds pattering onto the ashphalt from my lips, and pushed me away.

"Leave me alone!"

As if it was my fault. Well, now she knew how it felt to be the one with the frogs. Not so glamorous, huh?

And then I felt like the worst sister in the world for even thinking that.

"Want a tissue?" Zac got one out of the glove box and offered it to her. Then he stepped back as if she were a ticking bomb that might be about to blow.

God, he was perfect. A warmth spread through me, despite the public disaster and the horrible uncertainty of our curse. What trick would it pull next? I was so conscious of him standing next to me that I almost didn't care. Almost.

When CJ had calmed down enough to stop spraying frogs everywhere we got into the little Mazda. I sneaked peeks at Zac's handsome face as he drove. Was he really as calm as he appeared? "I'm sorry, this probably isn't the way you planned to spend tonight."

A handful of diamonds pattered into my lap. Remembering my resentment of CJ's ability to speak, I felt a little guilty now that it was my turn to enjoy the diamond half of the curse. But only a little.

"Don't be sorry. I'm not." He glanced my way, his eyes full of promise. "I'm still with you, aren't I?"

I drew in a short, shocked breath and tried to stop a goofy smile from spreading across my face.

"Admittedly, it wasn't quite what I had in mind when I asked you to go to the formal with me," he added, "but at least life with you is never dull."

"Not lately, anyway," I agreed.

I checked on CJ. She was staring out the window, apparently lost in her own thoughts. Not happy ones, I was sure. Anger at that jerk Josh Johnson welled up in me again. He was just like that stupid prince in the fairy tale. I was convinced he'd only become interested in her because of the diamonds. Once they were gone it was all over, red rover.

I preferred my princes a little more gallant, and a lot less focused on the money. Like Zac. He took one hand off the wheel and reached over for mine. I looked down at our joined hands resting on my leg and smiled.

I was still smiling when we pulled up outside our house and I realised it was ablaze with light. We definitely hadn't left it that way.

"Uh-oh."

"What's wrong?"

"Someone's home." And there was only one person that could be. I groaned. "Looks like we're in trouble."

He let go of my hand long enough to put the car into park. "Want me to come in with you?"

CJ got out and slammed the door, leaving us alone for a few precious seconds.

"You are amazing, you know that?" I leaned closer, and this time nothing happened to ruin the moment. His lips were soft and warm. I closed my eyes, breathing in the delicious pine scent of him as the kiss deepened, leaving me breathless, heart hammering.

He pulled away after an endless moment, looking a little dazed.

"I'm sorry," I said. "Was that too pushy?"

"I've been wanting to do that all night," he admitted. "Though I have to say I was hoping for a more romantic setting."

True, I'd been picturing a romantic moment on the dance floor instead of a stolen kiss in the front seat of the little Mazda, but I wasn't complaining. Outside, CJ shifted restlessly on the footpath. Time to face the music.

"I'm sorry. I have to go."

"Give me your phone."

I pulled it out of my bag and watched as he put his number into my Contacts.

"Call me tomorrow."

"I will," I promised.

I waved as he drove off, then floated up the driveway as if I was treading on air. Zac had kissed me, and I couldn't care less what was coming out of my mouth any more. His mum might get a surprise, though, when she found a few diamonds kicking round the floor of her car tomorrow.

It wasn't until we got inside and came face to face with Mum that my happy mood started to fade. Her mouth was a hard, furious line.

"Where the hell have you two been?" Her gaze took in fancy dresses and elaborate hairstyles in one scathing sweep. "I don't even need to ask, do I? It's obvious. You've been to the formal, after I specifically grounded you both." She glared at CJ, then turned on me. "I might have expected that of your sister, but you! I thought you had more sense than to encourage her."

I boggled at the injustice of it. Hello? She *was* talking about CJ, wasn't she? Surely she knew her own daughter well enough to know that nobody talked CJ out of something she'd set her mind on. And how come there were different standards for the two of us? How was that fair?

"Did you learn nothing from last weekend's disaster?" she went on. "It's a dangerous world out there for the daughters of a warder. You're supposed to be safe at home with Kyle, and instead you're running around completely unsupervised. How can I protect you if I don't know where you are? If I can't even trust you to do as you're told?"

"Like you even care!" CJ was just as angry, but she had presence of mind enough to grab my hand before she started yelling. "We've been spewing frogs and diamonds all week and we've hardly even seen you. You're so busy with your precious warders. This is all your fault!"

"Really? How is any of this my fault? Was I the one who cursed you?"

"Would we have been cursed if we weren't your daughters? We're just collateral damage in some stupid war you're fighting."

Outside, the little Mazda drove away, the noise of its engine dwindling into the distance. I wished I was in it still, with that beautiful pine-scented boy. In the harsh light of the foyer that dreamy moment was already slipping away. But tomorrow … tomorrow I would ring him. We had the whole two weeks of the holidays ahead.

"This war was fought and won long ago. It's our job to make sure it doesn't break out again. Do you really want to live in a world where this kind of thing can happen any time? Because that's what it used to be like. Humans were nothing more than playthings to them, subject to any ridiculous whim. No one was safe."

"It doesn't feel like it's over to me. But then, you haven't even asked me how I feel, have you, so you wouldn't know. You've never even said you were sorry this happened to us."

"Of course I'm sorry it happened to you!" Mum threw her arms up in a gesture of frustration. "But it's not all about you, Crystal! I'm a warder, and there's a lot going on right now, more than you know. I have a lot of responsibilities. Do you even know what that word means? Because you sure don't act like it lately."

Mum slammed into the kitchen and got herself a glass of water. I got the funniest feeling she was trying to hide the fact that she was crying. Mum never cried. Dad was the teary one in our family, always losing it at soppy movies. Mum could remain dry-eyed no matter how many cute puppies died or little kids lost their families.

"Mum? Are you okay?" I went after her, tugging CJ with me. "Has something else happened?"

We hadn't been expecting her home tonight, after all. If all these responsibilities were keeping her so busy, what was she doing here?

She turned to face us across the kitchen bench. There were tears in her eyes.

"I have to fly to Paris tomorrow. Something's happened to Dad."

My breath caught in my throat. My first thought was a plane crash, or maybe a car accident. But she hadn't said *Dad's had an accident.* I swallowed hard. "What's happened?"

She took a deep breath. Her hands gripped the benchtop so tight her knuckles went white. "He's been ... turned into a bear."

"A *bear?*"

"Oh crap," said CJ. "Which fairy tale is that?"

"If we're lucky, it'll be *East of the Sun and West of the Moon,* and he'll only be a bear by day. It's still daytime in Paris so we don't know yet."

Oh, God. Poor Dad. Tears stung my eyes as I sank down on the couch in a rustle of satin. CJ settled next to me. Mum hadn't seemed to notice yet that we were still holding hands.

"And if we're not lucky?"

She sighed, scrubbing wearily at her eyes. "Then it could be a longer term thing. But let's not get ahead of ourselves. I came home to pack. It's an early flight. I have to be at the airport by five. By the time I get over there we should know more, and hopefully I can make arrangements to bring him home, if nothing else."

"So he could be a bear forever?" I felt sick.

She tried to smile, but if it was meant to reassure us it failed miserably. Mum seemed to have aged ten years overnight. I'd never seen her look so lost and miserable. "I'm sure it won't come to that. Dena's very good, and Emmet is a great researcher. We'll find a way."

But they hadn't found a way to wake up Snow White yet, had they?

"Who's going to fix our collars now?" CJ said, more to me than Mum.

Mum stiffened. "What's wrong with them?"

CJ let go of my hand. "They don't work any more."

Three green frogs hopped across the tiles towards Mum.

"Dam*nation*." She closed her eyes. A split second later they flew open again. "Wait a minute—*you've* got the frogs?"

"That's right," I said. "And I've got the diamonds."

"How in God's name did that happen? What have you girls been *doing* tonight?"

"Nothing. We just went to the formal."

I gave her a brief outline of the evening, leaving out the part where Josh dumped CJ in front of the whole senior school. Mum didn't even know they'd been going out. I didn't mention kissing Zac either. There were some things you just didn't need to tell your mother.

She came and sat with us in the family room, looking shell-shocked.

"And they just started to get hot for no reason? You didn't damage them in any way?"

"Nope."

"Did anyone touch them apart from you? Were there any strangers there?"

"No and no." Not that the strangers thing made any difference. Puck had been disguised as someone we knew last time. "Do you think there was a Sidhe there?"

"I don't know. Puck's in custody, and we haven't seen any unusual activity on the monitors. But who knows any more? All the rules have changed." She rubbed her face wearily. "It could just be that the collars reached the end of their useful life. They were only ever meant to be a stopgap measure. Dad would know."

But of course we couldn't ask Dad now. Her shoulders slumped. Maybe that was why the Sidhe had targeted him. He seemed the most useful of the warders.

"How did they get to Dad in Paris, then, if there was no activity on the monitors?"

"Good question." Mum considered me thoughtfully. "For that matter, how did they get to Sergei when he was on that plane? Sidhe can't travel on planes, there's too much iron and too little space for them to tolerate it." She sighed, a deep, defeated sound. "Perhaps someone set a time-delayed spell. More likely it's just further proof that we have a traitor or two among us."

That was sucky: that someone could deliberately be hurting

the people they worked with, trying to destroy the organisation they had supposedly dedicated their lives to. No wonder Mum looked so despondent.

"I hate magic," CJ said into the silence. "Why couldn't you guys be accountants or something?"

"We can't change who we are, Crystal. It's our duty to continue our ancestors' work. We're the only ones who can protect humanity from the Sidhe."

"Did Dad find out if the cauldron's safe?" I asked.

"I don't think he had time. That's another reason for me to go to Paris." She stood up and stretched. "But right now I have to go pack. And so do you two."

"Are we coming to Paris too?"

"No." Mum gave us the disappointed face again. Nothing had such power over me as that look. I felt like a worm. No, lower than a worm. "Since I obviously can't trust you girls to do the right thing, you'll have to move into HQ so Dorian can keep an eye on you while I'm gone. I'm not having you running around unsupervised any more."

"But Mum, we could help!"

"Consequences, Crystal." Mum gave her a steely glare. "You should have thought of them before you defied me."

I could barely keep my eyes open as the big car purred through the dark streets. We'd dropped Mum at the airport so early it was still practically the middle of the night, but she was too steamed up about last night to leave us alone for a moment. She should have known no self-respecting teenager would get up to anything before breakfast. Too early. But she wasn't taking any chances, so we got dragged out of bed about five minutes after we went to sleep.

Simon was wide awake, though no more cheerful than usual, so there was no chitchat. I was kind of glad it wasn't Kyle this morning; I still felt guilty over the trick we'd played on him last night. I hoped Mum hadn't chewed him out too.

CJ wasn't even pretending to be alert; her head leaned at an uncomfortable angle against the window beside her, eyes shut. We were nearly at HQ; I watched the night-time city slide by past the windows, quieter than I'd ever seen it. It was too late even for late-night partygoers, and too early for anyone else. A garbage truck clanked along the street, seizing its chance to be king of the road, orange lights flashing a warning, though there was no one to see except us, and we were quickly past.

The Rocks huddled like a ghost town under the dark arch of the Harbour Bridge. Not even the windows of HQ were lit as we slipped quietly into the garage. There were only a couple of cars there before us; our footsteps echoed hollowly off the concrete walls as we made our way to the lift.

Simon led the way through half-lit corridors to the kitchen, where he offered us toast or cereal. CJ shook her head. She hadn't said a word all morning, not even to say goodbye to Mum. Her eyes were red and swollen, as if she'd spent more of the night crying than sleeping. I'd brought the silk scarf downstairs this morning, thinking to tie us together so we could talk freely, but she'd pushed me away with a vehement shake of her head. That seemed like cutting off your nose to spite your face to me, but arguing with CJ was a waste of breath, so I'd just shoved it in my pocket in case she changed her mind later.

I poured myself a big bowl of cereal and yawned. I hadn't slept so well myself, alternating between fretting over Dad and replaying every moment with Zac in my head.

I slid my foot over to touch CJ's before I spoke—I didn't want to be fishing diamonds out of my cornflakes. A girl could choke to death on one of those suckers. She didn't look up from her own bowl, but at least she didn't pull her foot away.

"So what's the plan for the rest of the day?" I asked Simon. I wanted to help. There must be something we could do.

"We'll have to check with Warder Kincumber. He's usually up around six thirty. I'll bring your bags up to the guest quarters when you've eaten, and you can get settled in while you're waiting."

The guest quarters was where we'd stayed before. There were four bedrooms off a central lounge area. Last time CJ and I had shared a tiny room that barely fit two single beds. Hopefully we could spread out a bit more if we were going to be here for the whole holidays.

God, I hoped Mum and Dad came back before then. I didn't want to spend two weeks wondering what was going on in Paris, with Simon looking over our shoulders every minute. I checked my watch, but it was too early yet to ring Zac. I was busting to talk to him again. And maybe do a little more than talk. The memory of that kiss made my lips tingle, though some of the shine had gone off it now. I couldn't stop thinking about Dad, wondering what he was thinking—if he could even think any more—and hoping he was okay.

Another guy came into the kitchen. He wore a Star Trek T-shirt and an apologetic expression. He could have been late twenties, but it was hard to be sure because his light brown hair was well and truly receding, which made him look older.

"Sorry, am I interrupting?"

"We're just grabbing some breakfast," said Simon. "Come in. Have you met the girls? Crystal and Violet, Emmet Branson."

The guy whose file we'd looked at.

"Hi," I said, and caught a diamond with my spoon. Oops. I pressed my foot back against CJ's.

Emmet's eyes widened. "You must be Warder Reilly's daughters. May I?"

He reached over and plucked the diamond from my spoon. A soggy flake of cereal clung to it, which he wiped off onto his shirt, leaving a damp milky patch. Then he examined the diamond from every side, turning it over and over as if he'd never seen one before.

Simon shoved a packet of cornflakes across the table towards him. "You going to have some breakfast?"

"Oh, right. Thanks." Emmet looked as if he'd forgotten what he'd come in for. He laid the gem down, wiping his milky fingers on his shirt, and got himself some cereal and a glass of juice. I wondered if his T-shirt had always been quite so mottled, or if he made a habit of wiping odd things on his clothes.

"I don't normally see you here at this hour," Simon said.

"No, well, we're very busy at the moment." Emmet kept sneaking little glances at me and CJ as he ate. He had a kind of apologetic air about him, as if he felt like he shouldn't be here. "I was here until late last night, too. Warder Bhutra and I are trying to adapt Warder Reilly's theories to help Kerrie Davidson."

"Any luck?" Simon couldn't disguise the eagerness in his voice. Right. Kerrie Davidson was Snow White. I looked at CJ, sure she'd see this as more evidence of Simon's interest in the sleeping girl, but she stared miserably at her breakfast.

Emmet shook his head and picked up the diamond again.

"Forgive me for asking," he said to me, "but why aren't you wearing your father's collars?"

"Because they don't work any more."

"Really?" His eyebrows shot up. "What, both of them?"

"Uh-huh."

"That's odd. Do you have them with you?"

"In our bags."

"Mind if I have a look?"

"I'd love you to. I hope you can fix them."

"We'll drop by your lab in a little while," Simon said.

"Great."

After breakfast we headed for the guest quarters. Someone had already delivered our bags.

"I'll leave you to unpack," Simon said. "I'll be back soon and we'll take those collars to Emmet and Warder Bhutra."

"You don't have to come back," I said, spitting diamonds all over the floor. "Just tell us where it is. I'm sure we can find our way around."

"It's no trouble," he said, though his face told a different story. Mum must have given him strict instructions not to let us go anywhere alone. This was going to be a nightmare.

By the time we got to Emmet's lab, Dorian Kincumber was there too. Must be a day for getting up early.

"Good morning, ladies." He smiled, but not in a particularly welcoming way. Here was someone else who didn't seem too pleased at being saddled with us. Well, the feeling was mutual. "Have you met Warder Bhutra? Dena, this is Crystal and Violet Reilly."

A small Indian woman with a thick grey plait even longer than Sona's smiled and said hello. Her smile was more genuine than Dorian's.

I smiled back, pleased to find that for once I wasn't the shortest person in the room.

"May I see those, please?"

We gave her our collars, and she handed one to Emmet. She had thick black-rimmed glasses hanging on a chain around her neck. When she put them on her dark eyes blinked huge behind their lenses.

"Oh, dear," she said after a moment.

"What?" I glanced at Emmet; he was frowning. "What's the problem? Can you fix them?"

"No. Not fix them. Replace them, maybe."

"Why? What's happened?" Dorian sounded grumpy. Maybe he wasn't a morning person.

"These collars didn't *fail*. They were destroyed."

"Destroyed? By whom?" Dorian shot me a suspicious look. Yeah, right, as if I'd destroy the damn thing myself, when it had been the only thing stopping me spraying frogs everywhere.

"I'd have to assume one of the High Sidhe," Dena said. "How did this happen?"

So I told the whole story of our night at the formal again, just as I'd told it to Mum. Her eyes widened when I got to the part where we swapped frogs and diamonds—she obviously hadn't realised that had happened too. By the time I'd finished she was shaking her head.

"So it could have been any one of two or three hundred people?" She looked at Dorian. "And I assume our Sidhe guest is still in residence?"

"Puck? Of course. So swamped in iron he wouldn't even be able to touch his magic."

"So there is at least one other out there with his shaping abilities, and we have no idea what shape they're wearing now."

"But there's been no activity on the monitors," said Dorian. "And I thought we plugged all the leaks?"

Simon shifted uneasily. "We did, sir."

"Then how can we have another escapee?"

"Perhaps," the tiny Indian woman suggested, "there was always more than one. We assumed Puck was working alone because he was the only one we saw, but there may be others out there who have managed to hide their aether from us. Perhaps many others."

Dorian paled. "Surely not. The walls are still strong. This is madness."

He realised we were all staring at him, and managed to force a smile. "At any rate, I'm afraid this is bad news for you, young ladies."

Uh-oh. "Why?"

"Everyone you saw last night—virtually anyone you know— could potentially be a Sidhe. Unless we can discover who it was, I can't let you have any contact with anyone outside this organisation until your parents come home. Your mother would kill me if anything further happened to you while you were under my care."

"No contact?" I repeated. Surely he couldn't mean none at all. I had a very important phone call to make, as soon as a certain floppy-haired boy might be awake. "What about the phone? We can still talk to our friends on the phone, right?"

He was already shaking his head before I'd finished. "No, no, no. I know you young people think the world will end if you are parted from your phones and your tweeting and what-have-you, but I'm afraid I must insist. In fact, I'll ask you to hand your phones over right now." He coughed, as if broaching a delicate subject. "Your mother did warn me not to … ah …" *Trust us?* "… leave anything to chance."

To my surprise, CJ handed hers over without a quibble. In fact, she hardly seemed to have listened to a word that had been said. I felt my own face heating as I tried to hang on to my anger and my dignity.

"I really don't see how a phone call or a text is going to do any harm." I clutched at my phone. I had to talk to Zac. He was the only bright thing left in my world.

Dorian held out his hand, his smile turning chilly. "And that is precisely why you need to be guided by me. You know nothing about magic."

Everyone was staring. Face flaming, I smacked the phone into his palm. Maybe he was right, but he didn't have to be such a *jerk* about it.

Chapter Twenty-One

CJ lay on the lounge in the guest quarters, a book propped against her raised knees and the TV burbling quietly in the background.

"Are you okay?" I let my fingers rest against her arm, not wanting to make her feel worse with a shower of diamonds.

"Fine." She didn't take her eyes off the book.

I hesitated. Clearly she wasn't fine; neither of us was. I was itching to know what was happening in Paris, but Mum wouldn't even arrive there until tomorrow. I was starting to feel we'd got off lightly with our toads and diamonds. Poor Dad was a bear. What if he stayed that way forever? That sick feeling you get before exams churned away in my stomach, making me wish I hadn't eaten quite so much breakfast.

I tried to focus on something positive instead. I could still talk to Zac. Mobiles weren't the only phones in the world.

"You know, we could always use the landline to call someone."

Though all my numbers were in my contact list, including

that precious one for Zac. Still, I could look up his home number in the White Pages online—or just ask on Facebook. There were plenty of computers I could use in the building, and Sona would give me his number.

CJ shrugged. "You can if you want. I don't want to talk to anyone."

I could see her point. Ashleigh would enjoy any conversation about last night a hell of a lot more than CJ would, and who else would she call? Not Josh, that's for sure.

But what if Dorian was right? How would I know if the boy I'd been kissing was the real Zac or a Sidhe impersonator? It's not as if they came with warning labels. And he *had* looked different last night; I'd thought so the minute I laid eyes on him standing on my doorstep. Older, more mature, and about five billion times hotter. Had that really all been the suit and a good haircut, or was it magic?

I sighed. And then there was Mum to consider. We were already well and truly on her bad side. How pissed would she be if we got ourselves into more trouble through not doing what Dorian said? As if she didn't have enough on her plate already, with Dad to worry about on top of everything else. Would it really kill me if I didn't speak to Zac for the next two weeks?

Part of me started jumping up and down screaming *yes! God, yes!* He'd been the only good thing about last night, the start of something wonderful. I couldn't wait to pick up where we'd left off. Surely I would have known if it wasn't the real Zac kissing me? He'd been so kind, just like his normal self. Would a Sidhe impersonator have bothered to tell me he liked frogs? And then I remembered the way he'd admired Miss Moore. Would a boy who was falling for me have been quite so blatant in his admiration for someone else? God, this was doing my head in.

"Do you know how many fairy tales there are involving bears?" CJ slammed her book shut and glared at me.

"Um … no? What are you reading?"

She showed me the cover—it was a book of fairy tales from around the world. "I checked that one Mum mentioned—*East of the Sun, West of the Moon*. Guy gets cursed, turns into a white bear by day, only turns human at night. His wife's not supposed to see his human form, so they always go to bed in the dark. Only one night she lights a candle and peeks, and then of course everything's screwed up and he has to leave. She goes on this epic journey to find him and save him from marrying an ogre."

"Does he turn human in the end?"

"Yeah, but I don't think it's going to help us. We'd need a whole bunch of old women to give us golden presents and a ride on the north wind."

"Damn."

An ad for a current affairs program came on.

"Tonight we have an exclusive interview with a QANTAS stewardess who was on the flight with the man who became an ogre."

The footage we'd seen before, of poor Sergei bursting out of the arrivals gate roaring and confused, played again, followed by the now-familiar "Snow White" shots, and a brief close-up of my face, screwed up in anger, with a frog caught in mid-air. I shuddered. Was there ever a more unflattering way to become famous?

"We ask the question: is there a magic war going on? Don't miss our in-depth coverage at 7:30 tonight."

Ad break over, the morning chat show resumed.

"And in breaking news," the sleek hostess informed the camera, "we have unconfirmed reports of the sudden appearance of a polar bear in central Paris."

"So it's not just an Australian thing?" her co-host joked. "That's a relief! I was starting to feel persecuted."

"Apparently not," she said. "We'll bring you the latest on that as soon as we know."

A polar bear. Poor Dad. My stomach coiled into an anxious knot. Mum would still be on the plane. What had happened to him?

"What else did you find?" I grabbed CJ's book and scanned the table of contents. Just about every culture had a story involving a bear. There was everything from *Goldilocks and the Three Bears* to the Greek myth of Callisto, who was turned into a bear and ended up in the sky as the constellation Ursa Major. "Wow, there's so many. How are we ever going to find something to help Dad?"

She shook her head. "I don't know. But we have to try. We can't just sit around here and hope that someone figures it out."

I felt so helpless; I couldn't stand to sit still any longer. "It would help if we knew which fairy tale it was." But how could I find out?

I left CJ hunched over the book and went out into the corridor. It was mainly office space up here, plus the guest quarters and the library. Dorian had rooms here, too, but I'd had quite enough of him for one morning. I got into the lift, telling myself I'd go down to the ground floor and see if Emmet had made any progress with our collars, but I punched the button for Basement instead.

The vault was down here, and other areas I hadn't explored yet. I stepped out of the lift and shivered. It felt colder, probably because it was underground. There were none of the big arched windows that let the sunlight stream in to the upper floors. Here I felt closed in, the stark corridors lit by fluorescent bulbs. My feet tapped down tiled floors, no plush carpet here.

I peeked into several rooms whose purposes I couldn't guess, though they were fitted out like some kind of laboratories. There was a room with a keypad at the door for access. I tried the handle, but it was locked. When I put my ear to the door I heard the hum of computers through the wood. Perhaps that was where they kept the servers.

Or maybe it was something completely weird. Dorian was right: I knew nothing about magic, and even though these people didn't have magic as such, they had some strange set-ups, and all these tools that combined their potential for magic with the aether stored in the vault. I'd been reading in *The Gilded Cage* about the way they'd created the prison that kept the Sidhe's world anchored here in Australia, with them trapped inside—or supposedly trapped; that didn't seem to be working so well any more. Probably the explanation made a lot more sense if you understood magic; there were a lot of references to things I didn't understand, like aetheric flows and condensors. From the description I gathered that condensors came in several sizes, and I had the feeling that that odd box on a tripod I'd seen in the vault the day they'd interviewed Puck was one. Whatever they did, they seemed to be bad news for Sidhe.

Just ahead was the corridor that led to the vault, where they stored all the remaining aether, as well as any magical items the seekers found in their travels. If I was completely honest with myself, this was where I'd really been heading the whole time. The place itself fascinated me—it held aether, the raw material of magic—but more than that I wanted to see its new resident again.

I'd seen him on Mum's computer screen, during the hook-up when Dad and Dorian questioned him, and that brief moment in the corridor. Admittedly, he'd appeared disappointingly normal, but I knew that appearances couldn't be trusted with the Sidhe.

Maybe I could trick him into telling me which fairy tale had attacked Dad. Maybe, if I could just get the chance to talk to him, I could find out something useful, something to help Dad and Kerrie and poor Sergei—and even us. What was behind all these attacks? I couldn't shake the feeling there was more to it than simple vengeance for locking them up all those years ago. If that was all, why had Puck been hanging around the Cathedral when he was captured? And yet the warders seemed so certain that the Spear the Cathedral protected was safe. How did they know?

I rounded the corner and stopped short. A young woman I didn't know sat on a chair outside the double doors that led to the vault. She sat up straighter when she saw me, the look of boredom on her face replaced with speculation.

What should I do? Of course they would have a guard on the vault now that Puck was in residence. She wasn't going to let me go wandering in. But if I left now it would look really suspicious. Even standing here like this was making me look guilty as hell.

Oh well. As long as I could manage not to blush I could

probably talk my way out of trouble. I started towards her again.

The doors behind her were made of heavy glass, with big rounded metal handles. The room behind them wasn't the vault itself—that was another room further on—but a big area full of work desks and odd machinery. Apparently the whole area was specially fortified with iron and "dampener", whatever that was, to prevent any aether leaking out. So Gretel had said, when she'd given us a quick tour. Several smaller rooms opened off the main one, most of them full of Sidhe artefacts, safely locked away where they could do no harm. They'd converted one of these into a temporary cell for Puck, and all the dampener stopped him from accessing the aether in the vault, which was a relief. I could just see his cell from the main doors, but I didn't have time for more than a quick glance before the guard rose and blocked my view.

"Can I help you?" she asked.

"I was just looking for Warder Bhutra. Have you seen her?"

The woman's eyes widened at the sight of diamonds dripping from my lips. I was getting better at catching them now; it was a pain to have to go scrabbling around the floor picking them up.

"You passed the lab back in the main corridor. She might be there. She hasn't come down this way this morning."

She was having trouble meeting my eyes, too distracted by the gems glittering in my hand. I caught movement out of the corner of my eye and saw Dorian come out of one of the side rooms beyond the glass doors.

He looked as surprised to see me as I was to see him, and hurried over to where I stood with the guard.

"What are you doing?" His voice was curt as he shut the door behind himself. He sounded even crosser than when he'd taken our phones that morning. Bet he was already regretting having promised to keep an eye on us.

"Just … looking for Warder Bhutra." Even to me it sounded lame.

"Well, go look somewhere else. You shouldn't be poking around on this level, particularly not so close to the prisoner."

Why, was Puck going to bewitch me through the walls? And if so, shouldn't Dorian be worried on his own behalf?

"What were you doing in there?" I asked, craning to see around him. Was that room he'd come out of the one where Puck was being held?

"I visit the prisoner every day, not that it's any of your business."

Okay, so it was.

"Just for a chat?" That seemed like an odd risk to take.

"If my chatting can help us, then I'll keep doing it," he said. "Where's Simon? I thought he was meant to be keeping an eye on you?"

Oops. Hope I hadn't got Mr Grumpy in trouble. That would be him *and* Kyle in less than twenty-four hours. Good job, Vi.

"Don't you need to lock that?" I asked, gesturing at the door into Puck's cell.

"It's iron. He can't touch it."

Well, that was interesting. So I wouldn't need a key to see Puck. I could just walk right in—if I was brave enough. Or stupid enough. It was hard to tell the difference sometimes.

He took my elbow and marched me back toward the lift. Gretel and Ronnie came out of the room I'd picked as the server room. Sure enough, I glimpsed banks of high-powered computers and servers with their lights blinking green and red as the door closed behind them.

"Oh, Gretel!" Dorian clutched at her like a drowning man. *Please save me from this nosy teenager.* "Would you mind taking Violet upstairs with you? And see that she doesn't come back. I don't wish to be disturbed."

Without waiting for an answer—though I suppose you can't really say no when the boss asks you to do something—he turned and headed back towards the vault.

"Ah—okay?" she said to his retreating back. Then she grinned at me. "What were you doing?"

"Nothing. Just looking around." I wasn't about to tell the truth, even to Gretel. She'd report me and there would go any chance of talking to Puck. "I don't think he likes me."

"Dorian doesn't like most people," Ronnie said cheerfully. "Don't take it personally."

Then she headed the other direction while we turned toward the lift.

"Sorry," I said to Gretel as the lift pinged and we got in. "You've probably got a million things to do. I seem to be getting in everybody's way."

"Don't worry about it." She grinned as I fumbled diamonds. My hands were getting pretty full now. Should have brought a bag with me. "You need a hand there? I was going to head upstairs and grab a coffee soon anyway. You want one?"

Gratefully I offloaded a handful of diamonds onto her. I wasn't a big coffee fan, but I went with her to the kitchen anyway. At least she was a friendly face.

They had a big café-style coffee machine on the bench, all gleaming steel and glass. Coffee seemed to be brewing or percolating or whatever it did all day. I grabbed a juice from the fridge, while Gretel closed her eyes and breathed out an ecstatic *ahhhh!* after her first sip. Must have been good coffee.

"So where's your sister?" she asked, inspecting me over the rim of her cup.

"We don't always hang together just because we're twins, you know."

She held up a placating hand. "I know, I know. I'm a twin too, remember?"

"Sorry. I'm a little stressed." I pushed my diamonds into a neat pile on the wooden tabletop; they glittered under the bright kitchen lights.

"I know." She smiled sympathetically. "We all are, but I guess you've got more reason than most, huh?"

"I feel so useless!" I burst out. "Just hanging around here doing nothing while everyone else is trying to save the world."

"How's CJ? She stressed too?"

I shrugged. "Wouldn't you be? As if everything wasn't bad enough already, now poor Dad's a polar bear. It hasn't been the greatest twenty-four hours."

She gave me a sympathetic look. "I heard about the collars. How did that happen?"

I gave her a brief rundown of our last twenty-four hours. I even told her about kissing Zac, and how I was still tossing up whether to try contacting him or not. By the time I was finished the pile of diamonds had grown considerably. If they'd been real I probably could have bought a small island, or maybe a nice private jet.

"Look, I'm not going to tell you what to do." Well, that made a nice change from the rest of the adult world. "But if it was me, I wouldn't call him. Truly. Just in case. We don't know what we're dealing with here, but it's dangerous. You've seen what the Sidhe can do with just a little opportunity. Let's not give them any more. Come with me—I want to show you something."

I followed her to a small office with three desks. She sat behind one of them and pulled a visitor's chair over for me.

"Look at this."

On her screen she called up a map of the world. Like the one on the big screen in the monitor room, this map showed glowing lights—but these lights weren't confined to Australia. The whole North American continent was ablaze, as was most of Europe, parts of China, all over Asia, even some in Africa. The only big empty parts were the places where no one lived, like huge swathes of Russia and some African deserts.

"I'm guessing this isn't good news? What is this—aether all over the world now?"

"No, thank God, not that bad. But almost—this shows the spread of belief in magic. I've been mapping my results from monitoring internet traffic to where discussions of magic and fairies are occurring."

"Wow. That's a lot of people talking about magic."

"Yep." She stared at the screen and chewed at her lip anxiously. "That much belief is like a shot in the arm for the Sidhe. It'll give them more power than they've had in centuries."

"Enough to break out?"

"I don't think so. No more than they've done already, anyway. Belief alone won't destroy their prison."

"Then what will?"

She sighed. "I wish I knew. Then we might be able to figure out what the hell they're doing."

Chapter Twenty-Two

Nearly two weeks later, CJ and I had become experts on bears in fairy tales, but were no closer to finding a solution for Dad. I still hadn't managed to see Puck, though I'd tried a couple of times. I hadn't rung Zac either. Every time I'd walked past a phone the first couple of days I'd been like a smoker trying to quit. *Just one! One call won't hurt. Then I'll be good.* My hand would twitch toward the phone, and my heart would start racing. But then I'd think of how much shit I'd be in if something else went wrong because of that one phone call, and every time I chickened out.

After a few days of that, the fact that I hadn't called *was* the problem. What must Zac have thought when I didn't ring the first day? He probably thought I'd changed my mind. And how would he react now if I did? For that matter, how could I explain the situation we were in? *Oh, yeah, there's a whole organisation dedicated to keeping the world safe from magic, and my parents just happen to be running it, and by the way my dad's a bear and we have a fairy locked up in the basement. Plus anyone we know could be a fairy in disguise, which is why I can't actually see you in the holidays. No, I'm not crazy, thank you very much for asking.* Yeah, that was a conversation I couldn't see myself having. Instead I'd spent the last two weeks reading every book of fairy tales I could find in the library, sneaking moments on borrowed computers to scour the internet with CJ for information on bears in general and fairytale ones in particular, and just wandering around talking to people when it all became too overwhelming. Oh, and trying to come up with a reasonable explanation for when I finally saw Zac again at school.

I tried not to get underfoot. Everyone seemed too busy to chat, though I caught rumours of investigations. Traitors and magic leaks were whispered about, but no one wanted to let me in on the secrets. It was driving me nuts. We were getting nowhere with our bear research and, for all the activity around HQ, no one else seemed any closer to finding answers either.

Mum had found Dad in the Paris zoo. He seemed to recognise her, and had the zookeepers confused, because he was the friendliest polar bear they'd ever seen—but he was still a bear. He didn't turn human again at night, and Mum was still wading through the complicated arrangements to have him shipped to Australia, posing as a cashed-up buyer from Taronga Zoo. Forging documents hadn't seemed to be a problem. I just hoped nobody thought to check with anyone else at Taronga.

When I needed a break, I often visited in Kerrie's room. Sometimes Emmet was there, running another experiment, or Dena, but there was always someone sitting with her regardless, just in case she woke up or her situation changed, and that person was often happy to chat to pass the time.

Often it was her brother Bryan, but when his duties as a

warder kept him away it could be anyone, and I'd met a lot of the staff this way. This afternoon it was Kyle, and he was telling me the latest diplomatic hurdle Mum had come up against in her efforts to bring Dad home. It annoyed me that he knew more about it than I did—I was her daughter! Why wasn't Dorian telling me this stuff instead of leaving me to find it out on my own? But mainly I was just glad to hear it at all.

"At least your Dad's a fairytale bear," Kyle said.

"What do you mean?"

"Well, he's not aggressive, like a real polar bear. He seems to have retained his humanity underneath the bear skin."

"Like Warder Nabukov." The ogre still knew who he was, though he was so distressed at his transformation he had to be kept sedated, and spent a lot of time asleep. You could hear the thunderous snores from his room as you passed in the corridor.

"Yes. If your Dad had become a real bear they might have had to shoot him."

I shuddered. Dad had been found sitting quietly in the courtyard outside the Louvre as the first early birds turned up for work at the famous gallery. Despite the screams, he hadn't moved, except to lie down meekly when a policeman with a gun appeared. Thank God he hadn't attacked anyone. In fact, he probably would have climbed calmly into the zoo truck when it finally arrived, but they'd shot him with a tranquilliser gun anyway, thoroughly confused by the bear's unbearlike behaviour. I'd seen the footage of the "capture".

Me and six billion other people. Could there be a person left on the planet who hadn't seen it? The fairytale attacks were the only thing anyone talked about on TV any more, and the internet had suddenly sprouted a thousand "experts", all pushing their own agenda. Predictably, some were convinced it meant the end times were here, and were busy exhorting the world to repent before Jesus returned and damned them to hell for all eternity. There was still a vocal minority that thought it was all an elaborate hoax, and there were various explanations put up as to who had done it and why. But an increasing number of people were starting to believe in magic, and Gretel was looking more and more worried as the days passed and her map of belief kept lighting up like a Christmas tree.

"Why do you think the Sidhe are attacking us with fairy tales?" I asked Kyle.

He sprawled in an armchair by Kerrie's bed, looking glad for the chance to sit down. Everyone at HQ looked tired these days—well, except Kerrie herself, of course. Snow White looked beautiful, absolutely prince-ready. There were no monitors in the room; no tubes or drips. The magic itself kept her alive as it kept her unconscious. She needed nothing more.

"Why not? Just because they can, most likely."

"I wish we could ask Puck. We've got a Sidhe sitting right there, and we can't use him."

"It wouldn't do you any good. You can't trust anything they say. He'd have you convinced you could breathe underwater, and laugh as you drowned." He frowned, giving me that *this is serious* face that adults all do when they're trying to convince you to listen to them—even though he was only a handful of years older than me. "The Sidhe aren't like us. Don't ever make the mistake of thinking they are, just because they look like us. They think, and feel, in completely alien ways."

Wow. That was probably the longest speech I'd ever heard out of Kyle. He had a tendency to fade into the background when others were around. Simon seemed to do most of the talking when they were together.

"Did you know her?" I nodded at the still figure in the bed. "Before this happened, I mean."

"I knew *of* her, but I'd never met her. Simon knew her when they were both in Perth; he said she was a lot of fun. Great sense of humour."

Well, what do you know? I wouldn't have thought Simon would know a great sense of humour if it jumped up and bit him on his grumpy arse. I looked at Kerrie again. She lay so still, never moving in her sleep, not even a twitch. It was hard to imagine her as a living breathing person, telling jokes, having a few drinks at the pub on a Friday night after work. She'd become a symbol, an archetype: the classic damsel in distress.

What was her favourite food? Did she like romantic comedies or action movies? Or maybe both?

"I heard a rumour," Kyle continued, "that Simon was pretty keen on her at one stage, but he got sent out on field work for a month, and by the time he got back she'd hooked up with someone else, so it never came to anything."

"Really?" Poor Mr Happy. So CJ was right. Was that the reason he always seemed angry at the world? Was there a broken heart beating in that poor disappointed breast? That seemed way too romantic for the grumpy seeker I knew.

Kyle frowned at me. "Don't tell anyone I told you that."

Don't tell your sister I told you that, he meant. He hadn't gotten into trouble the night of the formal, but he didn't trust CJ any more.

"Maybe he should try kissing her, then. She might wake up."

His frown deepened. "I wouldn't suggest that to him, if I were you. Let's just leave it to the experts. People who don't know what they're doing mucking around in it could just make it worse."

And by "people who don't know what they're doing", he meant me? Oh, nice one, Kyle. What did he expect? Of course I knew nothing—no one would *tell* me anything! But at least I was trying, not just sitting around staring at a comatose girl going *oh, gosh, this is sad.* It was like the whole organisation was paralysed by the fairytale curses.

If the Sidhe could see us from inside their prison, they must have been laughing their heads off.

Simon eventually persuaded Dorian to let us leave HQ under his supervision, proving that maybe he wasn't always such a grump. There were only two more days left before Term 4 started, Mum and Dad still weren't home, and we'd all but given up hope of finding a way to help Dad. The only bright spot in our dark days was that Emmet had handed over our new collars and we could speak freely again.

Maybe he was going a little stir-crazy himself, since he'd mainly been confined to HQ keeping an eye on us, but it was still nice of Simon to offer. I didn't care too much about his motivations as long as I got to escape the atmosphere of gloom at HQ for a couple of hours.

We headed out into a bright spring afternoon. The Rocks was full of tourists—tall German backpackers and big groups of excitable Japanese lugging enormous cameras—and everything seemed new and wonderful. Actually, it *was* pretty new, since we'd hardly had a chance to see Sydney yet, and I felt like a tourist myself, gawking at buildings and checking out the Akubra hats, boomerangs, and T-shirts in the tourist shops. For a little while I could forget the dark clouds that hung over us.

There was a bustling craft market set up in the heart of The Rocks. They'd closed off part of the main street and set up awnings across the road. Underneath, throngs of people browsed everything from clothes to pottery, kangaroo balls on key rings to delicate stitched artworks.

"Can we look?" CJ begged.

Shopping was a cure for just about anything, and CJ needed a break just as much as I did.

"There's too many people." Simon looked around uneasily, as if he expected a Sidhe to leap out of the crowd any minute and turn him into a toad.

"Please! Just for a few minutes? We'll stay right with you."

It was hard to resist those big blue eyes of CJ's. Tougher men than Simon had crumbled before.

"Five minutes, then."

She plunged into the crowd and we hurried to keep up with her.

"Look at these!" She held up a candle that looked like a ball of stained glass, or a miniature Tiffany artwork. It was beautiful. When I looked closer I could see some of the candles on display showed tiny street scenes; some were even adaptations of famous paintings. "They smell divine."

The next stall had dreamcatchers and wind chimes, threaded

with feathers and beautiful glass beads. Already Simon looked like a man who regretted his decision.

"Five minutes," he said again.

CJ flitted on through the stalls, the most animated she'd been since the night of the formal. It was nice to see her smile again.

"Keep up," said Simon. "We don't want to lose her in the crowd."

He forged ahead, calling to CJ to wait, and I strolled after them, trying to take it all in. I'd just stopped to look at some silver jewellery when a voice behind me said, "Hello, Violet."

I jumped. "Oh, hi, Miss Moore."

Why did she have to sneak up on me like that? My history teacher looked as glamorous as ever, in skin-tight black jeans and a deep burgundy top with the most plunging neckline I'd ever seen. Even I had trouble keeping my gaze out of her cleavage; the old guy manning the necklace stall had no chance. I doubt he had the faintest idea what her face looked like. A silver pendant nestled in the deep curve of her breast, a feather worked in the finest detail.

"How are you enjoying the holidays?" I asked, willing my heart rate to return to normal. Not that I cared, but she was staring at me expectantly, so I blurted out the first thing that came into my head. She had a knack of unsettling me; I never felt comfortable around her. I'd never managed to shake the bad impression of that first bloodthirsty Ancient History class.

"Very much," she said. "How about you? Have you bought anything at the market?"

"No, I'm just looking. Still new here. We're just getting to know our way around."

"Me too." She pulled a handful of origami figures out of one of her shopping bags. "Look what I found down the other end. Aren't they amazing?"

I'd never seen such intricate folding. There were birds, dolphins and even something that looked a little like a bear. It was probably meant to be a koala. All done in beautiful Japanese papers.

"Here, have one." She offered me one of the birds.

"No, that's okay," I didn't want anything of hers, despite how pretty it was. "I wouldn't want to deprive you."

"Nonsense. I've got plenty. You can't just window shop at your first markets—you need a souvenir." She pressed the little bird into my hand.

"Thanks." Her eyes were so intent on me, it seemed impossible to say no. My mouth just wouldn't form the word. Instead I found myself nodding stupidly and tucking the little thing into my pocket under her watchful gaze. Well, I'd just have to throw it out when she'd gone.

"You're welcome. Enjoy the rest of your holidays—I'll see you on Monday back at school."

I watched her walk away, irritated by the nagging feeling that I'd meant to do something when she'd gone. What was it? My head felt thick, as if I'd just woken up. She disappeared into the crowd while I stood there, trying to remember. I could see Simon's head peering this way and that, anxiously looking for me, so in the end I gave up and went to join the others. It couldn't have been that important.

"There you are," he said when I caught up with them. "I think we'd better move on. There's something I want to show you."

He shouldered his way out of the throng of shoppers and we tagged along in his wake. He led us away from George Street, up the hill toward the sandstone cutting under the road that led onto the Harbour Bridge. Dad had pointed it out on our first trip to HQ, said it had been partly built with convict labour. The Argyle Cut, it was called. Now we weren't flashing past in a car, I could actually see the chisel marks in the stone. Crazy to think that convicts had put them there. That was such a long time ago, though I guess it didn't seem that way to the warders, who were dealing with problems that began centuries ago—but it seemed like a long time when you were seventeen. I wondered what it would have been like to be seventeen back then. No internet. No phones. I was certainly glad I lived in *this* century.

Though I could have done without the threat of fairy invasion.

"Where are we going?" CJ asked as we dodged around another group of Japanese tourists, huddled together over a map.

"To Observatory Hill."

Simon led us past galleries and cute little stone cottages, past steakhouses and pubs where the clientele spilled onto the footpath along with a rich beery smell, through the Argyle Cut, and up a steep flight of stone steps so old the passage of feet had worn a hollow in the middle of each step.

"What's at Observatory Hill?"

"An observatory." Well, derr. "A famous piece of Sydney history—but also a vital piece of magical history. You won't find that mentioned on any of the tourist guides, though."

At the top of the stairs we crossed a road and entered a park. The observatory itself was a handsome old building with a green copper dome. Like most of the historic buildings in the area it was built from the local sandstone, and glowed a warm honey gold in the afternoon sun.

"What's that yellow thing on top of the tower that looks like an upside down Chupa-chup?" I asked.

"That's the time ball. It's the whole reason the observatory was built here. Every day they raise the ball up the spike, and at one o'clock exactly they let it drop. It's important for navigation to know the exact time. From up here all the ships in the harbour could see it, and they used it to set their chronometers to the right time before they started a long journey." He smiled, an expression you didn't see too often on his face. It made him look a different person. "And from Australia, every sea journey is a long one."

"But what's that got to do with the observatory? Couldn't they have just built the tower by itself?"

"The observatory is how they know the correct time. It's the astronomer's job to set the time from observing the movement of the sun and stars." He shook his head. "Of course, sightings of the stars aren't what they used to be, now a big modern city's grown up around the observatory. Too much light pollution. But anyway, that's only the mundane history."

It was peaceful up here, an oasis away from the crowded narrow streets of The Rocks. Hardly anyone was about, just a man walking his dog and a family on a picnic rug under the trees. It didn't seem like the kind of place to feature prominently in magical history.

Simon led us across the grass away from the observatory. We passed a war memorial and stopped at a stone bust.

"Hans Christian Andersen," I read.

"The Dutch guy who wrote all those fairy tales?" CJ asked. We'd certainly read our fair share of fairy tales over the last two weeks.

"Danish, actually," said Simon.

"What's he doing here?"

"It's ironic, really. He's only a new arrival—a present from the Danish royals in 2005—but they managed to put him almost exactly on the spot where the anchor once stood."

"What anchor?" CJ asked. She was gazing out at the view and was only half listening. She probably thought he meant some ship's anchor, but I'd been doing my reading, and I knew what he meant. Finally, someone was talking to us about the secrets of *The Gilded Cage*.

"The Spear of Lugh. It formed the southeast anchor of the great condensor built by the warders when they relocated the Sidhe prison."

"When they moved it to Australia?"

"Yes. It didn't move the Sidhe world anywhere—that exists on another plane altogether. Another dimension, if you want to call it that. But having the prison in the Northern Hemisphere made it too easy for them to worm their way out again. The first condensing was supposed to destroy all the existing portals between our two worlds—but there were a lot. Every second damn hillock in Ireland alone was a fairy hill, or an entryway to their world. That's how they got their name: 'Sidhe' means 'people of the hills' in Gaelic. After Cottingley the warders decided to move it, to stop the random escapes. There always seemed to be another portal that they'd missed."

"And that's what condensors do? Suck aether away?"

"Aether and Sidhe. If the warders wanted to they could condense Puck right back where he came from."

He was pacing out a circle with the bust of Hans Christian Andersen roughly at its centre, checking something on his phone and adjusting his perimeter as he went.

"What are you doing?"

"Checking the seals," he said.

"You have an *app* for that?" Warding had certainly come into the twenty-first century.

"The app shows me the markers. I could find them myself, but it takes longer. It doesn't check them; I have to do that. It takes latency to feel their resonance. We still haven't managed to come up with anything electronic that will do the job."

"What about the Hendrix counter?"

"That measures the presence of aether. If the seals are holding, there shouldn't be any."

I watched him curiously. He was pacing anti-clockwise, and I suddenly remembered something I'd read about entering fairy hills by circling them widdershins.

"And what are the seals sealing exactly?"

"The power of the Spear of Lugh. It's an ingenious system really—it uses the Sidhe's own magic against them. The power of the four anchors is sealed into the earth at the four anchor points. The original spell linked the anchors into a net that created one giant portal to suck the aether and all the Sidhe out of the world. The second spell moved the prison and made sure of it. Now the residual power's enough to hold that portal closed so the Sidhe can't get out." He grimaced. "At least, that's the theory. Obviously things haven't been working so well in practice lately."

"Obviously." One hand went to the collar I wore around my neck as living proof. At least Emmet's version had less pointy bits than the quick job Dad had knocked up the first time.

"How many times do you have to walk round that circle?" CJ asked. Clearly she would rather be somewhere else. Probably back at the markets.

"Seven times. Seven is a powerful number in magic."

"People must wonder what the hell you're doing sometimes," I said, but he didn't reply.

He stopped, frowning, and glanced down at his phone, then continued on more slowly. On the next revolution he paused again at the same place and sniffed the air. Curiouser and curiouser.

"What? Is something wrong?" I trotted over and sniffed too. "I can't smell anything except … um … burnt toffee?" That same smell had been in Josh Johnson's bedroom the night Puck cursed us.

"Burnt *toffee?*" CJ rolled her eyes. "What have you been smoking? All I can smell is car exhaust."

Simon gave me a strange look. "Burnt toffee's a pretty good description, actually. Are you sure?"

I nodded, mystified.

"That's the smell of aether," he said. "And if you can smell it even when you're wearing that collar, your latency must be off the charts."

CJ looked away and I felt a quick pang of guilt. But it wasn't my fault! And if all latency meant was that I could smell a bit of aether, it wasn't anything to be jealous of either.

"But why is there aether here? There shouldn't be, should there? What does it mean?"

His expression was bleak. "It means someone's been messing with the seals."

"Who? A Sidhe?"

"No. There's too much iron here. It must be one of us. One of the seekers."

"Don't look so horrified," CJ said to me. "They've been talking about a traitor for weeks."

"I know, I know. I just don't get why any human would be trying to let the Sidhe back in."

"We can worry about why later." Simon's mouth was a grim line. "But if we don't find out who and how soon, we're going to be up to our armpits in bloody fairies."

Chapter Twenty-Three

Late that night I was still tossing restlessly, unable to sleep. I wasn't used to sleeping in air-conditioned buildings: I'd get too cold and pull all the blankets up, only to overheat and have to throw them off again. In the other bed CJ was breathing softly, one hand thrown up beside her face, fingers gently curled. Her dark hair fanning across the pillow reminded me of Kerrie's, and I shivered.

Emmet and Dena were no closer to a solution for the warder's pretty sister. Dad was still a bear, though Mum had finally succeeded in getting clearance to bring him back to Sydney. They were due to arrive late Tuesday, which would be the second day of school. Sergei was still an ogre, and CJ and I at least had our collars, but the underlying problem remained. We were just lucky that ours manifested itself in a way the collars could fix. In the other victims the magic was buried too deep for such easy solutions.

I pulled my clothes back on, let myself out of the visitors' suite and padded down the dark hallway. There were night lights on for security in some of the offices, but the hallway was only lit by the streetlights coming in the big arched window at the end. I pressed the button to call the lift—might as well go down to the kitchen and grab something to eat. I wasn't even the tiniest bit sleepy.

The chime of the lift arriving sounded so loud in the stillness that I jumped. I stepped inside and raised my hand to press "G". For an instant it hovered there, and then I pushed "B" instead. What the hell, it was worth a try.

The dungeon level, as I thought of it, was darker than level 1. No windows. I padded down the hallway, my bare feet making no noise on the cool tiles. The faint hum of servers greeted me as I passed the computer room, then faded as I approached the corner leading to the vault.

I took a deep breath, then peeked round the corner. Too much to hope that there would be no guard there just because it was the middle of the night. The side corridor blazed with light and, sure enough, a guard sat in the chair just outside the double glass doors at the end of the corridor.

Despite the bright lights, though, the guard was asleep.

I took a hesitant step around the corner. Wow, that looked uncomfortable. The man's head rested against the wall, tilted back almost at a right angle to his neck. How could anyone sleep like that?

I crept down the corridor. He would wake up, for sure, and then what was I going to say? It was the middle of the night, and here I was, sneaking around after Dorian had specifically told me to stay away. I couldn't have looked more guilty if I tried. Yet my feet kept moving, inching me silently closer to the sleeping guard, like I had some kind of death wish. Not even the thought of Mum's disappointment at me getting into more trouble held me back.

What the hell was I doing here anyway? Puck was probably asleep, just like I was supposed to be, and even if he was awake, it wasn't as though he was going to get a sudden urge to reveal the whole Sidhe plan because I asked him nicely. In fact he'd probably think I was just a stupid kid, and I'd already had it up to here with people thinking that. But Dad needed me. He might be arriving home on Tuesday, but he was still a bear, and likely to remain that way forever if we couldn't come up with some kind of breakthrough. His condition made our frogs and diamonds look like a walk in the park. Someone had to do something.

The guard snuffled in his sleep and his head jerked to the side. I froze halfway through a step. *Please don't wake up. Please.* I waited, heart hammering in my throat, until his head sagged back to its original position and his breathing evened out again.

Okay, if I was really doing this, it was time to get it over with. My nerves couldn't take the strain.

I paused, hand on the glass door. *Hope the damn thing doesn't creak.* The guard was so close I could have touched him. I held my breath as I eased the door open, watching his sleeping face the whole time, but the door made no noise, and he didn't even twitch. I slipped inside and let the door whisper shut, relief making my knees tremble.

I stopped just inside the door. The lights were low in here and it took a moment for my eyes to adjust after the brightness of the corridor. The dimness was punctuated by bright dots of red, yellow, and green coming from the various monitors and machines in the room. They hummed quietly to themselves, a sleepy night-time song.

I picked my way across the room to the door to the side room where Puck was being held. A small window was set into it, but there were no lights on inside the makeshift cell. Strain as I might, with the light from the corridor behind me I couldn't see anything in that glass but my own reflection.

Suddenly a face loomed there, white and shocking. Bloody hell! I jumped back, swallowing a cry of surprise.

"You scared me," I said, trying not to sound accusing, though my heart was doing its best to hammer its way out of my chest.

The face grinned. It was an odd face. There was nothing about it that didn't look fully human—no pointy ears or winged eyebrows—and yet something in its expression managed to hint at an inhuman otherness. He still looked as he had the day we saw him in the corridor—a young man with dark hair falling across his face.

"I should be the one who's scared." His voice was muffled by the door between us, but I could hear him clearly enough, though he stood back at least a metre. Dorian had said the iron of the door would hurt him. Maybe that was as close as he could bear. "I'm the one who's being spied on in the middle of the night."

"I'm not spying!" My voice sounded loud in the empty room. I made an effort to lower it. "I was just trying to see if you were awake."

"Well, I am, as you can see." He moved away, disappearing into the darkness until he switched on a lamp by his bed.

Then I saw why he'd come no closer to the door. He couldn't: he was chained by a manacle around one ankle to a bracket on the wall. The chain was long enough to allow some movement, but not much.

He spread his arms wide in a mocking gesture. "Welcome to my kingdom. Won't you come in and join me?"

I laid a hand against the door. Opening it would be stupid. I could talk to him just as easily from out here. There was no reason to put myself in danger.

But he was chained up, and that chain looked like it meant business. No doubt it was made of iron.

He sat on the bed and crossed his legs. His jeans rode up enough to show the manacle, padded with some kind of thick wadding. Even so, I could see ominous black lines spreading up his leg from it. His foot was a nasty purplish colour and swollen.

I shoved open the door and marched in.

"What's wrong with your foot?"

"It's the blood sickness." His eyes glittered strangely in the half-light from the lamp. "Your iron poisons me."

I felt a flash of sympathy. Damn it, I shouldn't be wasting sympathy on him—it was his fault CJ and I were in this mess. His fault that pretty Kerrie might never wake up. And probably his fault too that my Dad was now a polar bear. I folded my arms across my chest and hardened my heart against him.

"Why did you come here?" I asked.

"Because your so-charming warders invited me. It was an invitation most difficult to refuse." He moved his leg and the chain rattled. "Now ask me why I don't leave."

I shifted impatiently. I could see what everyone meant about it being hard to get a straight answer out of these people. "I don't mean why did you come *here*, to this cell. Why did you leave your world and come back to ours?"

"But what is this distinction you draw?" He leaned forward, his gaze pinning me to the door. With the lamp behind him his face was in shadow, but his eyes glittered, red lights dancing in their depths. Creepy bastard. "Who was here first, child? It is *all* our world."

"I'm not a child." Mature, I know, but I had no answer to the rest of it, and his eyes were weirding me out. They made me think of demon possession and a bunch of half-remembered stories of things that go bump in the night. Maybe coming here wasn't one of my better ideas.

"Of course you are. I can feel it in you. All that power, longing to get out, but they won't even tell you you've got it, will they? The adults all want to keep you in the dark, keep you powerless. They like it that way."

I opened my mouth, but nothing came out. How the hell did he know that? It was true. No one, not even our own parents, had told us a thing about magic and the world they inhabited until it came knocking down the walls of our reality. They still hadn't mentioned my latency, or CJ's lack. The only reason I knew most of what I did was because I'd tricked Simon into giving me *The Gilded Cage*.

The Sidhe man laughed and patted the bed. "Come, sit down. I won't bite. They warned you about me, didn't they? And they were right to. It's all true. But at least you know where you stand with me. You should be more afraid of the things they didn't tell you about themselves."

"I'm fine here." I might be young, but I wasn't stupid. I leaned back against the door. Its solid iron weight reassured me. "Go on then, tell me what they should have. And while you're at it, tell me how to turn my Dad back into a man. Which fairy tale is he from?"

He laughed, showing even white teeth. "You don't even know the right questions, do you? Ask them how they anchored their great trap."

"They used the four treasures." I was confident of that one, at least.

"Then why are the treasures not needed any more? How did they transfer the power from our treasures to their anchors? Ask them about the blood they spilled. Ask them why they shun their own people who are born defective."

"What do you mean, defective?"

"Ask them. See what answer you get. And while you're there, ask them what else that collar around your neck does."

Goose bumps rose on my arms.

"It stops your curse from making me an outcast," I snapped.

He shook his head. Half hidden behind his hair, his eyes gleamed in the dim light from the lamp. "No, child. That's not all it does."

I swallowed, fighting down my uneasiness. It was so quiet in the little room, as if we were the only two people awake in all the world. Why had I come here alone? I should go; he was doing this deliberately, trying to get to me. Trying to drive a wedge between me and the warders. Dancing all around, refusing to give me a straight answer to anything. But I couldn't help myself; I had to ask.

"What else? What else does it do?"

"Take it off." He sat perfectly still, a statue of a man, but I couldn't shake the feeling he was a predator, and I was the dopey herbivore that was about to become lunch. "Take it off and you'll see."

"And then you'll tell me how to help my father?" There'd be a few diamonds to tidy away before I left, that was all. He couldn't hurt me, surrounded by iron.

"Then you might be able to help your father without any assistance from me."

Without taking my eyes off him, I reached behind my neck and undid the clasp that fastened it.

"So? Nothing's changed." With my free hand I caught the diamonds that fell.

"Can't you smell it?"

Oh, my God. There it was again. Burnt toffee. I groped behind me for the door handle. There was aether in the room, and he was a Sidhe. I had to get out.

"Be calm. You are in no danger. The aether is within *you*."

I froze, half in, half out of the room. He still hadn't moved from the bed. I was torn between flight and a desperate desire to know more. Dad needed help. If Puck so much as lifted a finger, I was out of there …

I took a deep breath to settle my nerves. Let's hope this cat could survive its curiosity one more time.

"You mean the aether from your curse? That's what I can smell? Then how come I couldn't smell it before?"

"You've been wearing that collar constantly for what? A week? More? The curse, as you call it, doesn't go away. The collar merely suppresses it. The aether, unexpressed, has built up to noticeable levels now. That is all."

With the door half open, the noise of the machines in the other room was more obvious. Somewhere a clock ticked away the night, loud in the darkness.

"And your point is—? That's what it's meant to do. You said the collar did something else as well." *And you implied it was something bad.*

He shook his head wonderingly. "You truly are ignorant, aren't you? Do they not teach you how to think in those schools you go to? You have latent powers, yes? Very strong ones, too, if I am any judge of these things. They have lain unused because there was no aether to make use of. And now there is. In you."

My God. He was saying I was a walking vault, full of the raw material of magic. And that my "powers", whatever they were, were now within reach. I sucked in a shaky breath. From latency to what? Magician? Mage? Someone who could turn a bear back into a man?

"Is it any wonder your warder friends were so quick to get that collar on you, before you discovered what you could do?"

"That's not true. Dad was trying to help us. To get rid of your stupid curse." And now these Sidhe bastards had punished him for it. I clung to the truth. It *was* the truth, wasn't it?

"Of course he was." He smiled agreeably. "And if it also suited his other purposes, why, who can blame him?"

"I don't believe you. I can't do magic."

"Ah. But have you tried?"

Well, of course I hadn't. The thought had never even occurred to me. Why would it? He watched me, patient as a cat stalking a bird.

"I don't know how to," I said at last, drawn into the conversation despite my best intentions. *Go back to bed*, my conscience insisted, *you know the Sidhe are liars*. But conscience stood no chance against the onslaught of curiosity. How could anyone be expected to walk away from a conversation like this? He was making so much sense. And the possibility that he was right, that I might be able to work magic and save Dad, took my breath away. I would do anything to have my father back.

"It's like everything," he said. "It takes practice, but once you have the way of it, it feels as natural as breathing. Do you have something small? A hair clip? A coin?"

My hair sprang free in wild curls around my head. It should be obvious even to a man that there was nothing restraining it. I felt in my pocket for a coin and my fingers brushed something. I pulled it out: the little origami bird Miss Moore had given me at the market, red and gold and intricately folded. Funny, I'd forgotten all about that.

"That will do very well," he said. "I cannot demonstrate, since the aether lies within you. Only you can access it. You must imagine this bird changing colour, becoming a green bird perhaps, or pink. Something quite different from its reality. See it in every perfect detail. Some think magic is a matter of willpower, but they are wrong. Magic comes from the heart. You must pour your heart into this little bird, and if your heart is true, the bird will follow your heart's desire."

Right. Pour my heart into an origami bird.

He smiled a little at the look on my face. "Don't be discouraged if nothing happens on the first try, or even the hundredth. Your power is like a muscle that must be exercised to make it strong."

Okaay.

What are you doing, you idiot? Don't listen to him! But I had to. How else was I going to help Dad? I stared at the bird, feeling like an idiot. How did you communicate your heart's desire to a piece of folded paper? Part of me suspected he was pulling my leg, and any minute now would burst out laughing at the poor foolish human who thought she could do magic. But the other part … Magic. He was saying I could do *magic*.

By now I had a good handful of diamonds, so I shoved them into my pocket and took a deep breath. *Concentrate.*

I frowned at the bird, focusing on it until I felt myself going cross-eyed. *Come on, bird. Be green.*

Nothing happened. The paper stayed resolutely red.

"Not like that," Puck said. "Not with the will. With the heart."

I eyed him suspiciously, but he still kept a straight face. I sighed. The beginnings of a headache gnawed at my temples. With the heart, then.

Please, little bird. I would love *you to be green.* I longed for green, the fresh green of maidenhair fern uncurling, the deep emerald glow of the beautiful dress I'd worn to the formal. The look in Zac's eyes when he saw me in it. I ached for a drop of green, no more, just a drop, to prove that there was something special in me, that I wasn't just a distant second to CJ's glittering first all the time. Something that would bring that look to Zac's face again. Something that could free Dad from his curse.

The smell of burnt toffee filled the room. Inside me, something … shifted. With a rustle of paper, the origami bird lifted from my hand.

Chapter Twenty-Four

The bird blazed with a sudden blinding light, and I fell back against the wall, hands raised to shield my eyes. A gust of air buffeted me, the sound of wings loud in the silence. Squinting against the glare I saw Puck stand, and something moved at his feet.

Then the light faded, and I saw a black bird, bigger than a crow, pecking at the manacle around his ankle. A raven? Sparks flew out of the lock and the manacle slipped to the floor with a metallic clunk. *Oh, shit.*

I lunged for the door, but the bird flew at my face, driving me back. The damn thing pecked me in the head. I screamed and lashed out with my fists. I felt feathers and claws, and then a lucky blow connected squarely with its body and I knocked it aside.

I leapt up, arms raised to protect my head, but the bird darted from the room. Puck was gone. I staggered out into the main room in time to see the double doors swing shut.

"Hey!"

I sprinted after him, flinging the doors wide, and nearly tripped over the body of the guard sprawled across the floor. The doors crashed back against the wall, and Puck looked back as the noise echoed off the walls and grinned at me. The bird flew ahead of him. I stopped to check the guard's pulse; it was strong, but he was out cold. Puck must have done something to him. Hopefully we didn't have another Snow White on our hands.

Puck took the fire stairs and I leapt up. The guard wasn't going anywhere, which left it up to me to stop him, though God knows what I could do if I managed to catch up. But I had to try. He was so fast. He burst out of the stairwell on the ground floor as I took the steps two at a time. I chased him down the corridor to the foyer. Where to now? The automatic doors that led out on to the street were locked for the night.

I saw him there, silhouetted against the sliding glass doors by the light coming in from outside. Trapped. I slowed down, now, finally realising the futility of the chase. What could I do? Ask him nicely to come back to his cell? I was very conscious of the dark, and how alone I was in the still corridors. Everyone else in the building was asleep.

"Well, I enjoyed our little chat." Something was wrong with his silhouette. He was shrinking, changing shape. "Thank you so much for your assistance."

Behind him the doors whispered open and somewhere behind me an alarm began to shrill. He turned and bounded into the street, a strange, stunted figure now. The raven cawed harshly and winged after him. I ran to the door, but already he was at the corner, moving with superhuman speed. Chasing him was pointless.

My heart was pounding. The running, the fear. I put my hand to my head and felt blood where the raven had pecked me. I backed away from the doors and they slid shut. The clanging alarm was making it hard to think, but I couldn't just stand here. People would be coming. Dena and Bryan were sharing the guest quarters with us, and Dorian would be in his rooms.

I couldn't let them find me here.

My whole body started to tremble with reaction. I'd just turned a piece of folded paper into a raven. And that raven had somehow used magic to pick the lock that was holding Puck prisoner. What would they do, those warders, if they found out I was capable of doing that? What would they think if they knew I'd aided Puck, even unintentionally, in his escape? Would they even believe that it *was* unintentional? After all, I'd been creeping around down there at two o'clock in the morning, sneaking past the guard, who was now conveniently unconscious. It was going to look pretty suspicious.

And it wasn't as if hiding my part in it was going to hurt anyone. The fact was, he'd escaped. *How* didn't really matter.

I felt a sudden great longing for Mum. She'd believe me. She'd know what to do now. But she was on the other side of the world, and I had to handle this on my own.

I had to hide somewhere. Probably the first thing they'd do would be to check the prisoner. When they'd gone down there I could sneak past and pretend I'd been in my bed the whole time. Except …

Oh, hell. The diamonds.

My pocket was full of them, but I knew I'd screamed when the bird attacked me. Had I said anything? I couldn't remember;

it was a blur of panic. But even a scream would have produced a diamond, and if there was a big fat jewel sitting in the middle of the empty cell, I might as well just hand myself over now.

I ran back to the fire stairs and headed down to the basement again. My legs felt weak and wobbly, as if they couldn't support my weight. My bare feet slapped against the concrete steps. Time was not my friend.

No one else was in the stairwell yet. How long would it take them to wake up, realise what the alarm meant, and head down here? I hurdled the guard's body and skidded across the main room. My eyes were well-adjusted to the dark now.

The lamp still burned in Puck's cell. A single black feather rested in the middle of the floor, right next to a fat diamond. I scooped them both up and put them in my pocket. Then I got down on my hands and knees and checked under the bed, to see if I'd kicked any under there in my tussle with the bird. There was nothing, but when I turned to leave I spotted another one behind the door.

I swooped on it and headed out, but halfway across the big room I heard the hollow bang as someone slammed the door to the stairs. Oh, no. The room was cluttered; I dived behind a desk and crouched there, trying to control my breathing.

I heard running feet in the corridor, then a muttered exclamation as they found the guard. My mouth was so dry I couldn't swallow. Someone came in; I saw feet go past my hiding spot. One of the men.

"Oh, my Lord." Bryan's voice. Then he ran out into the corridor, shouting for Dena.

She obviously wasn't on this floor; the door to the stairs thudded closed again.

I scrambled out from behind the desk. I didn't want to be here when they came back. They might have a better look around.

I ran down the corridor, heart pounding, expecting that damn door to open again any minute and the warders to pop out and catch me here red-handed. But it stayed closed, thank God, and I ran past it, trying office doors as I went.

I found one that was unlocked and let myself in, locking it behind me. I fumbled my collar back on, my hands shaking so much it took three tries to get the clasp done up. What should I do? I couldn't use the stairs, and I daren't try the lift, but I had to get back up to my bedroom. What if Dorian was up there now, checking to see CJ and I were all right? I shuddered.

There was no other way up.

While I hesitated the stairwell door banged open again. This time two sets of feet pounded down the corridor towards the vault. I eased my door open and risked a peek out. Bryan and Dena disappeared around the corner.

I chewed my lip for a moment, but there was really no other choice. I had to risk it. I took a deep breath and bolted for the stairs on shaky legs.

I made it into the stairwell. Concrete steps had never looked so good. I grabbed the door and eased it closed behind me. As I did, I heard Bryan's voice in the corridor again.

Another second and I would have been caught.

The stairs were quiet. No one here but me—for now. I took them two at a time, thankful for my bare feet. I made no noise as I sprinted upward. When I was almost at the top I heard the basement door open and Bryan begin to climb.

As slowly as I dared, I turned the handle of the door to level 1, trying not to make any noise as I opened it. There was no time to check what was on the other side. I stepped through, hoping I wouldn't come face to face with Dorian.

No one was there. I pulled the door shut, again trying to make no noise as I turned the handle, but the lock made a faint click as I closed it. It couldn't be helped. I was out of time.

I was outside Kerrie's room when the door to the stairwell banged open, so I turned and grabbed her door handle. Bryan checked at the sight of me.

"I was just going to see if Kerrie was okay," I said. "Why is the alarm going off? Is there a fire?"

"No. No fire." His face was set in grim lines as he came over and opened the door himself. We both looked in. Nothing had changed. Kerrie still lay sleeping the sleep of the dead. "Our prisoner has escaped and the seeker on duty is hurt. Dena's with him now, and I'm checking everyone's okay up here. The Sidhe will be long gone by now. We won't find him."

Sergei had slept through the excitement. We could hear his snores from the corridor, but Bryan still opened his door and had a look.

"Where's Dorian?" I was surprised he hadn't showed up yet.

"He went home for the night to see his wife. He's not usually here on the weekends, just lately, with everything that's been going on ... Rebecca was starting to miss him."

Wow. I hadn't even known he had a wife. And she actually missed him! Just goes to show there really is someone for everyone. He didn't seem like a family man. I'd just assumed he lived here permanently.

Back in the guest quarters, CJ was standing uncertainly in the middle of the lounge area.

"What's going on?"

She was looking at me, but Bryan answered. "Puck's escaped. You girls stay here, I'll go give Dena a hand."

He left.

"Where have you *been*?" she burst out as soon as the door closed behind him. "I woke up when the alarm started ringing, and you weren't in your bed. What have you done?"

I loved how she automatically assumed it was my fault. But she hadn't given me away to Bryan. Twins first, always. My legs gave way at last and I sank down on the nearest couch.

"I went to see Puck …"

"What the hell for? Are you mad?"

"I thought maybe I could find out something to help us. To help Dad."

She rolled her eyes, but flopped down next to me.

"And then he …" How did I tell her the next bit? *And then he taught me to do magic and I created a bird that freed him? Oops, pity about that, but hey, magic powers are really cool. Shame you don't have any.* Oh, hell no. "And then he tricked me … into taking my collar off and sort of … used the aether in my curse to help him escape." Which was kind of true.

She slumped back against the couch. "Oh, shit. Did anyone see you?"

"No. But now I feel really bad." *You have no idea how bad.* "He's out there again and it's all my fault."

And then the stress of it all caught up with me and I burst into tears.

CJ put her arms around me. "You idiot."

I turned and sobbed into her shoulder.

"You couldn't leave it alone, could you? You just had to go shoving your nose into it. You know what Mum would say, don't you?"

I nodded and mumbled into her shoulder: "Curiosity killed the cat."

"That's right."

She hugged me tight as I cried, and I felt her drop a kiss on my hair.

"Don't you get my shirt wet," she said.

We all sat around the big table in the kitchen, and a gloomier bunch of faces you've never seen. Bryan had his phone on loudspeaker in the centre of the table, and he and Dena were talking to Dorian, who was on his way in though it was only five o'clock in the morning. His wife wasn't going to be happy.

CJ and I were eating breakfast. I was too churned up to have any real appetite, but I didn't want to draw attention to myself, so I chewed dutifully on my cereal and listened to the conversation.

"What about aether?" Dorian was saying. "Did you check the levels in the vault?"

"Of course," said Dena. "It hasn't moved. Capacity's unchanged since he's been in there."

"And the artefacts," said Bryan. "Not a one missing. Every last damn whistle and hair comb accounted for."

"I don't understand where he got the power from then."

Frustration was clear in his voice, as it was on the faces of the two warders at the table with us. Dena hunched over a cup of coffee; its delicious scent filled the room, but did nothing to shift the worried frown from her face. Bryan's fingers tapped an endless rhythm on the table top as he thought.

Both of them had already said what Dorian was saying now. The conversation was going round in circles. No one had any idea how the prisoner could have escaped.

No one except me, of course.

"Maybe he always had it," Bryan said at last.

"Then why wait? What did he gain from staying in captivity all this time if he could have walked free whenever he wanted to?"

The gloom deepened as all three contemplated this. None of the answers to that question were likely to be comforting.

I almost wished I could reassure them that they were barking up the wrong tree. Almost. My free hand toyed with my collar. When I realised what I was doing I pulled it away.

Is it any wonder your warder friends were so quick to get that collar on you, before you discovered what you could do?

I couldn't tell them anything. Not until I was sure what the reaction would be. And what had Puck meant about "defectives"? Surely nothing happened to them. Simon's twin was fine—happily married and working as a solicitor, according to Gretel. I looked across at CJ's tousled head, bent over her bowl. Mum and Dad wouldn't let anything bad happen to her. But why didn't they tell us about magic?

"I'll be there in ten," Dorian said, his voice fading in and out. Must be going through a tunnel. "Get as many of the seekers in as you can. If they do a sweep with Hendrix counters before the trail gets muddied by too many civilians we might be able to pick him up."

That seemed unlikely to me, but hey, I knew that urge to be doing something, anything, whatever the chances of success, just to feel you were trying.

"If you like," I said to Bryan, "I can sit with Kerrie while you guys are busy."

He smiled, his first of the morning. "Thank you. I'd appreciate it. I'll send someone in to relieve you when more of the staff arrive."

His gratitude made me feel guilty. Well, guilti*er*. I was already feeling bad enough over Puck. At least the guard had woken up and seemed to be fine, if a little confused about what had happened. Really I just wanted an excuse to stay out of Dorian's way.

Kerrie's room was dark. I opened the blind and settled in the armchair, watching the light gradually seep into the room as the sun rose. It was a disused office, with the empty desk pushed aside to make room for the hospital-style bed she lay in. She still had a band-aid on the back of one hand where she'd had an IV drip when she was in hospital. They hadn't realised then that nothing was necessary to keep her alive except the magic that filled her.

Her temperature never varied, she was neither hot nor cold. She didn't need food or water. No one had to bathe her or empty bedpans. She just was. Not even her eyelids flickered, as people's sometimes did when they dreamed. She was perfectly still, like a wax effigy of a woman. When Bryan realised she had no need of a hospital's care he'd had her transferred, over the strenuous objections of the doctors, to this room, where at least Emmet and Dena might be able to help her.

If she did dream, I wondered what she would dream about. I curled my legs under me and rested my head against the back of the chair. The night had exhausted me. I could go to sleep right now and dream of my perfect man. He was probably still asleep at this hour, dark hair flopped across his face, long eyelashes resting on tanned cheeks. Now there was someone I'd like to kiss awake. What had he been up to for the last two weeks? I would get to ask him tomorrow. I couldn't decide if I was more scared or excited at the thought.

Tomorrow this nightmare of a holiday would come to an end and we would go back to school. And the next night Mum and Dad would be home. Well, not home, precisely. Obviously Dad wasn't really going to Taronga Zoo, but he couldn't come home either. Imagine the neighbours if a polar bear moved in next door. He'd probably end up here, down the hall from Sergei. The thought made me miserable. My Dad, locked up like another freak in sideshow alley. But maybe—just maybe—I might be able to help him.

"Wake up, sleepy head."

I jumped at a gentle hand on my shoulder. The room was flooded with bright daylight, and I had a crick in my neck from leaning back against the chair. I must have fallen asleep. Simon grinned down at me. I looked at him suspiciously. What, had I been dribbling or something? I rubbed my hands over my face just to be sure.

"What time is it?" I asked. "Aren't you supposed to be out checking the streets for traces of aether?"

"Done that. It's ten o'clock. How long have you been in here?"

"Since about six. Did you find anything?"

"No. There's too many people about now. The aether's dispersed, and there's nothing big showing on the monitors."

Maybe he'd used up all his stolen aether busting out of his chains, but how was he hiding his own? He'd certainly showed up all right on the monitors the day he'd been caught.

"So he got away?"

"Yes."

He perched on the end of Kerrie's bed and rested his hand briefly on her foot, in an oddly tender gesture.

"You can head off now, if you like. I'll sit with her for a couple of hours."

I stood up and stretched, rolling my head from side to side, trying to work out the kinks. He took no notice of me; his eyes were on the girl in the bed.

"You like her, don't you?"

That got his attention. He gave me the usual grumpy frown. I expected a swift "none of your business". Instead, he shrugged and looked away.

Well, that was encouraging. What would CJ do if she were here? I may as well go all the way. What was he going to do? Act all grumpy with me?

"Why don't you just kiss her?" Maybe I could do some good to make up for last night's efforts.

"What?" He threw me a startled look.

"Kiss her." *You know you want to.* "Why not? If you like her, maybe you're the one to break the spell."

He shook his head. "She doesn't love me."

"So? Snow White didn't know her prince from a bar of soap. First thing she knew, she's waking up in his arms. *Her* love didn't have anything to do with it."

Only his.

The words hung between us, as real as if I'd spoken them aloud.

He looked back at her, his face alive with longing. *Magic comes from the heart. Throw your heart at it.* And what was love but the greatest magic of all?

His Adam's apple moved as he swallowed. He looked at me, clearly torn.

"That could be an awkward conversation," he said.

"Awkward shmawkward. It's just a kiss." I felt Zac's lips on mine again, saw the hope and longing in his eyes. Was any kiss ever just a kiss? So much meaning in one little action. "Just kiss her. No one needs to find out. I won't tell anyone—cross my heart and hope to die. If nothing happens, what have you lost? But if it works ..."

If it worked he'd just saved the woman he loved from a living death.

He got off the bed and moved toward her, but still he hesitated.

"Would you like me to leave?" Maybe he'd rather not have an audience for this.

"No, stay. It's just a kiss."

He didn't sound like he believed that any more than I did. He leaned forward and gave her a quick peck on the cheek. Nothing happened.

"You've got to *mean* it, Simon."

He glared at me, his tanned face flushed crimson. Then he turned back and lowered his lips to hers with exquisite tenderness. They lingered there for a long moment, his hand cupping her face, then he straightened and gazed down at her.

"Nothing." His voice was tinged with bitterness.

"No, wait!" I sprang forward. "Her chest moved! She's breathing."

Side by side, we stared down at her. The movement of the sheet covering her was so small we wouldn't have noticed it if we hadn't been watching so intently.

"See!"

It was true. Simon drew in a shaky breath, and Kerrie's eyelids fluttered.

"Oh, my God," he breathed.

Her eyes opened. They were a beautiful blue, deep as the summer sea. She blinked a couple of times, then a tiny frown creased her brow. One hand fought free of the blankets and she turned her head on the pillow.

"W-water?" she croaked.

Simon leapt back. "I'll go!"

I could hear him shouting for Bryan in the corridor. A moment later they were both back, with Dena and Dorian crowding into the small room behind them.

"Kerrie! Thank God!" Bryan came forward to throw his arms around his sister, his eyes bright with happy tears.

Behind him stood Simon, a glass of water at the ready.

Bryan looked at me and then Simon, joy in his face. "How did this happen?" He helped Kerrie sit up, then took the water from Simon and held it for her while she drank.

Simon didn't come any closer. His face was still unnaturally pink.

He threw me a warning glance. "It just happened."

"That's right." This was one lie I could happily tell. "She just woke up."

Chapter Twenty-Five

Next morning I was up before the sun. Again. No magic disasters this time, just plain old nerves about going back to school and seeing Zac again. What if I'd just built the whole thing up in my head into something bigger than it really was? Maybe it was just a heat-of-the-moment kiss and he didn't actually want to take it further. Maybe he was glad I hadn't called. How the hell could I know when I hadn't talked to him for two whole weeks?

Two weeks had never seemed so long.

But I could talk to him at school, even if I wondered whether everyone I met was a Sidhe in disguise. What was any Sidhe going to do to me in the middle of so many witnesses? Although there'd been plenty of witnesses at Josh Johnson's party, and look what had happened after that …

Sick of tossing from side to side and punching the pillow in a failed effort to get back to sleep, I got up at ten to six and wandered out to the guest lounge. The other bedroom doors were all closed. Kerrie was asleep behind one of them now, a wax effigy no longer. She hadn't wanted to go to bed last night. Last

I'd heard she was telling Bryan she'd slept long enough. I thought she was scared to go back to sleep in case she couldn't wake up again. I reckoned I would have been, too, if I'd just lost three weeks of my life.

I stretched out on the couch and turned the TV on with the volume way down. I didn't want to watch it; I just wanted the company of the flickering colours on the screen. Apart from the whole Zac thing, I had a lot to think about.

My collar was on the coffee table; I hadn't put it on yet this morning. I told myself that was because it was uncomfortable, but I was a terrible liar. Even *I* didn't believe me. Really I was contemplating magic: specifically, whether I could do it again. And I knew I couldn't work magic with the collar on.

The sensible thing, of course, would be not to try. After all, it hadn't turned out so well last time. I'd been trying to change the colour of a piece of paper and ended up with a real live bird. God knows what could happen if I tried again.

But if I didn't try, I had no hope of ever helping Dad. It seemed a big step, from turning a paper bird into a real one, to turning a bear back into a human, but what other options did we have? CJ and I hadn't been the only ones working on the problem, and no one was even close to a solution. Sensible wasn't cutting it; someone had to be daring.

I sighed, and caught the resulting diamond without even thinking about it. It sure was easier with diamonds instead of frogs. I placed it on the coffee table and considered it. Maybe I could change its colour? How about a blue diamond instead?

I took a deep breath and tried to clear my mind. *Not the will. Throw your heart at it.*

Long moments passed. I heard Kerrie murmur in her sleep. Nothing.

Maybe I didn't want it enough. I waited for that feeling of something shifting inside me that I'd experienced when the bird came to life. Nothing happened. It had seemed so easy last time.

Or maybe it was because the diamond itself was a magical construct, and the two magic forces were kind of cancelling each other out. Something else might be better. Dammit, I didn't *know* anything.

My eye fell on the vase of flowers on the coffee table. I picked a white rose at random and pictured it turning red. *Wanted* it to turn red, as hard as I could.

"What are you doing out here?" CJ came out of the bedroom, yawning, collar already in place though she still wore her pyjamas. She settled on the lounge opposite, then noticed my collar on the table between us and frowned.

"Why aren't you wearing your collar?" Her voice was much sharper, almost accusing. "I thought you would have been more careful after what happened last time you took it off."

I clipped it round my neck. Was the white rose showing a tiny blush of colour? "Who was I going to talk to, the TV? There—happy now?"

"No, not really. After all the times you yelled at me about not wearing it when *I* had the diamonds, and now you're just as bad. Hypocrite much, Vi?"

"Why are you so grumpy this morning?"

"I'm not grumpy. Just stating a fact. And why are you staring at those flowers like you're trying to drill holes in them with your laser vision?"

I jumped, and tried to pretend I hadn't. "I'm not."

CJ gave me a shrewd look. She knew me too well. "You're up to something, aren't you?"

I kept my gaze on her face and made sure not to look anywhere near the damn flowers. It was torture—like when someone tells you not to think of an elephant and suddenly you can't get elephants out of your mind.

"Of course not. What can I get up to lying on the lounge? I just couldn't sleep, so I came out here. I was being *nice*. I didn't want to disturb you. Obviously it didn't work."

She shrugged. "I couldn't sleep either. I was just lying there, imagining everyone at school staring at me, all whispering behind my back. The worst thing is when you walk into a room and everyone stops talking, and you know they were just talking about you."

"It won't be that bad."

She looked at me. I really was a terrible liar.

"Okay, it might be bad, but you've just got to get it over with. By the end of the week they'll have forgotten and they'll all be talking about something else."

"Maybe. Just wait till they realise it's our dad who's turned into a polar bear. We'll never hear the end of it. This whole thing is such a mess."

"You can say that again. And everyone here's running around suspecting each other of helping the Sidhe. It's a wonder they can get anything done at all."

"Do you think there really is a traitor?"

"Gotta be. After all these years, the Sidhe wouldn't suddenly come up with a way to escape. They must have had outside help."

"But who would do that? Who do you think it is?"

I shrugged. "Search me. I mean, we don't know many people in the organisation, do we? Could be anyone."

"Dorian said it must be one of the seekers. That they're the only ones with enough latency." She said "latency" as if it left a bad taste in her mouth.

"Them and the warders," I said, "though obviously it's not one of them. But how do they know you'd need latency to do it, when they don't know what's been done?"

She pulled her knees up to her chin and hugged them. "Maybe they do know, and they're just not telling us."

Hmmm. That seemed quite likely, actually. They guarded information as if it was more precious than gold around here. Telling us something we didn't *need* to know would probably kill them.

"Just as well it's not our problem. All we have to deal with today is going back to school."

She sighed. "I wish we didn't have to go back."

I tried to think of something to cheer her up. "At least Josh won't be there."

He'd be starting his HSC exams soon. I hope he failed miserably, like the loser he was.

"Yeah. At least Josh won't be there." She didn't sound any happier. "I really thought he liked me. I feel like such an idiot, as if everyone will be laughing at me. And now you're going to say *I told you so*, aren't you? That it was the diamonds he was after all along."

"Wouldn't dream of it," I said.

"Was it so stupid to think he might like me for myself? I'm a nice person, aren't I?"

"My favourite sister. You're pretty hot, too. Not my type, but pretty hot all the same."

"Thanks, Vile."

"Welcome."

And then she caught me looking at the flowers again. She sat bolt upright.

"You *are* up to something. What are you doing? It's something magic, isn't it?" The accusing tone was back in her voice.

"Don't be stupid," I said.

"You're such a bad liar. Fine. Be like that. I don't suppose Miss All-Powerful Latency would want to share anything with her useless sister. Go and tell your new best friend Simon. He thinks you're so amazing."

She flounced back to our room and slammed the door.

Ouch. I wished Simon hadn't been quite so awestruck when I'd smelled the aether at Observatory Hill. CJ hadn't said anything at the time, but she'd obviously been stewing on it ever since. I knew, the minute I laid eyes on that file, that this would be a problem. CJ *never* settled for second-best.

And if she knew I could actually do magic …

I peered at the white rose. There was the faintest blush of pink at the very edge of the petals—so faint that I couldn't be sure it hadn't been there all along. So much for my supposed powers. Maybe CJ had nothing to be jealous of after all.

Simon actually sang along to the radio as he drove us to school. The difference was astonishing, like aliens had kidnapped Mr

Grumpy and left this smiling stranger in his place. But maybe this was the real Simon. We'd only known him since Kerrie was cursed, after all.

I wanted to ask if he'd spoken to Kerrie since he kissed her awake, but I knew that would go down like a lead balloon, so I kept my mouth shut and only winced occasionally as he hit a particularly bad note. He got full marks for enthusiasm, but holding a tune was not his forte.

At least someone in the car was happy. Kyle was his usual quiet self, but CJ stared stonily out the window, still mad with me. I was glad now I hadn't told her that Simon was the one who woke Kerrie. She would have dropped a hint that she knew by now, and there'd be two people here who hated me.

Or maybe three. I wasn't very happy with me either. Puck's escape still weighed heavily on my mind. The only bright spot on the horizon was the prospect of seeing Zac today.

And Sona, of course. Mustn't be one of those girls who forgot all about their friends the minute they hooked up with some guy. Although I'd hardly thought of Sona all holiday—just another thing to feel guilty about.

She didn't leave me in doubt long as to her feelings on our separation. I was barely through the door of the senior study before she pounced.

"Where have you *been*? I've been so worried!"

"Mum and Dad went away, so we had to go stay with someone else."

"I sent you a million texts, and you never answered one of them. I thought you were dead for sure—or turned into a toad or something equally horrific."

"Sorry. I didn't have my phone." Still didn't, in fact. Hopefully when Mum got home tomorrow Dorian would finally hand it back.

She blinked. "You didn't have your *phone*? How did you live?"

"Shut up. It wasn't that bad."

"But you've got it now, right?" She seemed fixated on the phone thing. As if being phoneless was the worst thing that could happen to anyone. She should try being in my shoes for a while.

"No, actually. It was kind of confiscated."

"Really? What did you do?"

Only then did it occur to me that this might not be the real Sona. Sure, she acted like it, but how could I tell? The senior study was packed—and any of these people could be a Sidhe wearing a false face. Could even be Puck. We'd never found out what happened to him.

I could hardly tell her my phone had been taken to protect me from magical doppelgangers when for all I knew she was one. I sighed. Damn, life got complicated.

"It's a long story. How was your holiday?"

Sona's grandparents were visiting from India, so there were many funny stories to tell. At least, the real Sona's grandparents were visiting. Was the real Sona standing here laughing about her grandfather's dreadful English or was this a Sidhe pretender?

God, I could go crazy thinking like this. I couldn't go on suspecting everyone.

Zac walked in, Ashleigh trailing behind him. Out of the corner of my eye I saw CJ tense, but I had no emotion to waste on her problems with Zac here. My heart leapt at the sight of him. He nodded to me and put his bag down on the other side of the room.

I swallowed. A feeling of dread squeezed my throat. He stayed chatting to Ashleigh. A nod? That was all the acknowledgement I got?

Oh, hell. He was mad that I hadn't contacted him all holidays. I knew it. I marched over to him, though my heart was stuttering with nerves, determined to put this straight right away.

"Hi, Zac."

"Hi." No dimple. Not even the hint of a smile.

"Did you—" I cleared my throat. Ashleigh stared at me as if I was some bug she'd like to squash. "Did you have a good holiday?"

No. This was all wrong. I didn't want to make meaningless small talk about the holidays. *Why are you being so cold?*

"It was okay." He shrugged. "I tried calling you, but …"

"I was tied up. With … the frog thing. You know."

How could I explain anything without explaining it all? I glared at Ashleigh. Why wouldn't she just get lost? This was hard enough without her standing there smirking and listening to every word.

"Right. Yeah."

He was really pissed. I'd never seen him like this, as if he just didn't care.

Or maybe this wasn't really him. Tears pricked my eyes as I heard Dorian's warning again in my head: *Everyone you saw— virtually anyone you know—could potentially be a Sidhe.* Why did everything have to be so bloody *complicated?*

"I just … my phone wasn't working."

Ashleigh folded her arms, as if she was just waiting for me to take myself off so she could resume her much more interesting conversation with Zac without interruption.

"Uh-huh."

He turned as if to go.

"I really wanted to call you!" I said desperately.

Ashleigh snorted. I could feel myself blushing furiously. Right now I was convinced Ashleigh was the damn Sidhe, and if I'd had a piece of iron handy I would have decked her with it.

He looked away, as if the conversation bored him. "Look, Violet, it's no big deal. You don't have to make excuses."

He'd called me Violet. He never called me Violet. And then he really did walk away, leaving me standing there with every eye in the room on me. I'd never felt so exposed, not even with my face all over the internet. I was hurting for him, and hurting for me. Not being able to explain, to make it right, was breaking my heart.

The bell rang for the first class. I got my bag and trudged out of the room with everyone else, unshed tears burning in my eyes.

Simon took one look at my face and lost his new smile. "What's wrong?"

"Nothing." *Everything.* My turn to be the grumpy one now.

CJ came up behind me and grabbed my arm. "Someone needs to hit that boy with the clue stick," she said tartly. "It's not as if there's nothing weird going on in your life right now. You'd think he might realise it's not all about him."

Coming from CJ, that was pretty funny. But it was nice to have her standing up for me. When it really mattered, no one cared for you as much as family. Twins first.

I gave her a wobbly smile. "Boys suck."

"Amen, sister."

Chapter Twenty-Six

I was glad, the next day, that CJ's Visual Arts class was coming with us on the excursion to the Art Gallery. She got on the bus and gave Zac a glare that would have stripped the skin off him if he'd been looking. Even though I was sitting next to Sona and she sat with a girl from her class, it was good to know she had my back. And tonight Mum and Dad would be home. I'd decided to tell Mum everything. Maybe she'd be able to help me bring my magic out again—she was a warder, after all. And she'd want to help Dad as much as I did.

Miss Moore and CJ's teacher, Miss Tan, got on the bus and did a headcount.

"Everyone got a clipboard and pen?" Miss Tan asked.

There were groans along the bus. "Can't we just go on an excursion without taking notes for once, miss?"

"And where would be the educational value in that?" she asked, passing worksheets to all her art students.

Miss Moore had a different set for the Ancient History class, of course. She strode down the aisle of the bus like a glamazon on the catwalk, handing them out. She was in a black pants suit today, her bright red stilettos the only pop of colour. I don't think I'd ever seen her in any colour other than red or black. I guess it made getting dressed for work easier.

Sona chattered all the way into town, only requiring the occasional contribution from me. Zac wasn't sitting anywhere near us, so she didn't realise there was anything wrong. I stared miserably at the back of his dark head. He hadn't caught the usual bus to school this morning either, as if he was trying to avoid me.

The bus dropped us at the base of the Gallery's wide steps. With those steps and the outsized Corinthian columns, the Gallery looked rather Hellenic itself, like an ancient Greek temple, although with massive sculptures of eighteenth century horsemen out the front rather spoiling the effect.

We trudged up the steps behind a crowd of excited primary schoolers squawking like a flock of parrots. They looked like Year 6; some of the boys had already started their growth spurts. Inside, a massive banner welcomed us to the Treasures of the Hellenic World exhibition, "direct from the Louvre", and Miss Moore led us down the stairs to the basement level where special exhibits were housed.

It was much darker down there than in the high-ceilinged open spaces of the entry level. My eyes took a moment to adjust to the dimness after the sunshine outside.

"Why's it so dark?" one of the primary kids complained as we entered the first room. "I can't even read the signs."

"These treasures are very old," his teacher replied. "Some of them were created seven centuries before Christ. They need to be protected, and bright light is bad for them."

"My mum says sunshine fades the curtains in my bedroom," one little girl piped up.

"That's right," the teacher said. "Too much light can damage things."

The exhibition space was divided into several smaller rooms, with each room featuring a particular ancient Greek culture. This first room was Mycenaean, and three beautiful bronze horses about thirty centimetres high had pride of place in a glass case in the centre of the room. The little kids milled around it for a moment before their teacher split them into smaller groups, each accompanied by a mum. Two little Asian boys got into a shoving contest with a kid whose hair was nearly the same colour as mine. The teacher made sure they were in different groups, then sent everyone off to separate rooms. The noise level dropped abruptly as they departed.

"All right, VA students," Miss Tan said, "I want you to move around the exhibit and find at least five pieces that speak to you, preferably not all from the same culture. Think about how form and function are combined in your chosen pieces, and what kind of decoration the artist uses. I believe there are some fine examples of Attic blackwork here. I want at least five sketches—" A few students groaned. "You don't have to sketch the whole thing. I would rather you capture ten artistic details—the curve of a handle, the scrollwork on a pot—than spend all your time rendering the picture on one vase. Got that?"

They agreed they had, with more or less enthusiasm, and headed off. I don't know what they were complaining about. I'd rather be drawing pots than filling in endless dates and details on worksheets, and I wasn't even an artist.

Miss Moore was much briefer. "You have two hours, people. Get cracking."

Sona and I headed straight for the Athenian room, which proved to be the biggest, and got to work. It turned out we did have some drawing to do, but only small things that related to our topic of everyday life in the ancient world. I managed a few lopsided amphorae that showed hoplites marching in a phalanx as I answered the questions about the duties of citizenship.

"Are they meant to be pregnant?" Sona asked doubtfully, peering at my work in the dimness of the room.

"They're soldiers, idiot."

"Then why do they have such big bellies?"

"That's their shields!"

She was working on the page about the Greek gods, and had drawn a stick figure with a bird, which I assumed was meant to be the bowl in the case in front of her that featured the god Apollo with a raven. More damn ravens.

"You're no Michelangelo yourself, you know," I pointed out.

"Yeah, well, there's a reason I didn't take Visual Arts as an elective."

Apart from the chatter of the primary school kids, the exhibition was pretty quiet, and even they were trying hard to keep their voices down, encouraged by constant shushing from their supervisors. The dim lighting fostered a quiet, contemplative mood in the rooms. It was hard to believe the great age of these things, that they represented the lives and works of people who'd lived so many centuries ago.

There were a few other adult visitors, but at this time of the morning on a Tuesday, the two school groups had the place pretty much to themselves. We spent half an hour in the Athens room then moved on to Sparta, which was a little smaller. Not surprisingly, there was a far greater emphasis on warfare in this room.

Zac was also here, and I nearly turned and chose another room instead. *Don't be stupid. He's in half your classes; you can't start avoiding him.* Besides, I didn't want to avoid him. Quite the opposite, in fact. The memory of our kiss was still vivid, and there was a Zac-shaped ache in my heart.

If the warders ever got their act together, and I could finally trust that people were who they appeared to be, I could explain it all to Zac. Everything would be different then. I stole glances at his bent head as I worked on my own worksheets. When he was looking down like that his eyelashes were super long and thick against his tanned cheeks.

Sona started chatting to Zac so I moved off to inspect a case full of pottery showing battle scenes. She hadn't realised yet there was anything wrong between us, but it wouldn't take her long if he refused to talk to me. Thank goodness she didn't know about the kiss. She'd seen our little confrontation in the senior study yesterday morning, but she hadn't put two and two together yet. Her family's visit from India seemed to be distracting her.

As I moved down the case, reading the descriptions of each vase and plate on display, a distinct smell hit me.

Uh-oh. This wasn't good. I looked around for Simon. He was standing against the wall looking just like a museum guard, a bored expression on his face. I caught his eye and beckoned him over.

"Can you smell something?" I whispered.

He sniffed, trying not to be too obvious. "No. Something like—?"

"Burnt toffee."

His eyes widened. Well, at least he wasn't bored any more. "Where?"

"In this room. I just noticed it."

Maybe I'd been smelling it for a while, and had just been distracted thinking about other things. I went back to the Athens room to check. CJ was there, busy sketching.

Nope. Nothing.

Back in the Sparta room, the scent seemed even stronger. I was surprised Simon couldn't smell it.

He raised an eyebrow questioningly, and I shook my head. "Just in here."

"Take off your collar," he said.

"What?" Things hadn't gone so well last time, as CJ had put it. I wasn't sure I wanted to do that out in public.

"It's blocking your senses." His voice was urgent. "Take it off and track down the aether."

Reluctantly, I fumbled with the clasp. "Why can't you smell it?"

"Don't know."

How very reassuring.

I removed the collar and the smell of aether overwhelmed me. Seriously? He couldn't smell *this*? It was much stronger than the traces I'd caught at Observatory Hill. What was going on?

Simon put his back against the case and watched the room while I followed my nose. The scent seemed strongest at the far end of the case, right in the darkest corner of the room.

"Here?" He joined me. "Damn, I wish I had a Hendrix counter. I can smell something, but it's very faint. Can you see anything odd?"

I shook my head. Now he expected me to *see* aether as well as smell it? What did he think I was? I put the collar back on so I could talk again.

There was nothing unusual in the room as far as I could tell. Nothing even about this particular corner of it. Half a dozen people wandered around, none of whom were doing anything even remotely suspicious, and a whole bunch of ancient artefacts sat in their cases looking old. There was certainly some ugly pottery in the case in front of me, but ugly was no crime. The Spartans definitely hadn't had the artistic flair of the Athenians. The pot on the end wasn't even decorated. It was just a squat black bowl shaped rather like a chamber pot.

A group of the primary school kids came in, using their best stage whispers, and clustered around the case where Sona and Zac were. The naughty redhead was among them. He waved at me and winked.

Odd kid. Was he seriously trying to pick up a high school chick? I turned back to Simon. I had more important things on my mind.

"What do we do?" I asked.

"I'll call HQ." He had his phone out already. "We have to get a Hendrix counter in here and possibly some dampener. One of the warders needs to take a look. If there's a leak we need to slap a seal on it fast before we have a full breach."

I nodded, not exactly sure what he was talking about, but getting his urgency. Something bad: check. Need back-up: check.

It was hard to think about Ancient History after that, but I turned back to the case while Simon issued instructions into his phone. As usual, there was nothing I could do to help. Given how catastrophic my "helping" had been so far, that was probably a good thing.

Hoplites on an aryballos from Sparta, 500—460 BC, read the description for the plain black pot. Huh. You'd think they'd get the labels right for a big exhibition like this.

"That's weird," I said.

"What?" Simon was instantly on the alert.

"Oh, nothing, they've just got the wrong label on this pot, see? It says there's hoplites on it and it's completely plain."

He gave me an odd look. "You can't see the figures on that?"

"What do you mean?"

"There are men wearing armour and carrying shields, marching all around the sides. The whole thing's covered. What do you see?"

"Nothing. It's a plain black pot."

"Not a decorated jug, with a handle?"

We stared at each other. Oh, this was bad. I took off the collar again, to see if it looked any different, but no.

The boy who'd winked at me had drifted away from his companions. He was behind Zac now.

I blinked. He was nearly as tall as Zac. That couldn't be right.

I looked closer, and my blood froze. He winked again, but now it was Puck's face leering at me.

"Hello, Violet."

"Simon, look out!"

Simon turned as Puck sprang forward. I screamed, and Simon shoved me out of the way.

And then the lights went out.

Every little kid in the place screamed. Some of the big ones too. Emergency lighting flickered on then off again, on and off like some maniacal strobe, as if something fought it. The flashing light showed glimpses of Simon struggling with the Sidhe man, Sona's shocked face, little kids scattering.

Kyle and CJ ran in from the next room, Miss Moore just behind them.

"Help him!" I yelled to Kyle.

He rushed forward, looking like a jerky robot in the flashes of light. And then, nothing. The next flash showed him crumpled on the floor. Miss Moore stood above him, the strangest look on her face.

In fact, she didn't look like Miss Moore at all any more. Her eyes burned red as she raised her arms and cried out in a language I didn't know her voice rolling like thunder around the room. Her black hair lifted in a wind that no one else felt, streaming behind her, whipping and snapping as if it were alive. And then ravens burst from its strands and dived straight at me. Dozens of them. Hundreds of them, their discordant voices rising even above the roaring of the wind.

I screamed and raised my clipboard above my head. Wings buffeted me. They were everywhere, pecking at my face, my shoulders, my arms with their savage, sharp beaks. Zac waded in to help, swinging his own clipboard with deadly accuracy. He smashed one bird clear across the room.

But it didn't seem to matter. They kept coming back. Their harsh cries filled the air and feathers flew. I was streaming blood from a dozen places, including a peck to the forehead that came dangerously close to my eye.

Miss Moore—or whoever she really was—raised both arms and the lights finally went out and stayed out. Blue fire crackled around her, like lightning gone mad. I felt a strange tugging sensation deep inside, and my knees sagged as weakness nearly overcame me. All of a sudden the clipboard felt too heavy to hold up. Behind me, glimpsed between a storm of black wings, the ugly little pot began to glow a deep blood red.

Simon staggered. The birds turned their attention to him, and he had trouble fending them off and Puck too. Puck charged him, and caught him low. Simon hurtled backwards and slammed into the display case.

Glass sprayed the room, and pots that were more than two thousand years old shattered into shards. Puck leapt forward and seized the glowing pot, which was untouched by the destruction. As his hands touched it I felt the strange weakness subside, and stood up straighter.

"I have it, mistress!" he crowed.

"Not for long, buddy."

Like a pro baseballer, Zac batted a bird straight at Puck's face with his trusty clipboard. Puck yelped and instinctively brought his hands up, dropping the pot. Zac dived forward and caught it before it hit the floor, earning himself some nasty gashes from the broken glass scattered everywhere.

He hurled the pot to me.

"Run!"

I darted forward and caught the glowing pot. A buzz like an electrical charge surged through my hands.

Ravens dive-bombed me as I ran. Miss Moore was still blocking the exit, framed in blue light that sizzled ominously.

She raised her hands—

And CJ cannoned into her with a wild yell. They fell to the floor in a spray of blue sparks.

"Run, Vi!"

So I did.

Chapter Twenty-Seven

Outside the exhibition there was a bottleneck as a throng of people all tried to push up the stairs at once.

A security guard saw me and the pot I carried. "Hey! Where are you going with that?"

He tried to push through the crowd toward me but the tide was against him. He made little headway against the rush of panicked people. I turned down another corridor. There must be another way out apart from the main stairs.

A raven darted out of the gift shop at me with a raucous cry. I held up the pot to protect my face and felt the impact of the bird's body, then a sizzle.

What the hell? I lowered the pot. Where was the bird?

The pot's blood-red glow brightened. I blinked. Had the pot *eaten* the raven? Nasty. Or maybe, since the raven was magical, the pot had gobbled up its magical essence. That was a slightly less horrifying way of looking at it. Handy, though, if I met any more ravens in the semi-darkness. Out here, at least the emergency lights were on.

A hand caught me from behind and I shrieked.

"Vi!"

It was Zac.

"Oh, thank God! You scared me." I looked past him hopefully. "Where's CJ? And Sona?"

"Don't know. I ran after you. Who the hell was that guy? And what happened to Miss Moore?"

Damn Puck, always turning up where mischief was involved.

"He's a Sidhe—more like, um … a fairy than a person. He's the one that cursed us with frogs and diamonds."

He took that better than I'd expected. I guess all the fairytale curses lately had kind of primed people to expect the unexpected where magic was concerned.

"And that wasn't Miss Moore. If there even is a real Miss Moore." Looking back, maybe I should have realised. Our Ancient History teacher's convenient broken leg. All those damn crows and ravens I kept seeing, and her so beautiful and warlike. I knew enough Celtic mythology to guess her identity now I'd seen her in action. "That was the Morrigan, the Celtic goddess of war."

Okay, that time his eyes boggled a bit, but I couldn't really blame him.

We found a set of fire stairs and raced up them to ground level. There was a big warning sign in bossy red letters on the door: *This door is alarmed.*

Yeah, you and me both, door.

Zac shoved it open and we burst out into the sunshine as the alarm began to shrill.

He took my hand and hurried me across the grass to the front of the building. Even in the middle of all this I felt a thrill of excitement at the touch of his hand.

"The Celtic goddess of war?" he asked. "Seriously?"

"Scout's honour."

His eyes gleamed with laughter, though the situation really wasn't funny. Far out. My life had plunged to new depths of insanity.

People were spilling down the front steps of the art gallery in a torrent of panic. I saw some of the primary schoolers in the crowd, and a couple of our classmates. But not Sona or CJ. I scanned the crowd for CJ's dark head, a knot of fear in my stomach. She'd thrown herself at the Morrigan so I could escape with the pot, and I had a feeling the Morrigan wasn't going to be too happy about that.

"I don't get it." Zac's face was a picture of confusion. "Where did that guy come from? He just appeared out of nowhere."

"The Sidhe can do that. They can disguise themselves as anyone. I could be one and you wouldn't even know. Or you could be." This was my chance. Surely we wouldn't be standing here having this conversation if he was one of them? He was bigger and stronger than me; he could have taken the pot if he wanted it. "That's why I couldn't contact you over the holidays. When the curses switched at the formal, everyone around us was a suspect. We didn't know who we could trust."

"Oh." He looked down at his feet.

Not quite the reaction I'd been hoping for.

"I guess it was Miss Moore—the Morrigan—all along, but we didn't know that at the time.

"So you ... wanted to ring me?"

"More than anything."

He looked up then, and his smile melted my heart. "And here I was thinking you were blowing me off."

"It's okay. I probably would have thought the same."

"I'll make it up to you." His voice was husky. "Scout's honour."

My hormones stood to attention, but now was not the time, with a magical pot glowing fiery red in my arms.

"We need to get this thing somewhere safe."

He glared at it as I led him away from the Art Gallery. "What the hell do they want with some Spartan pot?"

"If the Morrigan wants it, it's not some Spartan pot."

There was really only one thing it could be. The exhibition had come from the Louvre, after all, where our pot was still supposed to be, safely locked away. Somehow, someone had pulled a switch.

"It's the Dagda's cauldron."

We hurried along Art Gallery Road, away from the milling crowds. I kept looking over my shoulder, but there were no signs of pursuit yet. No sign of CJ either. Where could we go? The Rocks was too far, and I wasn't convinced HQ could provide much protection against one of the most dangerous of all the Sidhe anyway.

"Who's the Dagda?" Zac asked.

"The Morrigan's husband. The chief god of the Celts."

And his damn cauldron was heavy, but I didn't dare hand it to Zac to carry. The urge to keep it safe was almost primal. Its magic called to the aether in me, but it didn't make it any lighter. Damn it, if I had to be saddled with the job of saving one of the

Sidhe's four treasures, why couldn't it have been a lighter one? The Spear, maybe?

The Spear! Oh, my God, I was an idiot.

"I know where we can find safety!" I started to jog down Art Gallery Road as best I could with the heavy cauldron in my arms. "St Mary's Cathedral."

We'd passed it in the bus, just before arriving at the gallery this morning. It was right on the corner where Art Gallery Road began, a beautiful old collection of spires and towers that looked like it had come straight out of *The Hunchback of Notre Dame*.

"Let me carry that," Zac offered, but I shook my head and ploughed on.

I was panting and drenched in sweat by the time we got to the Cathedral. Its honeyed sandstone walls glowed in the sunlight. The entry was at the opposite end of the building, but I paused to get my breath as soon as we passed through the iron fence.

"What's that?" Zac was looking back the way we came.

I looked back too and saw a dark cloud gathering above the distant Art Gallery.

"Bad news," I said. Then I squinted at a running figure. "Hey, is that Sona?"

He shielded his eyes with his hand. "Yeah, I think it is. Sona!" He waved at her, and she waved back. "Over here."

Too late I remembered it might be Puck again, wearing another face. But she seemed genuine enough as she dashed across the road to join us. At least, she didn't try to grab the cauldron or attack us. But maybe she was just too out of breath.

"Hang … on." She bent over, hands on her knees, and panted for a moment.

I watched the cloud swirl above the Art Gallery, feeling like a sitting duck.

"Come on. We'd better get inside."

"Where are we going?" Sona asked, looking back fearfully. "What's going on?"

I gave Sona the short version as we hurried around to the entrance, which was at the top of a flight of stairs overlooking a large plaza. I took the stairs as fast as I could and gained the safety of the church at last.

The cauldron buzzed angrily against my hands and its crimson glow faded almost to nothing as I carried it through a door covered in a reassuring amount of iron scrollwork. The warders had said the Sidhe couldn't enter a church. Perhaps even their magical objects felt the hostility of Christianity.

We slid into a pew at the back and I laid down my burden with relief, stretching my aching arms.

"What now?" Zac asked. Sona still looked gobsmacked by my quick summary of events, and now I knew she was the real deal since she'd had no trouble entering the church.

"Don't know." I hadn't thought past reaching sanctuary. What could we do now but sit and wait to be rescued? Of all the times to be without my phone—I didn't know the phone number of a single person connected with HQ except for Mum and Dad, and they were in the air at the moment, out of contact. Everyone had assumed that Simon and Kyle would be with us if an emergency arose. Now I couldn't even tell anyone at HQ what was going on, or where we were.

The stained glass windows along the sides of the big cathedral dimmed as suddenly as if night had fallen in sixty seconds. Lights blazed inside the church, but the windows were black. Sona huddled closer to Zac, lost for words for a change.

I left them sitting there and wandered around the echoing interior, cauldron in my arms. Where was the Spear of Lugh? I couldn't see anything that looked like a spear, though I suppose it might have been disguised as a giant candelabra. There were a couple of those. There were a few spears in the paintings that hung on the walls, mainly held by Roman centurions, but no physical spears in sight.

I guessed it was good that I couldn't find it. If I couldn't, then hopefully the Sidhe couldn't either, if they did somehow get inside. The cauldron, subdued as it was by its surroundings, still glowed faintly to my sight. The spear was obviously better hidden.

There was a crash as something hit a window and I jumped.

"What was that?" cried Sona, eyes wide with fright.

As I hurried back to them it came again, and again, and soon it sounded as if it was hailing outside, as hundreds of bird bodies hurled themselves at the windows.

"It's the ravens. Don't worry, they can't get in." *I hope.* Silently I urged the windows not to shatter under the onslaught. There was lead running through the stained glass—pity it wasn't iron, but at least it should strengthen the windowpanes.

"Isn't there somewhere else we could go?" Sona asked. "Somewhere smaller?"

It was a big cathedral. The roof soared above us, arched and vaulted. The cavernous space was daunting, it was true. I felt exposed just sitting here in the pews.

Back near the entry stood a wrought iron gate, guarding a set of stairs carved from sandstone that led down beneath the floor of the church.

"What about this?"

The sign said it was the crypt, and tickets were available from the gift shop. Fortunately the gate wasn't locked. It creaked ominously when I pushed it open.

Sona pulled a face. "Do you think they have dead bodies down there?"

"I'd rather dead humans than live Sidhe."

We spiralled down the stairs and found a much larger space than I'd expected. It wasn't as big as the cathedral above, but you could have held a decent-sized church service down here. Carved pillars held up the vaulted arches of the ceiling, and a beautiful mosaic decorated the floor. Inlaid tiles formed the pattern of a giant Celtic cross bigger than a basketball court. The intricate Celtic knotwork would have been decoration enough, but there were also what looked like creation scenes from the bible in large circles at the points of the cross. The biggest circle, where the arms of the cross met, depicted a gorgeous glowing sun and moon. It was all very serene and beautiful. Not a body in sight. If they were here they were safely tucked away under the tiled floor. Down here the birds' assault on the windows was only a muffled noise. Nothing to be afraid of.

"Better?" I asked.

Sona nodded. After a moment the birds fell silent. That made me uneasy, wondering what the next development would be.

I didn't have to wait long.

"Violet," a voice boomed.

We all jumped.

"Is that Miss Moore?" Sona whispered.

Deep and resonant, the voice sounded like it belonged to someone as big as the cathedral itself. Must be magic.

"The Morrigan," I said.

"Violet, you clever girl," the Morrigan said. The voice reverberated off the walls, echoing through the whole cathedral. "What a good idea of yours to hide in there!"

She sounded so approving. Smug cow.

"You know I can't come in there, don't you? Of course you do! So I'm afraid you're going to have to come out."

As if. Wild horses couldn't drag me out there. I clutched the cauldron a little closer. Much as I hated relying on other people, I was in way over my head. Time to sit tight until the cavalry arrived.

"Why don't you come to the door and have a little peek? You'll be perfectly safe, but you need to know what the consequences of disobedience will be. Not for you, you understand. For your sister."

Oh, no.

My head whipped round, as if I could see up the stairs and through the walls.

"Don't listen to her, Vi," Sona said.

I looked at Zac, and saw the horror I felt mirrored in his face. She had CJ. Of course she did. Hadn't CJ thrown herself at the Morrigan, straight into her blue burning arms, so that I could escape?

I made a little noise of distress. Zac came over and put his arms around me, the cauldron glowing softly between us.

"I have to go up there," I said. "I have to see."

He nodded. "She might be lying."

But I could tell he didn't believe she was.

I took the stairs two at a time, Zac and Sona hard on my heels. At the cathedral's entrance, a nightmare scene met our eyes.

Every square centimetre of the huge plaza below was covered in ravens. The ground was black with them, heaving like the fur of some huge animal breathing. Every lamp post, every tree branch, every last seat and bike rack—everything we could see— had disappeared under a sea of black birds.

And all their beady eyes were staring right at us.

We stood just inside the doorway, gazing out in horror. Only the steps of the Cathedral themselves were clear. On the bottom one stood the Morrigan, CJ by her side. CJ didn't move or speak, but her eyes were wide with fear, and I could see the tracks of tears on her cheeks.

"There you are," said the Morrigan.

Blue fire sparked around her head. The sky above roiled with heavy thunderclouds, though the day had been sunny a few moments ago.

"I see you have the cauldron," she said. "Give it to me and I will let your sister live."

"That might not even be CJ," Zac whispered urgently.

True. And wouldn't I feel like a fool then, if I handed over one of the four great treasures to "save" Puck's miserable hide?

"I can't take that chance," I said.

Stuff noble gestures and saving mankind. If it was a choice between mankind and my sister, guess who lost out? The warders couldn't expect me to do any more. I'd done my best to save the cauldron. It was hardly my fault if they were so useless at protecting the damn thing that it ended up back in Sidhe hands. At least we still had the other three treasures.

"Give me a minute," I called to the Morrigan, then drew back out of sight.

"Don't take too long," she said. "I'm not a patient person."

We huddled in the foyer of the church, looking at each other in despair.

"What does it even *do*?" Zac asked. "What does she want it for?"

I shrugged. "She wants it because it's theirs, I guess, and we used it to force them out of our world a long time ago. Maybe they think they can use it to get back again." At this point I hardly cared.

"They seem to be back already," Sona pointed out.

"Only a couple of them, and they had outside help." And if I ever found out who that traitor was, I'd kill them myself. I was so sick of this whole stupid mess. Where were the warders when you needed them? They should have been dealing with this, not me. "As for what it does, it's a magic cauldron of never-emptiness. Whatever you want, it can dish out an endless supply."

"Anything? You mean like jewels and clothes and stuff?" Trust Sona to think of clothes.

"Only food, as far as I know."

I blinked as an idea came to me. The tales I'd read had only mentioned food, but that didn't prove anything. I put the cauldron down on the worn tiles of the foyer and turned all my longing on it. Threw my heart at it, as Puck might have said.

Then I reached in and pulled out three very peculiar pieces of equipment. The cauldron—not surprisingly—defied the laws of physics, since they were much bigger than the cauldron itself. Sona's eyes grew huge as I handed her one.

"On the count of three, Violet," the Morrigan called.

"What the hell are they?" Zac asked.

"One," said the Morrigan.

"No time!" I turned his over and showed him the On button. "As soon as I give her the cauldron, come out and blast her with these."

"Two!"

I grabbed the cauldron and ran to the door.

"I'm here!"

Behind me Zac and Sona moved into position. Out of the corner of my eye I saw Zac give me the thumbs-up.

"Just in time." The Morrigan lowered the wicked-looking knife she'd been holding at CJ's throat. A thin trickle of blood dribbled down my sister's neck where the knife must have nicked her. "Bring it to me."

I took one step out from the shelter of the cathedral. The ravens shifted and rustled, the sound like a great wind sighing through the plaza.

"Let her go."

"Bring me the cauldron."

Slowly I descended the steps, trying to watch her and the ravens at the same time. There was no sign of Puck. I hope that didn't mean Zac was right and he was standing in front of me pretending to be my tear-streaked sister.

When I was halfway down I moved to one side. All the ravens

turned their heads to track my movements. The hairs on the back of my neck rose. So creepy.

I set the cauldron down on the step beside a statue of some archbishop, then walked back to the centre.

"Now let her go," I said.

The Morrigan gave CJ a little shove. Dazed, she staggered up the steps to join me, but the Morrigan wasn't watching us any more. Her attention was on the cauldron.

"Now, Zac!"

I dragged CJ back up the steps as Zac and Sona leapt out of hiding and turned their condensors on.

Chapter Twenty-Eight

The Morrigan screamed, a piercing inhuman shriek of pain. Every raven in the plaza lifted into the air, the sound of all those wings like thunder. I bolted back inside for the third condensor, then ran down the steps.

"Form a triangle!" I yelled above the noise, and ran out into the plaza, buffeted by raucous, maddened birds, making a rough triangle with the Morrigan at the centre. I could hardly see where I was going, my vision filled with black feathers.

A dark rift opened in the stormclouds above, and screeching ravens disappeared into it. They twirled and writhed like a living tornado, sucked into the hole in the sky. The Morrigan's black hair stood on end, whipping around her head like snakes.

"It's working!" Zac's face split in a grin as he marched down the steps, his condensor trained on the Morrigan.

And it was … for one brief, glorious moment. Then the Morrigan raised her arms and blue fire shot from her fingertips. Zac yelped and dropped his condensor, now a blasted ruin. Sona's and mine followed in quick succession.

The Morrigan's eyes flashed red. "Is that all?"

I stepped back, suddenly alone in the middle of a plaza of angry ravens. More than half of them were gone, but enough remained to do some serious damage. They settled around me in a loose circle, their beady eyes malevolent.

The Morrigan's chest heaved as if she'd just run a marathon. Our attack might have weakened her, but it wasn't enough. Zac, CJ, and Sona clumped together on the steps, watching me anxiously, but the Morrigan paid them no attention. All her venom was focused on me.

"You thought you could defeat me?" she sneered. "You ridiculous child. I was working magic before your kind came down from the trees. You are less than nothing, little ape."

She paced toward me. The air felt charged, like it does when a storm's about to hit. Blue flames crackled through her hair. She took my chin in her hand and a jolt streaked from my jawbone to my feet. Up close, her face was no longer even remotely human, all trace of the glamorous Miss Moore gone. Red lights whirled in her eyes. My knees sagged so that only her hand held me up.

"The condensors were a good thought," she said, as if praising a dog for a trick well-performed. "Clever ape. But you should have wished for bigger ones. Those toys might work on my ravens, but they aren't strong enough for me."

She let me go, and I stumbled back. My jaw ached as if I'd been punched.

"It's a shame you're not prettier," she said. "I could use a thinker like you. A powerful latent, too. You might be quite strong if you ever reached your magic."

I said nothing, and she laughed. "You thought you had, didn't you? Silly girl. Did you like my raven? I spelled him into a piece of paper. It only took the slightest brush of the aether you carry to bring him to life. And you thought *you* had freed Puck." She frowned. "But now I think you have no more need of all that aether. You or your sister."

She waved her hand—the merest gesture—and I felt that shift inside that I'd felt the night the origami bird came to life. Which turned out to be *her* doing, not mine. The same kind of tugging I'd experienced at the Art Gallery just before Puck stole the cauldron. She must have been waiting for me, her little portable aether store, to provide the power to free the cauldron from whatever spells were concealing it.

And now she was accessing the aether inside me again, stealing it away. A strong smell of burnt toffee lingered on the air for a moment, and then faded, leaving me curiously empty. Something had been taken from me, but had it really been mine to start with? I knew it was too good to last.

With a crack, the collar I still wore burst into pieces and scattered at my feet. The nearest ravens took flight in alarm, then resettled, murmuring their annoyance. A glance across at the steps showed me the same thing had happened to CJ.

"So, you got what you wanted," I said. Nothing fell from my lips when I spoke. The curse had dissipated along with the aether. I should have been happier about that. "Take the cauldron and go."

"Oh, I don't think it's going to be quite that easy, little ape," she said. "You see, I want the whole world. And I'm not going anywhere until I have it."

Behind her, a figure carrying surveying equipment appeared around the side of the cathedral.

No, wait.

It was Gretel—and it wasn't surveying equipment at all, but a giant condensor, like the one they'd threatened Puck with back in the vault. What the hell was Gretel doing here? She was a techie, not a seeker. How had she known where to find us, anyway?

At the back of the plaza behind me I heard ravens croaking and shifting, a great rustle of wings. The Morrigan, enjoying her triumph over me, took no notice.

I hoped it meant there were seekers out there setting up more condensors. Otherwise, we were screwed.

"But the cauldron is a good place to start," said the Morrigan.

She turned and stalked toward it. Gretel was now in full view. *Come on, Gretel, now or never.*

The Morrigan raised a hand to blast her with blue fire. But Gretel flicked the switch and the big machine roared into life.

I spun round as ravens lifted screaming into the air, and saw what I'd most hoped for: two more condensors forming a giant triangle with the plaza at its heart.

The air was a whirl of black bodies and beating wings. Feathers rained down like black confetti as I bent over, hands over my head, and ran to join the others on the steps. The Morrigan fought her way to the cauldron, leaning forward as if into a howling headwind. Above us, ravens spiralled like a great inverted tornado into the sky and disappeared into a rent many times greater than the one we'd made with our handheld condensors.

I struggled toward the cauldron too, though Gretel was screaming something at me. I couldn't hear her over the howl of the wind and the cacophony of ravens. But I was too late. Before I could get close the Morrigan got her hand to it, with a cry of triumph that could be heard even over everything else.

But as she picked it up, the wind caught her too and tossed her into the sky in a streak of blue flame. She disappeared through the hole in creation with the last of her ravens, and the rent snapped closed with a boom that shook the plaza.

Black feathers wafted down as the roiling clouds shifted and the sun broke through. In a moment the sky was clear, as if none of it had ever happened.

We stared at each other in shock and relief.

"Oh my God, the frogs are gone!" CJ threw her arms around me. "Hallelujah!"

I hugged her back, my feelings a little more mixed than hers. Those few days when I'd thought I could do magic had been pretty special. At last, something I could do that she couldn't. Was it wrong to feel a little sad that I was back to being ordinary old Vi again?

At least I didn't have to wear that stupid collar any more. I grabbed Zac and Sona in a three-way hug. "Thanks, guys. You were great."

Gretel ran over to us. "Is everyone okay? God, Vi, that was close. I thought you were going to get sucked away with them."

I hugged her too. It was that kind of day.

"Gretel! You're a star! You came just in the nick of time."

Her face was a little pink, but she looked pleased with herself. She turned as the other two condensor operators joined us— Ronnie and Kerrie.

"Awesome job, ladies." They high-fived each other.

"But where are the seekers?" I asked. "And how did you know where to find us?"

"Well, the big old cloud of doom hanging over the cathedral was a bit of a giveaway," Kerrie said, laughing. She looked more alive than ever. I guess nuking a few Sidhe really perked a girl up.

"But before that I saw a huge concentration of aether forming here on the monitors," Gretel said. "Everyone else had taken off for the Art Gallery, so I rounded up the girls and headed here."

"Thank goodness you did."

Three vans pulled up as we spoke. A warder leapt out of each one, followed by a team of seekers. Simon was in the lead, looking a little worse for wear.

"Too late, boys," Gretel said. "Party's over." Then she turned to me. "What was that pot the Morrigan had?"

Oh, yeah. Some of my euphoria melted away.

"It was the Dagda's cauldron."

Her face paled. "Oh, shit. But … that's supposed to be in Paris!"

"I know." Yet here it was. Or rather, had been. Now it was in the Sidhe world, and God knew what that meant for the stability of the Gilded Cage. Nothing good, probably. The cauldron's power was at the heart of one of the four anchors, after all. I gave a mental shrug. That was a problem for another day. "But it was either lose the cauldron or leave the Morrigan running loose. I know which option I prefer."

She still looked shellshocked. "I just hope the warders feel the same way."

She went to meet them, squaring her shoulders. I turned back to my friends with a sigh. Zac's eyes were full of warmth. I felt my cheeks start to redden. Stupid blushes. Sona looked at the two of us with a knowing smile, but thankfully made no comment.

"Well, that was fun. Remind me not to go on any more school excursions with you," he said.

"Sorry."

"Don't apologise. I should be the one saying sorry." He shook his head. "I didn't realise how big this magic thing was, or how … involved you were in it."

There was a question in his eyes, but I didn't feel ready to go into detail. "Yeah. It's kind of a long story."

"Take your time. I'm not going anywhere." He moved closer, and my heart, which had only just stopped trying to beat its way out of my chest, started racing again. "I'm sorry I was such a jerk."

I shrugged, trying to pretend his nearness wasn't affecting me. I don't think he was fooled. "I'll forgive you. On one condition."

"What's that?"

I leaned close and whispered in his ear. "Kiss me again."

His arms circled me and I sagged against him in relief. It felt like coming home.

"You've got a deal," he said.

THE END

Thank you for reading! If you enjoyed *The Fairytale Curse*, please take a moment to leave a short review where you bought it. Your feedback helps other readers find the book, and I would be very grateful for your assistance in helping to spread the word.

Don't miss the thrilling sequel, *The Cauldron's Gift*, coming soon! For news on this, plus special deals and other book news, sign up for my newsletter.

Sign up by visiting my website, www.marinafinlayson.com.

Also by Marina Finlayson

THE PROVING TRILOGY

Twiceborn

The Twiceborn Queen

Twiceborn Endgame

Moonborn, a prequel novella to the trilogy

Acknowledgements

I had a whole bunch of beta readers helping me on this one: first and foremost, my resident teenagers, Jen and Alana. Thank you, girls for helping me bring Vi and CJ to life.

Thanks also to Michael Omer, Jen Rasmussen, Axel Blackwell, and Constance Whitley for their very helpful feedback.

About the Author

Marina Finlayson is a reformed wedding organist who now writes fantasy. She is married and shares her Sydney home with three kids, a large collection of dragon statues and one very stupid dog with a death wish.

Her idea of heaven is lying in the bath with a cup of tea and a good book until she goes wrinkly.